S0-BNJ-254

EYES
to
SEE

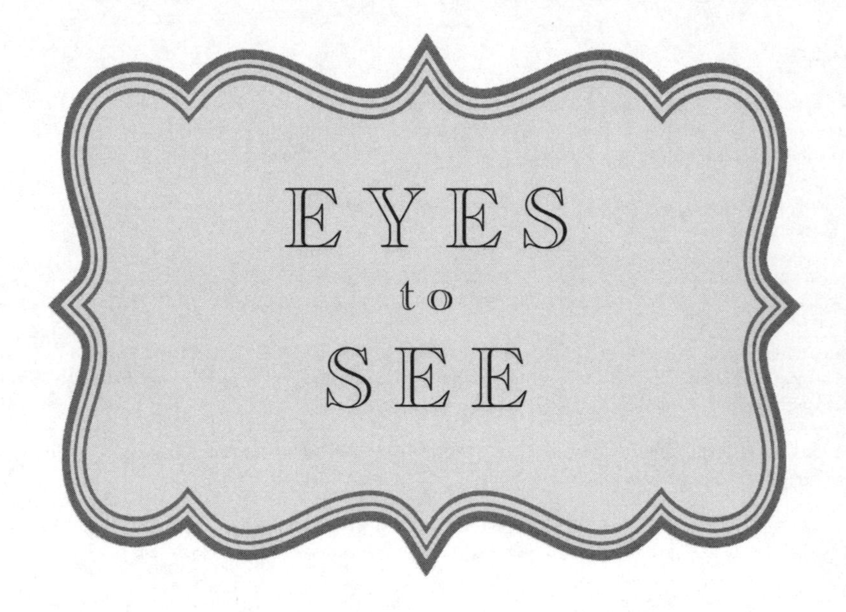

VOLUME *TWO*

Edited by

BRET LOTT

THOMAS NELSON
Since 1798

NASHVILLE DALLAS MEXICO CITY RIO DE JANEIRO BEIJING

Published in Nashville, Tennessee, by Thomas Nelson. Thomas Nelson is a registered trademark of Thomas Nelson, Inc.

Thomas Nelson, Inc., titles may be purchased in bulk for educational, business, fund-raising, or sales promotional use. For information, please e-mail SpecialMarkets@ThomasNelson.com.

Library of Congress Cataloging-in-Publication Data

Eyes to see / edited by Bret Lott.
p. cm.
ISBN 978-1-59554-276-2 (hardcover)
1. Short stories. I. Lott, Bret.
PN6120.2.E96 2007
808.83'1—dc22 2007036676

Printed in the United States of America

08 09 10 11 QW 6 5 4 3 2 1

CONTENTS

INTRODUCTION

I HAVE BEEN READING STORIES FOR MORE THAN FORTY-FIVE years now, and the longer I read the more I see what makes a great story a great story: precision.

By *precision* I don't mean merely the author's ability to make certain the colors of the rainbow follow their correct order, or that a '57 Chevy doesn't appear in Victorian England; I don't mean just getting the facts right. Those sorts of matters are easy to master. The truth is, even making certain that such fine-tuned details as the difference between a four-in-hand and a post chaise, or the words *gray* and *grey* (go look that one up!) is only a matter of study: you can find these distinctions in a book.

The precision I am here speaking of—the kind that makes the tales we love worthy of the room they take up in our hearts and minds—is a story's ability to pierce this present world in which we live and which we think we already understand, and through that piercing bring us to a deeper understanding of ourselves; the best stories reveal ourselves to ourselves, and ask us how then shall we live.

Precision in a story is that instant of understanding, given to us through the author's rendering in just the right way at just the right moment—this revelation of the self we have forgotten amidst the cluttered business of living our lives. In "Burnt Norton," the first poem of his monumental book *The Four Quartets,* poet and Christian

T. S. Eliot wrote of this preoccupation with ourselves that we are all "Distracted from distraction by distraction/Filled with fancies and empty of meaning."

Greats works of literature strip us of these distractions and, through the precision of the writer's vision, make our hearts stop for a moment in a kind of rebooting (if I may be allowed an analogy out of our computer age) of the heart and mind. The sharper and deeper and more full this complete stop—the more *precise* this moment—the better the understanding of ourselves that rushes in once that CPU (forgive me!) starts up again.

I give my rather wordy and, well, imprecise attempt at defining precision as a means to introduce this new collection of classic stories. The stories here all exhibit a lasting, indeed timeless precision, the authors' exact and exacting examinations of the deep territory of the soul revealing itself to us—as it does in the seemingly remote and fable-like world of George MacDonald's "The Broken Swords," in which three siblings survey a world they do not yet know will lead them from childhood to the knowledge of loss and of triumph.

Each story here gives us a glimpse of *ourselves,* no matter we are living here in the early morning of this new century, so that when the captain of the *Golden Mary* cries out inwardly, "O, what a thing it is, in a time of danger and in the presence of death, the shining of a face upon a face!" in Charles Dickens's "The Wreck of the *Golden Mary,*" we experience firsthand the loss he speaks thereof, even though it occurs on a lifeboat at sea more than 150 years ago; and when we encounter the moment of wonder and reverence when the narrator in Sarah Orne Jewett's "An October Ride" sees the "thin blue whiff of smoke still coming up from the great chimney," we are the ones who feel the tenuousness of our own histories, and how fleeting is the evidence we leave behind that we were ever here.

Elsewhere in this collection—and please don't worry that I am giving away any of the beauty and surprise you will encounter by citing such passages—you will find such exquisite instances of clarity and insight as Tolstoy's impetuous Ivan in "A Lost Opportunity," and the way in which his "sad affair rested with himself." Here, too, is John Updike's David in "Pigeon Feathers," an intensely ruminative boy who feels himself a "beautiful avenger," a tapestry of precise writing that allows us a window, through the characters drawn in its pages, into ourselves.

But beyond this quality of vision, beyond the granite-like gracefulness of these moments of illumination, their instances of *precision,* lies the fact each of these imagined sparks mimics in its own way the supremely and perfectly precise flame of illumination that occurs when Christ encounters others—those full stops that take place when He sees deeply into the lives around Him.

There is, for starters, His encounter with the woman at the well, and the fine point of how many husbands she has had and the fact the man she lives with now isn't even her spouse. Like anyone confronted with his or her sin, she attempts to divert the subject to the trivia of who worships at what hill where; but Christ's well-timed and piercing insight brings the woman from the small talk of a hot afternoon with this oddball Hebrew here at a Samaritan well to her rousting out all her townspeople with the call, "Come, see a man who told me everything I ever did. Could this be the Christ?"

And there is the moment of precision Christ reveals that leads to the opposite outcome, when the rich young ruler comes to Him and inquires, "Good teacher, what must I do to inherit eternal life?"

This is when Jesus answers him with what seems a little double-talk in asking why the young man calls Him good (He's Christ, we know from our own vantage point in history—of *course* He's good!); Christ then goes on to tell the man he must observe the commandments, the young man replying that he indeed has done all these things since childhood.

Then this, from the Gospel of Mark:

"Jesus looked at him and loved him. 'One thing you lack,' he said. 'Go, sell everything you have and give to the poor, and you will have treasure in heaven. Then come, follow me.'

"At this the man's face fell. He went away sad, because he had great wealth. Jesus looked around and said to his disciples, 'How hard it is for the rich to enter the kingdom of God'" (Mark 10, NIV).

What makes this story so memorable, so important and real—what makes this moment so *precise* as to change the man's life—is that Jesus' incision into the man's soul reveals to him and to Christ's gathered disciples the hollow fact of the man's life: though he may live according to the Law, he does not do so out of love. Instead, he has lived this way for his own benefit and, when faced with himself in this bright and cold and loving way (remember: "Jesus looked at him and loved him"), the rich young ruler walks away, unable to give himself up in order to find himself.

This sort of precision—the moment when the world turns upside down, for better, as with the Samaritan woman, or for worse, as with the rich young ruler who has obeyed the commandments all his life—is what turns mere words into Truth, and what makes Truth a measure against which we must examine our lives.

And it is by that measure the stories in this collection have been weighed: does each author speak, through the precision of his or her own language and imagination, the Truth of humankind? You will see in these stories that conversion isn't the question, and that change in the way these characters live is left to their own choice; you'll see here as well that change occurs, and that hearts and minds and souls are moved toward a deeper understanding of the one true God.

But above all you will see that these stories of triumph and loss, of longing and discovery, have a greater resonance than the sum of their words, and that the worlds they render reveal the Truth that man is lost without his creator God, and that man is found through his encounter with Him.

BRET LOTT
March 2008
Charleston, South Carolina

EYES
to
SEE

FREDERICK BUECHNER

CARL FREDERICK BUECHNER WAS BORN IN NEW YORK CITY IN 1926. He attended the Lawrenceville School in New Jersey, graduating in 1943 and entering Princeton immediately after. There he attended classes for a year, then took time to serve in World War II, returning in 1946 and graduating in 1947.

In 1950, he published his first novel, *A Long Day's Dying*, beginning one of the most impressive literary careers in American letters. This first book was met with wide critical acclaim, his artistry being compared to that of Henry James and Marcel Proust. Not long after this, Buechner, who had been raised in a secular household, began to attend Madison Avenue Presbyterian Church, where noted evangelical theologian George Buttrick served as pastor. Sensing the emptiness of his life, even with his literary success, Buechner experienced a turning toward Christ, and at Buttrick's suggestion, attended Union Theological Seminary where he studied under such theologians as Paul Tillich, James Muilenburg, and Reinhold Niebuhr. The rest is literary and evangelical history.

The author of such modern classics of Christian thought as *The Alphabet of Grace, Telling the Truth,* and *The Faces of Jesus,* Buechner continued to break ground with his fiction as well, especially with the publication of his

Leo Bebb novels, *Lion Country* (nominated for the National Book Award), *Open Heart, Love Feast,* and *Treasure Hunt,* books that explore through the life of Leo Bebb, a con man and man of God, the dichotomy of mankind and its distance from God.

OUR LAST DRIVE TOGETHER

BY FREDERICK BUECHNER

It was while my mother was staying with us in Vermont that the fatal phone call came. It was from Incoronata, the woman who for years had been her factotum and mainstay in the New York apartment that she rarely left except for occasional visits to us or trips to the doctor or the hearing aid people who were always selling her new models, none of which, she said, were any damn good.

Incoronata must have spent hours working herself up to it because I'd barely lifted the receiver when she dropped her bombshell. She said she was quitting. She said she'd had all she could take. She said there was nothing more to say. And then she said a good deal more.

She told me my mother said such terrible things to her that I wouldn't believe it if she repeated them. She said she had to work like a slave and never got a word of thanks for it, let alone any time off. She said her live-in boyfriend threatened to walk out on her if she stayed on the job a day longer because in her present state she was giving him ulcers. She was getting ulcers herself, she said. And no wonder. She said she had left the key to the apartment with one of the doormen because she would not be needing it again to let herself in. And that was that. She said she was on the verge of a nervous breakdown.

I could feel my scalp run cold at the thought of my mother's reaction and said everything I could think of to make Incoronata change her mind. I told her my mother was devoted to her no matter what terrible things she said. I told her the whole family was devoted to her. I told her that when people got old and deaf and started falling to pieces, they said things they didn't mean and then felt awful about it afterward. I said I didn't know how my mother could possibly manage without her, how any of us could. I said we would give her a raise and see to it that she got more time off. But by then she was so close to hysterics I don't think she even heard me.

So I changed my tactics and begged her at least to stay on till we could find somebody to replace her, at least to be there when we got back from Vermont to help my mother unpack and get resettled. But if she did that, Incoronata said, she knew my mother would find some way to make her stay, and with her nerves the way they were she simply couldn't face it. So there was nothing more to say, and we finally hung up.

The question then became how to break the news to Kaki, which was what her grandchildren called my mother as eventually all of us did. To have told her then and there would have been to ruin the rest of her visit for all of us, so we decided to wait till I had managed to find somebody else to replace her and then not breathe a word till we had gotten her back to her apartment where there would be another Incoronata waiting to welcome her and she would simply have to accept the new state of things as a fait accompli.

My brother Jamie, who lived in New York too, came up by bus to help with the historic drive back. There was the usual mound of luggage piled out on the lawn—the suitcases with bits of brightly colored yarn tied around their handles to identify them, the plastic and canvas carry-alls, the paper shopping bags from Saks and Bonwits stuffed with things like her hair dryer, her magnifying mirror, extra slippers, and so on. There was the square Mark Cross case she kept her jewelry in and the flowered duffel bag with her enormous collection of pills and assorted medicines together with a second like it which was full of all the things she needed for making up her face in the morning. She said it was all of it breakable so for God's sake not to put anything heavy on it and to be sure to put her long black garment bag in at the very end so it could lie flat on top of everything else and her best clothes wouldn't end up a mass of wrinkles.

We put her white plastic toilet seat extender behind her on the back seat like a wedding cake in case she needed it on the way. She kept her straw purse on her lap with things she might want during the journey like her smelling salts and Excedrin and the little flask of water in case she started to choke. She also had me put a can of root beer in the cup holder because she said root beer was the only thing that helped her dry throat. The final thing was to get Jamie to stuff her little velvet, heart-shaped pillow in behind the small of her back because she said he was the only one who knew how to do it properly.

She had one of her many chiffon scarves around her neck to keep off drafts and another one, just for looks, tied around her melon-shaped straw hat with her crescent-shaped diamond pin to hold it in place. For shoes she wore her usual suede Hush Puppies with crepe soles to prevent her from slipping and kept her cane within reach at her side. Before we started off I told her not to forget to fasten her seat belt, but she refused. She said she sat so low in her seat that the strap went across her face and almost knocked her dentures out, and that got all three of us laughing so hard I was able to click it into place without her even noticing.

Driving with Kaki was one of the best ways there was of visiting with her because with no other noises to distract her I could speak in my normal voice, and that meant that not only could we speak the kinds of things that can't be shouted but could do it like the old friends we were instead of the caricatures we became when almost nothing I said got through to her. Heading west through the rolling green farmland, I began to think of her again as the hero she had been all through my childhood when it seemed there was nothing she couldn't do, no company she couldn't charm, no disaster she couldn't pull us all through like my father's death in a garage filled with bitter blue fumes when I was ten and Jamie going on eight. I remembered how proud I was of how much younger and prettier and funnier she was than the mothers of any of my friends and how I loved being with her. I remembered the new life she had made for us in Bermuda in a pink house called the Moorings on the harbor across from Hamilton where Jamie and I could catch fish much too beautiful to keep and where we lived until 1939 when the war broke out and we had to go home.

At sixty miles an hour she seemed as mobile as I was, and I couldn't imagine her ever again having to hand herself across a room from chair back to chair back groaning that her knees bent the wrong way like a stork's and she had no balance and couldn't imagine what in God's name was wrong with her. What was wrong with her, of course, was that she would be ninety on her next birthday, but if ever I tried telling her that, she would put her hands over her ears and close her eyes tight shut. Sometimes she would scream.

Jamie was dozing in the back seat next to the toilet seat extender, and all was peaceful until she complained that the sun was getting in her eyes and giving her a terrible headache. She had her dark glasses on, but she said they were no damn good so I pulled her sun visor down, and she said any fool could see she was too low in her seat for that to be any damn good either. She told me to stop at the next service station we came to and get her a piece of cardboard or something to cover her half of the windshield. I explained if I did that I wouldn't be able to see the road properly, and she said she couldn't believe a man would treat his own mother the way I did.

Her next step was to take off the chiffon scarf she had around her neck and get Jamie to tie it on from behind like a blindfold. That seemed to work at first, but then she said she needed something heavier so he took off his jacket and draped it over the melon-shaped hat and the chiffon scarf. We said it made her look as if she was being kidnapped by terrorists, and she said we could laugh all we wanted, but as for her she failed to see the joke.

Not long afterward she said in a muffled voice that she was having trouble breathing. If it led to a heart attack, she supposed that would give us another good chuckle. But by this time we weren't driving into the sun anymore, so Jamie took off her various wrappings, and for a while she didn't say anything until we hit a stretch of rough pavement. Each time the car gave the smallest jounce, she sucked her breath in through her teeth like a hissing radiator. It was like me, she said, to pick out the worst road I could find when I knew what it did to her back.

It was toward the end of the journey as we were barreling down the Hudson River Parkway toward the Seventy-ninth Street exit that she told me she had to get to a bathroom in a hurry. I told her there was no way in the world we could find her a bathroom where we were, but if she could just hold out about twenty minutes longer, we would have her home. She told me she never dreamed that the child she'd almost died giving birth to would treat her like a dog the way I did, and it was at that point that I found myself having fantasies. I could pull the car over to the side of the road and just leave her there with all her belongings including the seat extender. I could move to another country. I could grow a beard and change my name.

She did hold out, as it happened, but by the time the doorman had helped her out of the car and into the elevator, she was in such a rush she didn't even notice that it wasn't Incoronata who opened the door to let us in. When she eventually came out of the bathroom, she still had her hat on her head with one end of the chiffon scarf trailing out behind her, and it was only then that she noticed that the person who was offering to take it off for her was a total stranger.

As briefly and calmly as I could, I explained what had happened to Incoronata, and to my surprise she didn't explode the way I'd been dreading but just stood there in the hallway looking old and dazed with her skirt pulled crooked. Incoronata's replacement, whose name turned out to be Sheila, was under five feet tall, and it wasn't until she had helped her lie down on the her bed and taken her shoes off that Kaki spoke to her for the first time.

"Get me a root beer out of the icebox," she barked and then, before Sheila left the bedroom, "That dyed hair doesn't fool me for a minute. She's seventy if she's a day. And if you think I'm going to have a dwarf taking care of me, you're out of your minds."

Kaki's bedroom was where she spent the last few years of her life, rarely leaving it except when Jamie and his wife came for supper. She had pasted gold stars on almost everything—the headboard of her bed, the picture frames, the lamp shades, the covers of books. Her chaise longue was heaped with pillows, and there was a pile of magazines on the carpet beside it and a fake leopard-skin throw at the foot. There was her bow-fronted antique desk that she loved telling she'd bought out from under the nose of a childhood friend who would have killed for it, and the dressing table where she used to do her face the first thing every morning until she took to having the powder and lipstick and eyebrow pencil and what have you brought to her on a tray while she was still in bed.

The glass-topped green bureau was loaded with colognes, hairsprays, eyedrops, cough syrup. There was a jar of almonds that she had read kept you from getting cancer and a bowl of M&M's that she said gave her energy. A number of pictures hung on the peach-colored walls including a watercolor of the Moorings with its whitewashed roof and the blue harbor beyond it. She said she'd never been so happy anywhere else. There was a framed piece of needlepoint she'd done with the word "JOY" on it and several ladybugs for luck. She kept her bedside telephone under a quilted tea cozy and beside it a little covered china dish for her teeth at night.

It was in this room that early one morning she died in her sleep. Little pint-sized Sheila was the one who phoned Jamie the news. He said that when he got to the apartment shortly afterward, she told him she had put one of Kaki's best nighties on her and the ribboned pink bedjacket that was her favorite. She had washed her face and hands and brushed her hair. When he turned to go in and see her, Sheila went and busied herself with something in the kitchen.

Kaki was lying on her bed with a fresh sheet pulled up all the way over her. He said that for a few moments he thought he would pull it back to have one last look at her face and then didn't. He just stood at the window for a while staring down at Seventy-ninth Street three stories below. The windowsill felt gritty to his touch. He noticed that one of the muslin curtains needed mending.

When the long black vehicle with side curtains pulled up at the awninged front entrance, he found himself remembering an exchange he and I had had with her once. She had told us for God's sake not to let them carry her out in a bag when the time came, and we had told her we wouldn't. Instead, I said, I would take her under one arm and Jamie would take her under the other and together we would walk her out between us, which had gotten all three of us laughing the way we did in the car when she said the seat belt strap almost knocked her dentures out.

Down below he could see the undertakers talking to the doorman. He went back and stood by the bed for a few moments, then reached down under the bottom of the sheet and pinched one of her toes.

"They're coming," he said.

G.K. CHESTERTON

BORN IN LONDON IN 1874 TO A MIDDLE-CLASS FAMILY, GILBERT Keith Chesterton was a journalist, poet, and biographer, but was most famous for his beloved "Father Brown" mystery stories, which he wrote between 1911 and 1936. An influential Christian writer and thinker, he was the author of, among other important works, *The Everlasting Man*, *Heretics*, and *Orthodoxy*.

While a student at University College and the Slade School of Art from 1893 to 1896, Chesterton experienced a crisis of uncertainty and depression, and left the university without a degree. He then worked for London publishers, and later renewed his Christian faith, due in no small part to Frances Blogg, the woman he courted and then married in 1901.

In 1909 Chesterton and his wife moved twenty-five miles west of London to the village of Beaconsfield, where he continued his writing life, and from which he traveled widely. In 1922 he converted from Anglicanism to Roman Catholicism.

During his lifetime he published sixty-nine books and received honorary degrees from Edinburgh, Dublin, and Notre Dame universities. Chesterton died on June 14, 1936, at his home in Beaconsfield.

THE PARADISE OF THIEVES

BY G.K. CHESTERTON

The great Muscari, most original of the young Tuscan poets, walked swiftly into his favourite restaurant, which overlooked the Mediterranean, was covered by an awning and fenced by little lemon and orange trees. Waiters in white aprons were already laying out on white tables the insignia of an early and elegant lunch; and this seemed to increase a satisfaction that already touched the top of swagger. Muscari had an eagle nose like Dante; his hair and neckerchief were dark and flowing; he carried a black cloak, and might almost have carried a black mask, so much did he bear with him a sort of Venetian melodrama. He acted as if a troubadour had still a definite social office, like a bishop. He went as near as his century permitted to walking the world literally like Don Juan, with rapier and guitar.

For he never travelled without a case of swords, with which he had fought many brilliant duels, or without a corresponding case for his mandolin, with which he had actually serenaded Miss Ethel Harrogate, the highly conventional daughter of a Yorkshire banker on a holiday. Yet he was neither a charlatan nor a child; but a hot, logical Latin who liked a certain thing and was it. His poetry was as straightforward as anyone else's prose. He desired fame or wine or the beauty of women with a torrid directness inconceivable among the cloudy ideals or cloudy compromises of the north; to vaguer races his intensity smelt of danger or even crime. Like fire or the sea, he was too simple to be trusted.

The banker and his beautiful English daughter were staying at the hotel attached to Muscari's restaurant; that was why it was his favourite restaurant. A glance flashed around the room told him at once, however, that the English party had not descended. The restaurant was glittering, but still comparatively empty. Two priests were talking at a table in a corner, but Muscari (an ardent Catholic) took no more notice of them than of a couple of crows. But from a yet farther seat, partly concealed behind a dwarf tree golden with oranges, there rose and advanced towards the poet a person whose costume was the most aggressively opposite to his own.

This figure was clad in tweeds of a piebald check, with a pink tie, a sharp collar and protuberant yellow boots. He contrived, in the true tradition of 'Arry at Margate, to look at once startling and commonplace. But as the Cockney apparition drew nearer, Muscari was astounded to observe that the head was distinctly different from the body. It was an Italian head: fuzzy, swarthy and very vivacious, that rose abruptly out of the standing collar like cardboard and the comic pink tie. In fact it was a head he knew. He recognized it, above all the dire erection of English holiday array, as the face of an old but forgotten friend name Ezza. This youth had been a prodigy at college, and European fame was promised him when he was barely fifteen; but when he appeared in the world he failed, first publicly as a dramatist and a demagogue, and then privately for years on end as an actor, a traveller, a commission agent or a journalist. Muscari had known him last behind the footlights; he was but too well attuned to the excitements of that profession, and it was believed that some moral calamity had swallowed him up.

"EZZA!" CRIED THE POET, RISING AND SHAKING HANDS IN A pleasant astonishment. "Well, I've seen you in many costumes in the green room; but I never expected to see you dressed up as an Englishman."

"This," answered Ezza gravely, "is not the costume of an Englishman, but of the Italian of the future."

"In that case," remarked Muscari, "I confess I prefer the Italian of the past."

"That is your old mistake, Muscari," said the man in tweeds, shaking his head; "and the mistake of Italy. In the sixteenth century we Tuscans made the morning: we had the newest steel, the newest carving, the newest chemistry. Why should we not now have the newest factories, the newest motors, the newest finance—the newest clothes?"

"Because they are not worth having," answered Muscari. "You cannot make Italians really progressive; they are too intelligent. Men who see the short cut to good living will never go by the new elaborate roads."

"Well, to me Marconi, or D'Annunzio, is the star of Italy" said the other. "That is why I have become a Futurist—and a courier."

"A courier!" cried Muscari, laughing. "Is that the last of your list of trades? And whom are you conducting?"

"Oh, a man of the name of Harrogate, and his family, I believe."

"Not the banker in this hotel?" inquired the poet, with some eagerness.

"That's the man," answered the courier.

"Does it pay well?" asked the troubadour innocently.

"It will pay me," said Ezza, with a very enigmatic smile. "But I am a rather curious sort of courier." Then, as if changing the subject, he said abruptly: "He has a daughter—and a son."

"The daughter is divine," affirmed Muscari, "the father and son are, I suppose, human. But granted his harmless qualities doesn't that banker strike you as a splendid instance of my argument? Harrogate has millions in his safes, and I have—the hole in my pocket. But you daren't say—you can't say—that he's cleverer than I, or bolder than I, or even more energetic. He's not clever, he's got eyes like blue buttons; he's not energetic, he moves from chair to chair like a paralytic. He's a conscientious, kindly old blockhead; but he's got money simply because he collects money, as a boy collects stamps. You're too strong-minded for business, Ezza. You won't get on. To be clever enough to get all that money, one must be stupid enough to want it."

"I'm stupid enough for that," said Ezza gloomily. "But I should suggest a suspension of your critique of the banker, for here he comes."

Mr Harrogate, the great financier, did indeed enter the room, but nobody looked at him. He was a massive elderly man with a boiled blue eye and faded grey-sandy moustaches; but for his heavy stoop he might have been a colonel. He carried several unopened letters in his hand. His son Frank was a really fine lad, curly-haired, sun-burnt and strenuous; but nobody looked at him either. All eyes, as usual, were riveted, for the moment at least, upon Ethel Harrogate, whose golden Greek head and colour of the dawn seemed set purposely above that sapphire sea, like a goddess's. The poet Muscari drew a deep breath as if he were drinking something, as indeed he was. He was drinking the Classic; which his fathers made. Ezza studied her with a gaze equally intense and far more baffling.

Miss Harrogate was specially radiant and ready for conversation on this occasion; and her family had fallen into the easier Continental habit, allowing the stranger Muscari and even the courier Ezza to share their table and their talk. In Ethel Harrogate conventionality crowned itself with a perfection and splendour of its own. Proud of her father's prosperity, fond of fashionable pleasures, a fond daughter but an arrant flirt, she was all these things with a sort of golden good-nature that made her very pride pleasing and her worldly respectability a fresh and hearty thing.

They were in an eddy of excitement about some alleged peril in the mountain path they were to attempt that week. The danger was not from rock and avalanche, but from something yet more romantic. Ethel had been earnestly assured that brigands, the true cut-throats of the modern legend, still haunted that ridge and held that pass of the Apennines.

"They say," she cried, with the awful relish of a schoolgirl, "that all that country isn't ruled by the King of Italy, but by the King of Thieves. Who is the King of Thieves?"

"A great man," replied Muscari, "worthy to rank with your own Robin Hood, signorina. Montano, the King of Thieves, was first heard of in the mountains some ten years ago, when people said brigands were extinct. But his wild authority spread with the swiftness of a silent revolution. Men found his fierce proclamations nailed in every mountain village; his sentinels, gun in hand, in every mountain ravine. Six times the Italian Government tried to dislodge him, and was defeated in six pitched battles as if by Napoleon."

"Now that sort of thing," observed the banker weightily, "would never be allowed in England; perhaps, after all, we had better choose another route. But the courier thought it perfectly safe."

"It is perfectly safe," said the courier contemptuously. "I have been over it twenty times. There may have been some old jailbird called a King in the time of our grandmothers; but he belongs to history if not to fable. Brigandage is utterly stamped out."

"It can never be utterly stamped out," Muscari answered; "because armed revolt is a recreation natural to southerners. Our peasants are like their mountains, rich in grace and green gaiety, but with the fires beneath. There is a point of human despair where the northern poor take to drink—and our own poor take to daggers."

"A poet is privileged," replied Ezza, with a sneer. "If Signor Muscari were English he would still be looking for highwaymen in Wandsworth. Believe me, there is no more danger of being captured in Italy than of being scalped in Boston."

"Then you propose to attempt it?" asked Mr Harrogate, frowning.

"Oh, it sounds rather dreadful," cried the girl, turning her glorious eyes on Muscari. "Do you really think the pass is dangerous?"

Muscari threw back his black mane. "I know it is dangerous:" he said. "I am crossing it tomorrow."

The young Harrogate was left behind for a moment emptying a glass of white wine and lighting a cigarette, as the beauty retired with the banker, the courier and the poet, distributing peals of silvery satire. At about the same instant the two priests in the corner rose; the taller, a white-haired Italian, taking his leave. The shorter priest turned and walked towards the banker's son, and the latter was astonished to realize that though a Roman priest the man was an Englishman. He vaguely remembered meeting him at the social crushes of some of his Catholic friends. But the man spoke before his memories could collect themselves.

"Mr Frank Harrogate, I think," he said. "I have had an introduction, but I do not mean to presume on it. The odd thing I have to say will come far better from a stranger. Mr Harrogate, I say one word and go: take care of your sister in her great sorrow."

Even for Frank's truly fraternal indifference the radiance and derision of his sister still seemed to sparkle and ring; he could hear her laughter still from the garden of the hotel, and he stared at his sombre adviser in puzzledom.

"Do you mean the brigands?" he asked; and then, remembering a vague fear of his own, "or can you be thinking of Muscari?"

"One is never thinking of the real sorrow," said the strange priest. "One can only be kind when it comes."

And he passed promptly from the room, leaving the other almost with his mouth open.

A day or two afterwards a coach containing the company was really crawling and staggering up the spurs of the menacing mountain range. Between Ezza's cheery denial of the danger and Muscari's boisterous defiance of it, the financial family were firm in their original purpose; and Muscari made his mountain journey coincide with theirs. A more surprising feature was the appearance at the coast-town station of the little priest of the restaurant; he alleged merely that business led him also to cross the mountains of the midland. But young Harrogate could not but connect his presence with the mystical fears and warnings of yesterday.

The coach was a kind of commodious wagonette, invented by the modernist talent of the courier, who dominated the expedition with his scientific activity and breezy wit. The theory of danger from thieves was banished from thought and speech; though so far conceded in formal act that some slight protection was employed. The courier and the young banker carried loaded revolvers, and Muscari (with much boyish gratification) buckled on a kind of cutlass under his black cloak.

He had planted his person at a flying leap next to the lovely

Englishwoman; on the other side of her sat the priest, whose name was Brown and who was fortunately a silent individual; the courier and the father and son were on the banc behind. Muscari was in towering spirits, seriously believing in the peril, and his talk to Ethel might well have made her think him a maniac. But there was something in the crazy and gorgeous ascent, amid crags like peaks loaded with woods like orchards, that dragged her spirit up alone with his into purple preposterous heavens with wheeling suns. The white road climbed like a white cat; it spanned sunless chasms like a tight-rope; it was flung round far-off headlands like a lasso.

And yet, however high they went, the desert still blossomed like the rose. The fields were burnished in sun and wind with the colour of kingfisher and parrot and humming-bird, the hues of a hundred flowering flowers. There are no lovelier meadows and woodlands than the English, no nobler crests or chasms than those of Snowdon and Glencoe. But Ethel Harrogate had never before seen the southern parks tilted on the splintered northern peaks; the gorge of Glencoe laden with the fruits of Kent. There was nothing here of that chill and desolation that in Britain one associates with high and wild scenery. It was rather like a mosaic palace, rent with earthquakes; or like a Dutch tulip garden blown to the stars with dynamite.

"It's like Kew Gardens on Beachy Head," said Ethel.

"It is our secret," answered he, "the secret of the volcano; that is also the secret of the revolution—that a thing can be violent and yet fruitful."

"You are rather violent yourself," and she smiled at him.

"And yet rather fruitless," he admitted; "if I die tonight I die unmarried and a fool."

"It is not my fault if you have come," she said after a difficult silence.

"It is never your fault," answered Muscari; "it was not your fault that Troy fell."

As they spoke they came under overwhelming cliffs that spread almost like wings above a corner of peculiar peril. Shocked by the big shadow on the narrow ledge, the horses stirred doubtfully. The driver leapt to the earth to hold their heads, and they became ungovernable. One horse reared up to his full height—the titanic and terrifying height of a horse when he becomes a biped. It was just enough to alter the equilibrium; the whole coach heeled over like a ship and crashed through the fringe of bushes over the cliff. Muscari threw an arm round Ethel, who clung to him, and shouted aloud. It was for such moments that he lived.

At the moment when the gorgeous mountain walls went round the poet's head like a purple windmill a thing happened which was superficially even more startling. The elderly and lethargic banker sprang erect in the coach and leapt over the precipice before the tilted vehicle could take him there. In the first flash it looked as wild as suicide; but in the second it was as sensible as a safe investment. The Yorkshireman had evidently more promptitude, as well as more sagacity, than Muscari had given him credit for; for he landed in a lap of land which might have been specially padded with turf and clover to receive him. As it happened, indeed, the whole company were equally lucky, if less dignified in their form of ejection. Immediately under this abrupt turn of the road was a grassy and flowery hollow like a sunken meadow; a sort of green velvet pocket in the long, green, trailing garments of the hills. Into this they were all tipped or tumbled with little damage, save that their smallest baggage and even the contents of their pockets were scattered in the grass around them. The wrecked coach still hung above, entangled in the tough hedge, and the horses plunged painfully down the slope. The first to sit up was the little priest, who scratched his head with a face of foolish wonder. Frank Harrogate heard him say to himself: "Now why on earth have we fallen just here?"

He blinked at the litter around him, and recovered his own very clumsy umbrella. Beyond it lay the broad sombrero fallen from the head of Muscari, and beside it a sealed business letter which, after a glance at the address, he returned to the elder Harrogate. On the other side of him the grass partly hid Miss Ethel's sunshade, and just beyond it lay a curious little glass bottle hardly two inches long. The priest picked it up; in a quick, unobtrusive manner he uncorked and sniffed it, and his heavy face turned the colour of clay.

"Heaven deliver us!" he muttered; "it can't be hers! Has her sorrow come on her already?" He slipped it into his own waistcoat pocket. "I think I'm justified," he said, "till I know a little more."

He gazed painfully at the girl, at that moment being raised out of the flowers by Muscari, who was saying: "We have fallen into heaven; it is a sign. Mortals climb up and they fall down; but it is only gods and goddesses who can fall upwards."

And indeed she rose out of the sea of colours so beautiful and happy a vision that the priest felt his suspicion shaken and shifted. "After all," he thought, "perhaps the poison isn't hers; perhaps it's one of Muscari's melodramatic tricks."

Muscari set the lady lightly on her feet, made her an absurdly theatrical bow, and then, drawing his cutlass, hacked hard at the taut reins of the horses, so that they scrambled to their feet and stood in the grass trembling. When he had done so, a most remarkable thing occurred. A very quiet man, very poorly dressed and extremely sunburnt, came out of the bushes and took hold of the horses' heads. He had a queer-shaped knife, very broad and crooked, buckled on his belt; there was nothing else remarkable about him, except his sudden and silent appearance. The poet asked him who he was, and he did not answer.

Looking around him at the confused and startled group in the hollow, Muscari then perceived that another tanned and tattered man, with a short gun under his arm, was looking at them from the ledge just below, leaning his elbows on the edge of the turf. Then he looked up at the road from which they had fallen and saw, looking down on them, the muzzles of four other carbines and four other brown faces with bright but quite motionless eyes.

"The brigands!" cried Muscari, with a kind of monstrous gaiety. "This was a trap. Ezza, if you will oblige me by shooting the coachman first, we can cut our way out yet. There are only six of them."

"The coachman," said Ezza, who was standing grimly with his hands in his pockets, "happens to be a servant of Mr Harrogate's."

"Then shoot him all the more," cried the poet impatiently; "he was bribed to upset his master. Then put the lady in the middle, and we will break the line up there—with a rush."

And, wading in wild grass and flowers, he advanced fearlessly on the four carbines; but finding that no one followed except young Harrogate, he turned, brandishing his cutlass to wave the others on. He beheld the courier still standing slightly astride in the centre of the grassy ring, his hands in his pockets; and his lean, ironical Italian face seemed to grow longer and longer in the evening light.

"You thought, Muscari, I was the failure among our schoolfellows," he said, "and you thought you were the success. But I have succeeded more than you and fill a bigger place in history. I have been acting epics while you have been writing them."

"Come on, I tell you!" thundered Muscari from above. "Will you stand there talking nonsense about yourself with a woman to save and three strong men to help you? What do you call yourself?"

"I call myself Montano," cried the strange courier in a voice equally loud and full. "I am the King of Thieves, and I welcome you all to my summer palace."

And even as he spoke five more silent men with weapons ready came out of the bushes, and looked towards him for their orders. One of them held a large paper in his hand.

"This pretty little nest where we are all picnicking," went on the courier-brigand, with the same easy yet sinister smile, "is, together with some caves underneath it, known by the name of the Paradise of Thieves. It is my principal stronghold on these hills; for (as you have doubtless noticed) the eyrie is invisible both from the road above and from the valley below. It is something better than impregnable; it is unnoticeable. Here I mostly live, and here I shall certainly die, if the gendarmes ever track me here. I am not the kind of criminal that 'reserves his defence,' but the better kind that reserves his last bullet."

All were staring at him thunderstruck and still, except Father Brown, who heaved a huge sigh as of relief and fingered the little phial in his pocket. "Thank God!" he muttered; "that's much more probable. The poison belongs to this robber-chief, of course. He carries it so that he may never be captured, like Cato."

The King of Thieves was, however, continuing his address with the same kind of dangerous politeness. "It only remains for me," he said, "to explain to my guests the social conditions upon which I have the pleasure of entertaining them. I need not expound the quaint old ritual of ransom, which it is incumbent upon me to keep up; and even this only applies to a part of the company. The Reverend Father Brown and the celebrated Signor Muscari I shall release tomorrow at dawn and escort to my outposts. Poets and priests, if you will pardon my simplicity of speech, never have any money. And so (since it is impossible to get anything out of them), let us, seize the opportunity to show our admiration for classic literature and our reverence for Holy Church."

He paused with an unpleasing smile; and Father Brown blinked repeatedly at him, and seemed suddenly to be listening with great attention. The brigand captain took the large paper from the attendant brigand and, glancing over it, continued: "My other intentions are clearly set forth in this public document, which I will hand round in a moment; and which after that will be posted on a tree by every village in the valley, and every cross-road in the hills. I will not weary you with the verbalism, since you will be able to check it; the substance of my proclamation is this: I announce first that I have captured the English millionaire, the colossus of finance, Mr Samuel Harrogate. I next announce that I have found on his person notes and bonds for two thousand pounds, which he has given up to me. Now since it would be really immoral to announce such a thing to a credulous public if it had not occurred, I suggest it should occur without further delay. I suggest that Mr Harrogate senior should now give me the two thousand pounds in his pocket."

The banker looked at him under lowering brows, red-faced and sulky, but seemingly cowed. That leap from the failing carriage seemed to have used up his last virility. He had held back in a hang-dog style when his son and Muscari had made a bold movement to break out of the brigand trap. And now his red and trembling hand went reluctantly to his breast-pocket, and passed a bundle of papers and envelopes to the brigand.

"Excellent!" cried that outlaw gaily; "so far we are all cosy. I resume the points of my proclamation, so soon to be published to all Italy. The third item is that of ransom. I am asking from the friends of the Harrogate family a ransom of three thousand pounds, which I am sure is almost insulting to that family in its moderate estimate of their importance. Who would not pay triple this sum for another day's association with such a domestic circle? I will not conceal from you that the document ends with certain legal phrases about the unpleasant things that may happen if the money is not paid; but meanwhile, ladies and gentlemen, let me assure you that I am comfortably off here for accommodation, wine and cigars, and bid you for the present a sportsman-like welcome to the luxuries of the Paradise of Thieves."

All the time that he had been speaking, the dubious-looking men with carbines and dirty slouch hats had been gathering silently in such preponderating numbers that even Muscari was compelled to recognize his sally with the sword as hopeless. He glanced around him; but the girl had already gone over to soothe and comfort her father, for her natural affection for his person was as strong or stronger than her somewhat snobbish pride in his success. Muscari, with the illogicality of a lover, admired this filial devotion, and yet was irritated by it. He slapped his sword back in the scabbard and went and flung himself somewhat sulkily on one of the green banks. The priest sat down within a yard or two, and Muscari turned his aquiline nose on him in an instantaneous irritation.

"Well," said the poet tartly, "do people still think me too romantic? Are there, I wonder, any brigands left in the mountains?"

"There may be," said Father Brown agnostically.

"What do you mean?" asked the other sharply.

"I mean I am puzzled," replied the priest. "I am puzzled about Ezza or Montano, or whatever his name is. He seems to me much more inexplicable as a brigand even than he was as a courier."

"But in what way?" persisted his companion. "Santa Maria! I should have thought the brigand was plain enough."

"I find three curious difficulties," said the priest in a quiet voice. "I should like to have your opinion on them. First of all I must tell you I was lunching in that restaurant at the seaside. As four of you left the room, you and Miss Harrogate went ahead, talking and laughing; the banker and the courier came behind, speaking sparely and rather low. But I could not help hearing Ezza say these words—'Well, let her have a little fun; you know the blow may smash her any minute.' Mr Harrogate answered nothing; so the words must have had some meaning. On the impulse of the moment I warned her brother that she might be in peril; I said nothing of its nature, for I did not know. But if it meant this capture in the hills, the thing is nonsense. Why should the brigand-courier warn his patron, even by a hint, when it was his whole purpose to lure him into the mountain-mousetrap? It could not have meant that. But if not, what is this disaster, known both to courier and banker, which hangs over Miss Harrogate's head?"

"Disaster to Miss Harrogate!" ejaculated the poet, sitting up with some ferocity. "Explain yourself; go on."

"All my riddles, however, revolve round our bandit chief," resumed the priest reflectively. "And here is the second of them. Why did he put so prominently in his demand for ransom the fact that he had taken two thousand pounds from his victim on the spot? It had no faintest tendency to evoke the ransom. Quite the other way, in fact. Harrogate's friends would be far likelier to fear for his fate if they thought the thieves were poor and desperate. Yet the spoliation on the spot was emphasized and even put first in the demand. Why should Ezza Montano want so specially to tell all Europe that he had picked the pocket before he levied the blackmail?"

"I cannot imagine," said Muscari, rubbing up his black hair for once with an unaffected gesture. "You may think you enlighten me, but you are leading me deeper in the dark. What may be the third objection to the King of the Thieves?" "The third objection," said Father Brown, still in meditation, "is this bank we are sitting on. Why does our brigand-courier call this his chief fortress and the Paradise of Thieves? It is certainly a soft spot to fall on and a sweet spot to look at. It is also quite true, as he says, that it is invisible from valley and peak, and is therefore a hiding-place. But it is not a fortress. It never could be a fortress. I think it would be the worst fortress in the world. For it is actually commanded from above by the common high-road across the mountains—the very place where the police would most probably pass. Why, five shabby short guns held us helpless here about half an hour ago. The quarter of a company of any kind of soldiers could have blown us over the precipice. Whatever is the meaning of this odd little nook of grass and flowers, it is not an entrenched position. It is something else; it has some other strange sort of importance; some value that I do not understand. It is more like an accidental theatre or a natural green-room; it is like the scene for some romantic comedy; it is like. . . ."

As the little priest's words lengthened and lost themselves in a dull and dreamy sincerity, Muscari, whose animal senses were alert and impatient, heard a new noise in the mountains. Even for him the sound was as yet very small and faint; but he could have sworn the evening breeze bore with it something like the pulsation of horses' hoofs and a distant hallooing.

At the same moment, and long before the vibration had touched the less-experienced English ears, Montano the brigand ran up the bank above them and stood in the broken hedge, steadying himself against a tree and peering down the road. He was a strange figure as he stood there, for he had assumed a flapped fantastic hat and swinging baldric and cutlass in his capacity of bandit king, but the bright prosaic tweed of the courier showed through in patches all over him.

The next moment he turned his olive, sneering face and made a movement with his hand. The brigands scattered at the signal, not in confusion, but in what was evidently a kind of guerrilla discipline. Instead of occupying the road along the ridge, they sprinkled themselves along the side of it behind the trees and the hedge, as if watching unseen for an enemy. The noise beyond grew stronger, beginning to shake the mountain road, and a voice could be clearly heard calling out orders. The brigands swayed and huddled, cursing and whispering, and the evening air was full of little metallic noises as they cocked their pistols, or loosened their knives, or trailed their scabbards over the stones. Then the noises from both quarters seemed to meet on the road above; branches broke, horses neighed, men cried out.

"A rescue!" cried Muscari, springing to his feet and waving his hat;

"the gendarmes are on them! Now for freedom and a blow for it! Now to be rebels against robbers! Come, don't let us leave everything to the police; that is so dreadfully modern. Fall on the rear of these ruffians. The gendarmes are rescuing us; come, friends, let us rescue the gendarmes!"

And throwing his hat over the trees, he drew his cutlass once more and began to escalade the slope up to the road. Frank Harrogate jumped up and ran across to help him, revolver in hand, but was astounded to hear himself imperatively recalled by the raucous voice of his father, who seemed to be in great agitation.

"I won't have it," said the banker in a choking voice; "I command you not to interfere."

"But, father," said Frank very warmly, "an Italian gentleman has led the way. You wouldn't have it said that the English hung back."

"It is useless," said the older man, who was trembling violently, "it is useless. We must submit to our lot."

Father Brown looked at the banker; then he put his hand instinctively as if on his heart, but really on the little bottle of poison; and a great light came into his face like the light of the revelation of death.

Muscari meanwhile, without waiting for support, had crested the bank up to the road, and struck the brigand king heavily on the shoulder, causing him to stagger and swing round. Montano also had his cutlass unsheathed, and Muscari, without further speech, sent a slash at his head which he was compelled to catch and parry. But even as the two short blades crossed and clashed the King of Thieves deliberately dropped his point and laughed.

"What's the good, old man?" he said in spirited Italian slang; "this damned farce will soon be over."

"What do you mean, you shuffler?" panted the fire-eating poet. "Is your courage a sham as well as your honesty?"

"Everything about me is a sham," responded the ex-courier in complete good humour. "I am an actor; and if I ever had a private character, I have forgotten it. I am no more a genuine brigand than I am a genuine courier. I am only a bundle of masks, and you can't fight a duel with that." And he laughed with boyish pleasure and fell into his old straddling attitude, with his back to the skirmish up the road.

Darkness was deepening under the mountain walls, and it was not easy to discern much of the progress of the struggle, save that tall men were pushing their horses' muzzles through a clinging crowd of brigands, who seemed more inclined to harass and hustle the invaders than to kill them. It was more like a town crowd preventing the passage of the police than anything the poet had ever pictured as the last stand of doomed and outlawed men of blood. Just as he was rolling his eyes in bewilderment he felt a touch on his elbow, and found the odd little priest standing there like a small Noah with a large hat, and requesting the favour of a word or two.

"Signor Muscari," said the cleric, "in this queer crisis personalities may be pardoned. I may tell you without offence of a way in which you will do more good than by helping the gendarmes, who are bound to break through in any case. You will permit me the impertinent intimacy, but do you care about that girl? Care enough to marry her and make her a good husband, I mean?"

"Yes," said the poet quite simply.

"Does she care about you?"

"I think so," was the equally grave reply.

"Then go over there and offer yourself," said the priest: "offer her everything you can; offer her heaven and earth if you've got them. The time is short."

"Why?" asked the astonished man of letters.

"Because," said Father Brown, "her Doom is coming up the road."

"Nothing is coming up the road," argued Muscari, "except the rescue."

"Well, you go over there," said his adviser, "and be ready to rescue her from the rescue."

Almost as he spoke the hedges were broken all along the ridge by a rush of the escaping brigands. They dived into bushes and thick grass like defeated men pursued; and the great cocked hats of the mounted gendarmerie were seen passing along above the broken hedge. Another order was given; there was a noise of dismounting, and a tall officer with cocked hat, a grey imperial, and a paper in his hand appeared in the gap that was the gate of the Paradise of Thieves. There was a momentary silence, broken in an extraordinary way by the banker, who cried out in a hoarse and strangled voice: "Robbed! I've been robbed!"

"Why, that was hours ago," cried his son in astonishment: "when you were robbed of two thousand pounds."

"Not of two thousand pounds," said the financier, with an abrupt and terrible composure, "only of a small bottle."

The policeman with the grey imperial was striding across the green hollow. Encountering the King of the Thieves in his path, he clapped him on the shoulder with something between a caress and a buffet and gave him a push that sent him staggering away. "You'll get into trouble, too," he said, "if you play these tricks."

Again to Muscari's artistic eye it seemed scarcely like the capture of a great outlaw at bay. Passing on, the policeman halted before the Harrogate group and said: "Samuel Harrogate, I arrest you in the name of the law for embezzlement of the funds of the Hull and Huddersfield Bank."

The great banker nodded with an odd air of business assent, seemed to reflect a moment, and before they could interpose took a half turn and a step that brought him to the edge of the outer mountain wall. Then, flinging up his hands, he leapt exactly as he leapt out of the coach. But this time he did not fall into a little meadow just beneath; he fell a thousand feet below, to become a wreck of bones in the valley.

The anger of the Italian policeman, which he expressed volubly to Father Brown, was largely mixed with admiration. "It was like him to escape us at last," he said. "He was a great brigand if you like. This last trick of his I believe to be absolutely unprecedented. He fled with the company's money to Italy, and actually got himself captured by sham brigands in his own pay, so as to explain both the disappearance of the money and the disappearance of himself. That demand for ransom was really taken seriously by most of the police. But for years he's been doing things as good as that, quite as good as that. He will be a serious loss to his family."

Muscari was leading away the unhappy daughter, who held hard to him, as she did for many a year after. But even in that tragic wreck he could not help having a smile and a hand of half-mocking friendship for the indefensible Ezza Montano. "And where are you going next?" he asked him over his shoulder.

"Birmingham," answered the actor, puffing a cigarette. "Didn't I tell you I was a Futurist? I really do believe in those things if I believe in anything. Change, bustle and new things every morning. I am going to Manchester, Liverpool, Leeds, Hull, Huddersfield, Glasgow, Chicago—in short, to enlightened, energetic, civilized society!"

"In short," said Muscari, "to the real Paradise of Thieves."

CHARLES DICKENS

PERHAPS THE MOST BELOVED AUTHOR EVER TO HAVE WRITTEN in English, Charles Dickens was born in 1812. His father, a clerk in the Naval Pay Office, poorly managed the family's funds and was imprisoned for debt in 1824; his entire family, save for young Charles, was forced to join him in "the poor house" of Marshalsea Prison. Charles, however, was put to work in a blacking factory.

Between 1824 and 1827, Dickens—his father now out of Marshalsea—was a day student at a school in London, and at fifteen he began working as an office boy for an attorney's office. These youthful experiences—child labor, his firsthand familiarity with poverty, the labyrinthine world of bureaucracy—formed the backbone of his imagination, and led to some of the greatest works of fiction we have, among them (though it seems ridiculous to make a short list) *David Copperfield, Great Expectations, The Pickwick Papers, Nicholas Nickleby, A Tale of Two Cities,* and *A Christmas Carol.*

Dickens was a fierce abolitionist and worked through his fiction to change child labor practices. His public readings in England, Scotland, Ireland, France, and America were always sold-out affairs, and readers were known to have waited in line each week to purchase issues of the periodicals in which his novels were serialized.

Universally regarded as a brilliant artist both during his lifetime and to this day, he was a tireless writer whose astounding output brought him great physical illness, resulting in a series of strokes late in his life. He died in 1870 at the family home, Gad's Hill, an estate he had purchased years before and which he had admired all during his childhood. He is buried in Westminster Abbey.

THE WRECK OF THE *GOLDEN MARY*

BY CHARLES DICKENS

The Wreck

I was apprenticed to the Sea when I was twelve years old, and I have encountered a great deal of rough weather, both literal and metaphorical. It has always been my opinion since I first possessed such a thing as an opinion, that the man who knows only one subject is next tiresome to the man who knows no subject. Therefore, in the course of my life I have taught myself whatever I could, and although I am not an educated man, I am able, I am thankful to say, to have an intelligent interest in most things.

A person might suppose, from reading the above, that I am in the habit of holding forth about number one. That is not the case. Just as if I was to come into a room among strangers, and must either be introduced or introduce myself, so I have taken the liberty of passing these few remarks, simply and plainly that it may be known who and what I am. I will add no more of the sort than that my name is William George Ravender, that I was born at Penrith half a year after my own father was drowned, and that I am on the second day of this present blessed Christmas week of one thousand eight hundred and fifty-six, fifty-six years of age.

When the rumour first went flying up and down that there was gold in California—which, as most people know, was before it was discovered in the British colony of Australia—I was in the West Indies, trading among the Islands. Being in command and likewise part-owner of a smart schooner, I had my work cut out for me, and I was doing it. Consequently, gold in California was no business of mine.

But, by the time when I came home to England again, the thing was as clear as your hand held up before you at noon-day. There was

Californian gold in the museums and in the goldsmiths' shops, and the very first time I went upon 'Change, I met a friend of mine (a seafaring man like myself), with a Californian nugget hanging to his watch-chain. I handled it. It was as like a peeled walnut with bits unevenly broken off here and there, and then electrotyped all over, as ever I saw anything in my life.

I am a single man (she was too good for this world and for me, and she died six weeks before our marriage-day), so when I am ashore, I live in my house at Poplar. My house at Poplar is taken care of and kept ship-shape by an old lady who was my mother's maid before I was born. She is as handsome and as upright as any old lady in the world. She is as fond of me as if she had ever had an only son, and I was he. Well do I know wherever I sail that she never lays down her head at night without having said, "Merciful Lord! bless and preserve William George Ravender, and send him safe home, through Christ our Saviour!" I have thought of it in many a dangerous moment, when it has done me no harm, I am sure.

In my house at Poplar, along with this old lady, I lived quiet for best part of a year: having had a long spell of it among the Islands, and having (which was very uncommon in me) taken the fever rather badly. At last, being strong and hearty, and having read every book I could lay hold of, right out, I was walking down Leadenhall Street in the City of London, thinking of turning-to again, when I met what I call Smithick and Watersby of Liverpool. I chanced to lift up my eyes from looking in at a ship's chronometer in a window, and I saw him bearing down upon me, head on.

It is, personally, neither Smithick, nor Watersby, that I here mention, nor was I ever acquainted with any man of either of those names, nor do I think that there has been any one of either of those names in that Liverpool House for years back. But, it is in reality the House itself that I refer to; and a wiser merchant or a truer gentleman never stepped.

"My dear Captain Ravender," says he. "Of all the men on earth, I wanted to see you most. I was on my way to you."

"Well!" says I. "That looks as if you WERE to see me, don't it?" With that I put my arm in his, and we walked on towards the Royal Exchange, and when we got there, walked up and down at the back of it where the Clock-Tower is. We walked an hour and more, for he had much to say to me. He had a scheme for chartering a new ship of their own to take out cargo to the diggers and emigrants in California, and to buy and bring back gold. Into the particulars of that scheme I will not enter, and I have no right to enter. All I say of it is, that it was a very original one, a very fine one, a very sound one, and a very lucrative one beyond doubt.

He imparted it to me as freely as if I had been a part of himself. After doing so, he made me the handsomest sharing offer that ever was made to me, boy or man—or I believe to any other captain in the Merchant Navy—and he took this round turn to finish with:

"Ravender, you are well aware that the lawlessness of that coast and country at present, is as special as the circumstances in which it is placed. Crews of vessels outward-bound, desert as soon as they make the land; crews of vessels homeward-bound, ship at enormous wages, with the express intention of murdering the captain and seizing the gold freight; no man can trust another, and the devil seems let loose. Now," says he, "you know my opinion of you, and you know I am only expressing it, and with no singularity, when I tell you that you are almost the only man on whose integrity, discretion, and energy—" &c., &c. For, I don't want to repeat what he said, though I was and am sensible of it.

Notwithstanding my being, as I have mentioned, quite ready for a voyage, still I had some doubts of this voyage. Of course I knew, without being told, that there were peculiar difficulties and dangers in it, a long way over and above those which attend all voyages. It must not be supposed that I was afraid to face them; but, in my opinion a man has no manly motive or sustainment in his own breast for facing dangers, unless he has well considered what they are, and is able quietly to say to himself, "None of these perils can now take me by surprise; I shall know what to do for the best in any of them; all the rest lies in the higher and greater hands to which I humbly commit myself." On this principle I have so attentively considered (regarding it as my duty) all the hazards I have ever been able to think of, in the ordinary way of storm, shipwreck, and fire at sea, that I hope I should be prepared to do, in any of those cases, whatever could be done, to save the lives intrusted to my charge.

As I was thoughtful, my good friend proposed that he should leave me to walk there as long as I liked, and that I should dine with him by-and-by at his club in Pall Mall. I accepted the invitation and I walked up and down there, quarter-deck fashion, a matter of a couple of hours; now and then looking up at the weathercock as I might have looked up aloft; and now and then taking a look into Cornhill, as I might have taken a look over the side.

All dinner-time, and all after dinner-time, we talked it over again. I gave him my views of his plan, and he very much approved of the same. I told him I had nearly decided, but not quite. "Well, well," says he, "come down to Liverpool to-morrow with me, and see the *Golden Mary*." I liked the name (her name was Mary, and she was golden, if golden stands for good), so I began to feel that it was almost done when I said I would go to Liverpool. On the next morning but one we were on board the *Golden Mary*. I might have known, from his asking me to come down and see her, what she was. I declare her to have been the completest and most exquisite Beauty that ever I set my eyes upon.

We had inspected every timber in her, and had come back to the gangway to go ashore from the dock-basin, when I put out my hand to my friend. "Touch upon it," says I, "and touch heartily. I take command of this ship, and I am hers and yours, if I can get John Steadiman for my chief mate."

John Steadiman had sailed with me four voyages. The first voyage John was third mate out to China, and came home second. The other three voyages he was my first officer. At this time of chartering the *Golden Mary*, he was aged thirty-two. A brisk, bright, blue-eyed fellow, a very neat figure and rather under the middle size, never out of the way and never in it, a face that pleased everybody and that all children took to, a habit of going about singing as cheerily as a blackbird, and a perfect sailor.

We were in one of those Liverpool hackney-coaches in less than a minute, and we cruised about in her upwards of three hours, looking for John. John had come home from Van Diemen's Land barely a month before, and I had heard of him as taking a frisk in Liverpool. We asked after him, among many other places, at the two boarding-houses he was fondest of, and we found he had had a week's spell at each of them; but, he had gone here and gone there, and had set off "to lay out on the main-to'-gallant-yard of the highest Welsh mountain" (so he had told the people of the house), and where he might be then, or when he might come back, nobody could tell us. But it was surprising, to be sure, to see how every face brightened the moment there was mention made of the name of Mr. Steadiman.

We were taken aback at meeting with no better luck, and we had wore ship and put her head for my friends, when as we were jogging through the streets, I clap my eyes on John himself coming out of a toyshop! He was carrying a little boy, and conducting two uncommon pretty women to their coach, and he told me afterwards that he had never in his life seen one of the three before, but that he was so taken with them on looking in at the toyshop while they were buying the child a cranky Noah's Ark, very much down by the head, that he had gone in and asked the ladies' permission to treat him to a tolerably correct Cutter there was in the window, in order that such a handsome boy might not grow up with a lubberly idea of naval architecture.

We stood off and on until the ladies' coachman began to give way, and then we hailed John. On his coming aboard of us, I told him, very gravely, what I had said to my friend. It struck him, as he said himself, amidships. He was quite shaken by it. "Captain Ravender," were John Steadiman's words, "such an opinion from you is true commendation, and I'll sail round the world with you for twenty years if you hoist the signal, and stand by you for ever!" And now indeed I felt that it was done, and that the *Golden Mary* was afloat.

Grass never grew yet under the feet of Smithick and Watersby. The riggers were out of that ship in a fortnight's time, and we had begun taking in cargo. John was always aboard, seeing everything stowed with his own eyes; and whenever I went aboard myself early or late, whether he was below in the hold, or on deck at the hatchway, or overhauling his cabin, nailing up pictures in it of the Blush Roses of England, the Blue Belles of Scotland, and the female Shamrock of Ireland: of a certainty I heard John singing like a blackbird.

We had room for twenty passengers. Our sailing advertisement was no sooner out, than we might have taken these twenty times over. In entering our men, I and John (both together) picked them, and we entered none but good hands—as good as were to be found in that port. And so, in a good ship of the best build, well owned, well arranged, well officered, well manned, well found in all respects, we parted with our pilot at a quarter past four o'clock in the afternoon of the seventh of March, one thousand eight hundred and fifty-one, and stood with a fair wind out to sea.

It may be easily believed that up to that time I had had no leisure to be intimate with my passengers. The most of them were then in their berths sea-sick; however, in going among them, telling them what was good for them, persuading them not to be there, but to come up on deck and feel the breeze, and in rousing them with a joke, or a comfortable word, I made acquaintance with them, perhaps, in a more friendly and confidential way from the first, than I might have done at the cabin table.

Of my passengers, I need only particularise, just at present, a bright-eyed blooming young wife who was going out to join her husband in California, taking with her their only child, a little girl of three years old, whom he had never seen; a sedate young woman in black, some five years older (about thirty as I should say), who was going out to join a brother; and an old gentleman, a good deal like a hawk if his eyes had been better and not so red, who was always talking, morning, noon, and night, about the gold discovery. But, whether he was making the voyage, thinking his old arms could dig for gold, or whether his speculation was to buy it, or to barter for it, or to cheat for it, or to snatch it anyhow from other people, was his secret. He kept his secret.

These three and the child were the soonest well. The child was a most engaging child, to be sure, and very fond of me: though I am bound to admit that John Steadiman and I were borne on her pretty little books in reverse order, and that he was captain there, and I was mate. It was beautiful to watch her with John, and it was beautiful to watch John with her. Few would have thought it possible, to see John playing at bo-peep round the mast, that he was the man who had caught up an iron bar and struck a Malay and a Maltese dead, as they were gliding with their knives down the cabin stair aboard the barque *Old England*, when the captain lay ill in his cot, off Saugar Point. But he was; and give him his back against a bulwark, he would have done the same by half a dozen of them. The name of the young mother was Mrs. Atherfield, the name of the young lady in black was Miss Coleshaw, and the name of the old gentleman was Mr. Rarx.

As the child had a quantity of shining fair hair, clustering in curls all about her face, and as her name was Lucy, Steadiman gave her the name of the Golden Lucy. So, we had the Golden Lucy and the *Golden Mary*; and John kept up the idea to that extent as he and the child went playing about the decks, that I believe she used to think the ship was alive somehow—a sister or companion, going to the same place as herself. She liked to be by the wheel, and in fine weather, I have often stood by the man whose trick it was at the wheel, only to hear her, sitting near my feet, talking to the ship. Never had a child such a doll before, I suppose; but she made a doll of the *Golden Mary*, and used to dress her up by tying ribbons and little bits of finery to the belaying-pins; and nobody ever moved them, unless it was to save them from being blown away.

Of course I took charge of the two young women, and I called them "my dear," and they never minded, knowing that whatever I said was said in a fatherly and protecting spirit. I gave them their places on each side of me at dinner, Mrs. Atherfield on my right and Miss Coleshaw on my left; and I directed the unmarried lady to serve out the breakfast, and the married lady to serve out the tea. Likewise I said to my black steward in their presence, "Tom Snow, these two ladies are equally the mistresses of this house, and do you obey their orders equally;" at which Tom laughed, and they all laughed.

Old Mr. Rarx was not a pleasant man to look at, nor yet to talk to, or to be with, for no one could help seeing that he was a sordid and selfish character, and that he had warped further and further out of the straight with time. Not but what he was on his best behaviour with us, as everybody was; for we had no bickering among us, for'ard or aft. I only mean to say, he was not the man one would have chosen for a messmate. If choice there had been, one might even have gone a few points out of one's course, to say, "No! Not him!" But, there was one curious inconsistency in Mr. Rarx. That was, that he took an astonishing interest in the child. He looked, and I may add, he was, one of the last of men to care at all for a child, or to care much for any human creature. Still, he went so far as to be habitually uneasy, if the child was long on deck, out of his sight. He was always afraid of her falling overboard, or falling down a hatchway, or of a block or what not coming down upon her from the rigging in the working of the ship, or of her getting some hurt or other. He used to look at her and touch her, as if she was something precious to him. He was always solicitous about her not injuring her health, and constantly entreated her mother to be careful of it. This was so much the more curious, because the child did not like him, but used to shrink away from him, and would not even put out her hand to him without coaxing from others. I believe that every soul on board frequently noticed this, and not one of us understood it. However, it was such a plain fact, that John Steadiman said more than once when old Mr. Rarx was not within earshot, that if the *Golden Mary* felt a tenderness for the dear old gentleman she carried in her lap, she must be bitterly jealous of the Golden Lucy.

Before I go any further with this narrative, I will state that our ship was a barque of three hundred tons, carrying a crew of eighteen men, a second mate in addition to John, a carpenter, an armourer or smith, and two apprentices (one a Scotch boy, poor little fellow). We had three boats; the Long-boat, capable of carrying twenty-five men; the Cutter, capable of carrying fifteen; and the Surf-boat, capable of carrying ten. I put down the capacity of these boats according to the numbers they were really meant to hold.

We had tastes of bad weather and head-winds, of course; but, on the whole we had as fine a run as any reasonable man could expect, for sixty days. I then began to enter two remarks in the ship's Log and in my Journal; first, that there was an unusual and amazing quantity of ice; second, that the nights were most wonderfully dark, in spite of the ice.

For five days and a half, it seemed quite useless and hopeless to alter the ship's course so as to stand out of the way of this ice. I made what southing I could; but, all that time, we were beset by it. Mrs.

Atherfield after standing by me on deck once, looking for some time in an awed manner at the great bergs that surrounded us, said in a whisper, "O! Captain Ravender, it looks as if the whole solid earth had changed into ice, and broken up!" I said to her, laughing, "I don't wonder that it does, to your inexperienced eyes, my dear." But I had never seen a twentieth part of the quantity, and, in reality, I was pretty much of her opinion.

However, at two p.m. on the afternoon of the sixth day, that is to say, when we were sixty-six days out, John Steadiman who had gone aloft, sang out from the top, that the sea was clear ahead. Before four p.m. a strong breeze springing up right astern, we were in open water at sunset. The breeze then freshening into half a gale of wind, and the *Golden Mary* being a very fast sailer, we went before the wind merrily, all night.

I had thought it impossible that it could be darker than it had been, until the sun, moon, and stars should fall out of the Heavens, and Time should be destroyed; but, it had been next to light, in comparison with what it was now. The darkness was so profound, that looking into it was painful and oppressive—like looking, without a ray of light, into a dense black bandage put as close before the eyes as it could be, without touching them. I doubled the look-out, and John and I stood in the bow side-by-side, never leaving it all night. Yet I should no more have known that he was near me when he was silent, without putting out my arm and touching him, than I should if he had turned in and been fast asleep below. We were not so much looking out, all of us, as listening to the utmost, both with our eyes and ears.

Next day, I found that the mercury in the barometer, which had risen steadily since we cleared the ice, remained steady. I had had very good observations, with now and then the interruption of a day or so, since our departure. I got the sun at noon, and found that we were in Lat. 58 degrees S., Long. 60 degrees W., off New South Shetland; in the neighbourhood of Cape Horn. We were sixty-seven days out, that day. The ship's reckoning was accurately worked and made up. The ship did her duty admirably, all on board were well, and all hands were as smart, efficient, and contented, as it was possible to be.

When the night came on again as dark as before, it was the eighth night I had been on deck. Nor had I taken more than a very little sleep in the day-time, my station being always near the helm, and often at it, while we were among the ice. Few but those who have tried it can imagine the difficulty and pain of only keeping the eyes open—physically open—under such circumstances, in such darkness. They get struck by the darkness, and blinded by the darkness. They make patterns in it, and they flash in it, as if they had gone out of your head to look at you. On the turn of midnight, John Steadiman, who was alert and fresh (for I had always made him turn in by day), said to me, "Captain Ravender, I entreat of you to go below. I am sure you can hardly stand, and your voice is getting weak, sir. Go below, and take a little rest. I'll call you if a block chafes." I said to John in answer, "Well, well, John! Let us wait till the turn of one o'clock, before we talk about that." I had just had one of the ship's lanterns held up, that I might see how the night went by my watch, and it was then twenty minutes after twelve.

At five minutes before one, John sang out to the boy to bring the lantern again, and when I told him once more what the time was, entreated and prayed of me to go below. "Captain Ravender," says he, "all's well; we can't afford to have you laid up for a single hour; and I respectfully and earnestly beg of you to go below." The end of it was, that I agreed to do so, on the understanding that if I failed to come up of my own accord within three hours, I was to be punctually called. Having settled that, I left John in charge. But I called him to me once afterwards, to ask him a question. I had been to look at the barometer, and had seen the mercury still perfectly steady, and had come up the companion again to take a last look about me—if I can use such a word in reference to such darkness—when I thought that the waves, as the *Golden Mary* parted them and shook them off, had a hollow sound in them; something that I fancied was a rather unusual reverberation. I was standing by the quarter-deck rail on the starboard side, when I called John aft to me, and bade him listen. He did so with the greatest attention. Turning to me he then said, "Rely upon it, Captain Ravender, you have been without rest too long, and the novelty is only in the state of your sense of hearing." I thought so too by that time, and I think so now, though I can never know for absolute certain in this world, whether it was or not.

When I left John Steadiman in charge, the ship was still going at a great rate through the water. The wind still blew right astern. Though she was making great way, she was under shortened sail, and had no more than she could easily carry. All was snug, and nothing complained. There was a pretty sea running, but not a very high sea neither, nor at all a confused one.

I turned in, as we seamen say, all standing. The meaning of that is, I did not pull my clothes off—no, not even so much as my coat: though I did my shoes, for my feet were badly swelled with the deck. There was a little swing-lamp alight in my cabin. I thought, as I looked at it before shutting my eyes, that I was so tired of darkness, and troubled by darkness, that I could have gone to sleep best in the midst of a million of flaming gas-lights. That was the last thought I had before I went off, except the prevailing thought that I should not be able to get to sleep at all.

I dreamed that I was back at Penrith again, and was trying to get round the church, which had altered its shape very much since I last saw it, and was cloven all down the middle of the steeple in a most singular manner. Why I wanted to get round the church I don't know; but I was as anxious to do it as if my life depended on it. Indeed, I believe it did in the dream. For all that, I could not get round the church. I was still trying, when I came against it with a violent shock, and was flung out of my cot against the ship's side. Shrieks and a terrific outcry struck me far harder than the bruising timbers, and amidst sounds of grinding and crashing, and a heavy rushing and breaking of water—sounds I understood too well—I made my way on deck. It was not an easy thing to do, for the ship heeled over frightfully, and was beating in a furious manner.

I could not see the men as I went forward, but I could hear that they were hauling in sail, in disorder. I had my trumpet in my hand, and, after directing and encouraging them in this till it was done, I hailed first John Steadiman, and then my second mate, Mr. William Rames. Both answered clearly and steadily. Now, I had practised them and all my crew, as I have ever made it a custom to practise all who sail with me, to take certain stations and wait my orders, in case of any unexpected crisis. When my voice was heard hailing, and their voices were heard answering, I was aware, through all the noises of the ship and sea, and all the crying of the passengers below, that there was a pause. "Are you ready, Rames?"—"Ay, ay, sir!"—"Then light up, for God's sake!" In a moment he and another were burning blue-lights, and the ship and all on board seemed to be enclosed in a mist of light, under a great black dome.

The light shone up so high that I could see the huge Iceberg upon which we had struck, cloven at the top and down the middle, exactly like Penrith Church in my dream. At the same moment I could see the watch last relieved, crowding up and down on deck; I could see Mrs. Atherfield and Miss Coleshaw thrown about on the top of the companion as they struggled to bring the child up from below; I could see that the masts were going with the shock and the beating of the ship; I could see the frightful breach stove in on the starboard side, half the length of the vessel, and the sheathing and timbers spirting up; I could see that the Cutter was disabled, in a wreck of broken fragments; and I could see every eye turned upon me. It is my belief that if there had been ten thousand eyes there, I should have seen them all, with their different looks. And all this in a moment. But you must consider what a moment.

I saw the men, as they looked at me, fall towards their appointed stations, like good men and true. If she had not righted, they could have done very little there or anywhere but die—not that it is little for a man to die at his post—I mean they could have done nothing to save the passengers and themselves. Happily, however, the violence of the shock with which we had so determinedly borne down direct on that fatal Iceberg, as if it had been our destination instead of our destruction, had so smashed and pounded the ship that she got off in this same instant and righted. I did not want the carpenter to tell me she was filling and going down; I could see and hear that. I gave Rames the word to lower the Long-boat and the Surf-boat, and I myself told off the men for each duty. Not one hung back, or came before the other. I now whispered to John Steadiman, "John, I stand at the gangway here, to see every soul on board safe over the side. You shall have the next post of honour, and shall be the last but one to leave the ship. Bring up the passengers, and range them behind me; and put what provision and water you can got at, in the boats. Cast your eye for'ard, John, and you'll see you have not a moment to lose."

My noble fellows got the boats over the side as orderly as I ever saw boats lowered with any sea running, and, when they were launched, two or three of the nearest men in them as they held on, rising and falling with the swell, called out, looking up at me, "Captain Ravender, if anything goes wrong with us, and you are saved, remember we stood by you!"—"We'll all stand by one another ashore, yet, please God, my lads!" says I. "Hold on bravely, and be tender with the women."

The women were an example to us. They trembled very much, but they were quiet and perfectly collected. "Kiss me, Captain Ravender," says Mrs. Atherfield, "and God in heaven bless you, you good man!" "My dear," says I, "those words are better for me than a life-boat." I held her child in my arms till she was in the boat, and then kissed the child and handed her safe down. I now said to the people in her, "You have got your freight, my lads, all but me, and I am not coming yet awhile. Pull away from the ship, and keep off!"

That was the Long-boat. Old Mr. Rarx was one of her complement, and he was the only passenger who had greatly misbehaved since the ship struck. Others had been a little wild, which was not to be wondered at, and not very blamable; but, he had made a lamentation and uproar which it was dangerous for the people to hear, as there is always contagion in weakness and selfishness. His incessant cry had been that he must not be separated from the child, that he couldn't see the child, and that he and the child must go together. He had even tried to wrest the child out of my arms, that he might keep her in his. "Mr. Rarx," said I to him when it came to that, "I have a loaded pistol in my pocket; and if you don't stand out of the gang-way, and keep perfectly quiet, I shall shoot you through the heart, if you have got one." Says he, "You won't do murder, Captain Ravender!" "No, sir," says I, "I won't murder forty-four people to humour you, but I'll shoot you to save them." After that he was quiet, and stood shivering a little way off, until I named him to go over the side.

The Long-boat being cast off, the Surf-boat was soon filled. There only remained aboard the *Golden Mary*, John Mullion the man who had kept on burning the blue-lights (and who had lighted every new one at every old one before it went out, as quietly as if he had been at an illumination); John Steadiman; and myself. I hurried those two into the Surf-boat, called to them to keep off, and waited with a grateful and relieved heart for the Long-boat to come and take me in, if she could. I looked at my watch, and it showed me, by the blue-light, ten minutes past two. They lost no time. As soon as she was near enough, I swung myself into her, and called to the men, "With a will, lads! She's reeling!" We were not an inch too far out of the inner vortex of her going down, when, by the blue-light which John Mullion still burnt in the bow of the Surf-boat, we saw her lurch, and plunge to the bottom head-foremost. The child cried, weeping wildly, "O the dear *Golden Mary*! O look at her! Save her! Save the poor *Golden Mary*!" And then the light burnt out, and the black dome seemed to come down upon us.

I suppose if we had all stood a-top of a mountain, and seen the whole remainder of the world sink away from under us, we could hardly have felt more shocked and solitary than we did when we knew we were alone on the wide ocean, and that the beautiful ship in which most of us had been securely asleep within half an hour was gone for ever. There was an awful silence in our boat, and such a kind of palsy on the rowers and the man at the rudder, that I felt they were scarcely keeping her before the sea. I spoke out then, and said, "Let every one here thank the Lord for our preservation!" All the voices answered (even the child's), "We thank the Lord!" I then said the Lord's Prayer, and all hands said it after me with a solemn murmuring. Then I gave the word "Cheerily, O men, Cheerily!" and I felt that they were handling the boat again as a boat ought to be handled.

The Surf-boat now burnt another blue-light to show us where they were, and we made for her, and laid ourselves as nearly alongside of her as we dared. I had always kept my boats with a coil or two of good stout stuff in each of them, so both boats had a rope at hand. We made a shift, with much labour and trouble, to got near enough to one another to divide the blue-lights (they were no use after that night, for the sea-water soon got at them), and to get a tow-rope out between us. All night long we kept together, sometimes obliged to cast off the rope, and sometimes getting it out again, and all of us wearying for the morning—which appeared so long in coming that old Mr. Rarx screamed out, in spite of his fears of me, "The world is drawing to an end, and the sun will never rise any more!"

When the day broke, I found that we were all huddled together in a miserable manner. We were deep in the water; being, as I found on mustering, thirty-one in number, or at least six too many. In the Surf-boat they were fourteen in number, being at least four too many. The first thing I did, was to get myself passed to the rudder—which I took from that time—and to get Mrs. Atherfield, her child, and Miss Coleshaw, passed on to sit next me. As to old Mr. Rarx, I put him in the bow, as far from us as I could. And I put some of the best men near us in order that if I should drop there might be a skilful hand ready to take the helm.

The sea moderating as the sun came up, though the sky was cloudy and wild, we spoke the other boat, to know what stores they had, and to overhaul what we had. I had a compass in my pocket, a small telescope, a double-barrelled pistol, a knife, and a fire-box and matches. Most of my men had knives, and some had a little tobacco: some, a pipe as well. We had a mug among us, and an iron spoon. As to provisions, there were in my boat two bags of biscuit, one piece of raw beef, one piece of raw pork, a bag of coffee, roasted but not ground (thrown in, I imagine, by mistake, for something else), two small casks of water, and about half-a-gallon of rum in a keg. The Surf-boat, having rather more rum than we, and fewer to drink it, gave us, as I estimated, another quart into our keg. In return, we gave them three double handfuls of coffee, tied up in a piece of a handkerchief; they reported that they had aboard besides, a bag of biscuit, a piece of beef, a small cask of water, a small box of lemons, and a Dutch cheese. It took a long time to make these exchanges, and they were not made without risk to both parties; the sea running quite high enough to make our approaching near to one another very hazardous. In the bundle with the coffee, I conveyed to John Steadiman (who had a ship's compass with him), a paper written in pencil, and torn from my pocket-book, containing the course I meant to steer, in the hope of making land, or being picked up by some vessel—I say in the hope, though I had little hope of either deliverance. I then sang out to him, so as all might hear, that if we two boats could live or die together, we would; but, that if we should be parted by the weather, and join company no more, they should have our prayers and blessings, and we asked for theirs. We then gave them three cheers, which they returned, and I saw the men's heads droop in both boats as they fell to their oars again.

These arrangements had occupied the general attention advantageously for all, though (as I expressed in the last sentence) they ended in a sorrowful feeling. I now said a few words to my fellow-voyagers on the subject of the small stock of food on which our lives depended if they were preserved from the great deep, and on the rigid necessity of our eking it out in the most frugal manner. One and all replied that whatever allowance I thought best to lay down should be strictly kept to. We made a pair of scales out of a thin scrap of iron-plating and some twine, and I got together for weights such of the heaviest buttons among us as I calculated made up some fraction over two ounces. This was the allowance of solid food served out once a-day to each, from that time to the end; with the addition of a coffee-berry, or sometimes half a one, when the weather was very fair, for breakfast. We had nothing else whatever, but half a pint of water each per day, and sometimes, when we were coldest and weakest, a teaspoonful of rum each, served out as a dram. I know how learnedly it can be shown that rum is poison, but I also know that in this case, as in all similar cases I have ever read of—which are numerous—no words can express the comfort and support derived from it. Nor have I the least doubt that it saved the lives of far more than half our number. Having mentioned half a pint of water as our daily allowance, I ought to observe that sometimes we had less, and sometimes we had more; for much rain fell, and we caught it in a canvas stretched for the purpose.

Thus, at that tempestuous time of the year, and in that tempestuous part of the world, we shipwrecked people rose and fell with the waves. It is not my intention to relate (if I can avoid it) such circumstances appertaining to our doleful condition as have been better told in many other narratives of the kind than I can be expected to tell them. I will only note, in so many passing words, that day after day and night after night, we received the sea upon our backs to prevent it from swamping the boat; that one party was always kept baling, and that every hat and cap among us soon got worn out, though patched up fifty times, as the only vessels we had for that service; that another party lay down in the bottom of the boat, while a third rowed; and that we were soon all in boils and blisters and rags.

The other boat was a source of such anxious interest to all of us that I used to wonder whether, if we were saved, the time could ever come when the survivors in this boat of ours could be at all indifferent to the fortunes of the survivors in that. We got out a tow-rope whenever the weather permitted, but that did not often happen, and how we two parties kept within the same horizon, as we did, He, who mercifully permitted it to be so for our consolation, only knows. I never shall forget the looks with which, when the morning light came, we used to gaze about us over the stormy waters, for the other boat. We once parted company for seventy-two hours, and we believed them to have gone down, as they did us. The joy on both sides when we came within view of one another again, had something in a manner Divine in it; each was so forgetful of individual suffering, in tears of delight and sympathy for the people in the other boat.

I have been wanting to get round to the individual or personal part of my subject, as I call it, and the foregoing incident puts me in the right way. The patience and good disposition aboard of us, was wonderful. I was not surprised by it in the women; for all men born of women know what great qualities they will show when men will fail; but, I own I was a little surprised by it in some of the men. Among one-and-thirty people assembled at the best of times, there will usually, I should say, be two or three uncertain tempers. I knew that I had more than one rough temper with me among my own people, for I had chosen those for the Long-boat that I might have them under my eye. But, they softened under their misery, and were as considerate of the ladies, and as compassionate of the child, as the best among us, or among men—they could not have been more so. I heard scarcely any complaining. The party lying down would moan a good deal in their sleep, and I would often notice a man—not always the same man, it is to be understood, but nearly all of them at one time or other—sitting moaning at his oar, or in his place, as he looked mistily over the sea. When it happened to be long before I could catch his eye, he would go on moaning all the time in the dismallest manner; but, when our looks met, he would brighten and leave off. I almost always got the impression that he did not know what sound he had been making, but that he thought he had been humming a tune.

Our sufferings from cold and wet were far greater than our sufferings from hunger. We managed to keep the child warm; but, I doubt if any one else among us ever was warm for five minutes together; and the shivering, and the chattering of teeth, were sad to hear. The child cried a little at first for her lost playfellow, the *Golden Mary*; but hardly ever whimpered afterwards; and when the state of the weather made it possible, she used now and then to be held up in the arms of some of us, to look over the sea for John Steadiman's boat. I see the golden hair and the innocent face now, between me and the driving clouds, like an angel going to fly away.

It had happened on the second day, towards night, that Mrs. Atherfield, in getting Little Lucy to sleep, sang her a song. She had a soft, melodious voice, and, when she had finished it, our people up and begged for another. She sang them another, and after it had fallen dark ended with the Evening Hymn. From that time, whenever anything could be heard above the sea and wind, and while she had any voice left, nothing would serve the people but that she should sing at sunset. She always did, and always ended with the Evening Hymn. We mostly took up the last line, and shed tears when it was done, but not miserably. We had a prayer night and morning, also, when the weather allowed of it.

Twelve nights and eleven days we had been driving in the boat, when old Mr. Rarx began to be delirious, and to cry out to me to throw the gold overboard or it would sink us, and we should all be lost. For days past the child had been declining, and that was the great cause of his wildness. He had been over and over again shrieking out to me to give her all the remaining meat, to give her all the remaining rum, to save her at any cost, or we should all be ruined. At this time, she lay in her mother's arms at my feet. One of her little hands was almost always creeping about her mother's neck or chin. I had watched the wasting of the little hand, and I knew it was nearly over.

The old man's cries were so discordant with the mother's love and submission, that I called out to him in an angry voice, unless he held his peace on the instant, I would order him to be knocked on the head and thrown overboard. He was mute then, until the child died, very peacefully, an hour afterwards: which was known to all in the boat by the mother's breaking out into lamentations for the first time since the wreck—for, she had great fortitude and constancy, though she was a little gentle woman. Old Mr. Rarx then became quite ungovernable, tearing what rags he had on him, raging in imprecations, and calling to me that if I had thrown the gold overboard (always the gold with him!) I might have saved the child. "And now," says he, in a terrible voice, "we shall founder, and all go to the Devil, for our sins will sink us, when we have no innocent child to bear us up!" We so discovered with amazement, that this old wretch had only cared for the life of the pretty little creature dear to all of us, because of the influence he superstitiously hoped she might have in preserving him! Altogether it was too much for the smith or armourer, who was sitting next the old man, to bear. He took him by the throat and rolled him under the thwarts, where he lay still enough for hours afterwards.

All that thirteenth night, Miss Coleshaw, lying across my knees as I kept the helm, comforted and supported the poor mother. Her child, covered with a pea-jacket of mine, lay in her lap. It troubled me all night to think that there was no Prayer-Book among us, and that I could remember but very few of the exact words of the burial service. When I stood up at broad day, all knew what was going to be done, and I noticed that my poor fellows made the motion of uncovering their heads, though their heads had been stark bare to the sky and sea for many a weary hour. There was a long heavy swell on, but otherwise it was a fair morning, and there were broad fields of sunlight on the waves in the east. I said no more than this: "I am the Resurrection and the Life, saith the Lord. He raised the daughter of

Jairus the ruler, and said she was not dead but slept. He raised the widow's son. He arose Himself, and was seen of many. He loved little children, saying, Suffer them to come unto Me and rebuke them not, for of such is the kingdom of heaven. In His name, my friends, and committed to His merciful goodness!" With those words I laid my rough face softly on the placid little forehead, and buried the Golden Lucy in the grave of the *Golden Mary*.

Having had it on my mind to relate the end of this dear little child, I have omitted something from its exact place, which I will supply here. It will come quite as well here as anywhere else.

Foreseeing that if the boat lived through the stormy weather, the time must come, and soon come, when we should have absolutely no morsel to eat, I had one momentous point often in my thoughts. Although I had, years before that, fully satisfied myself that the instances in which human beings in the last distress have fed upon each other, are exceedingly few, and have very seldom indeed (if ever) occurred when the people in distress, however dreadful their extremity, have been accustomed to moderate forbearance and restraint; I say, though I had long before quite satisfied my mind on this topic, I felt doubtful whether there might not have been in former cases some harm and danger from keeping it out of sight and pretending not to think of it. I felt doubtful whether some minds, growing weak with fasting and exposure and having such a terrific idea to dwell upon in secret, might not magnify it until it got to have an awful attraction about it. This was not a new thought of mine, for it had grown out of my reading. However, it came over me stronger than it had ever done before—as it had reason for doing—in the boat, and on the fourth day I decided that I would bring out into the light that unformed fear which must have been more or less darkly in every brain among us. Therefore, as a means of beguiling the time and inspiring hope, I gave them the best summary in my power of Bligh's voyage of more than three thousand miles, in an open boat, after the Mutiny of the Bounty, and of the wonderful preservation of that boat's crew. They listened throughout with great interest, and I concluded by telling them, that, in my opinion, the happiest circumstance in the whole narrative was, that Bligh, who was no delicate man either, had solemnly placed it on record therein that he was sure and certain that under no conceivable circumstances whatever would that emaciated party, who had gone through all the pains of famine, have preyed on one another. I cannot describe the visible relief which this spread through the boat, and how the tears stood in every eye. From that time I was as well convinced as Bligh himself that there was no danger, and that this phantom, at any rate, did not haunt us.

Now, it was a part of Bligh's experience that when the people in his boat were most cast down, nothing did them so much good as hearing a story told by one of their number. When I mentioned that, I saw that it struck the general attention as much as it did my own, for I had not thought of it until I came to it in my summary. This was on the day after Mrs. Atherfield first sang to us. I proposed that, whenever the weather would permit, we should have a story two hours after dinner (I always issued the allowance I have mentioned at one o'clock, and called it by that name), as well as our song at sunset. The proposal was received with a cheerful satisfaction that warmed my heart within me; and I do not say too much when I say that those two periods in the four-and-twenty hours were expected with positive pleasure, and were really enjoyed by all hands. Spectres as we soon were in our bodily wasting, our imaginations did not perish like the gross flesh upon our bones. Music and Adventure, two of the great gifts of Providence to mankind, could charm us long after that was lost.

The wind was almost always against us after the second day; and for many days together we could not nearly hold our own. We had all varieties of bad weather. We had rain, hail, snow, wind, mist, thunder and lightning. Still the boats lived through the heavy seas, and still we perishing people rose and fell with the great waves.

Sixteen nights and fifteen days, twenty nights and nineteen days, twenty-four nights and twenty-three days. So the time went on. Disheartening as I knew that our progress, or want of progress, must be, I never deceived them as to my calculations of it. In the first place, I felt that we were all too near eternity for deceit; in the second place, I knew that if I failed, or died, the man who followed me must have a knowledge of the true state of things to begin upon. When I told them at noon, what I reckoned we had made or lost, they generally received what I said in a tranquil and resigned manner, and always gratefully towards me. It was not unusual at any time of the day for some one to burst out weeping loudly without any new cause; and, when the burst was over, to calm down a little better than before. I had seen exactly the same thing in a house of mourning.

During the whole of this time, old Mr. Rarx had had his fits of calling out to me to throw the gold (always the gold!) overboard, and of heaping violent reproaches upon me for not having saved the child; but now, the food being all gone, and I having nothing left to serve out but a bit of coffee-berry now and then, he began to be too weak to do this, and consequently fell silent. Mrs. Atherfield and Miss Coleshaw generally lay, each with an arm across one of my knees, and her head upon it. They never complained at all. Up to the time of her child's death, Mrs. Atherfield had bound up her own beautiful hair every day; and I took particular notice that this was always before she sang her song at night, when everyone looked at her. But she never did it after the loss of her darling; and it would have been now all tangled with dirt and wet, but that Miss Coleshaw was careful of it long after she was herself, and would sometimes smooth it down with her weak thin hands.

We were past mustering a story now; but one day, at about this period, I reverted to the superstition of old Mr. Rarx, concerning the Golden Lucy, and told them that nothing vanished from the eye of God, though much might pass away from the eyes of men. "We were all of us," says I, "children once; and our baby feet have strolled in green woods ashore; and our baby hands have gathered flowers in gardens, where the birds were singing. The children that we were, are not lost to the great knowledge of our Creator. Those innocent creatures will appear with us before Him, and plead for us. What we were in the best time of our generous youth will arise and go with us too. The purest part of our lives will not desert us at the pass to which all of us here present are gliding. What we were then, will be as much in existence before Him, as what we are now." They were no less comforted by this consideration, than I was myself; and Miss Coleshaw, drawing my ear nearer to her lips, said, "Captain Ravender, I was on my way to marry a disgraced and broken man, whom I dearly loved when he was honourable and good. Your words seem to have come out of my own poor heart." She pressed my hand upon it, smiling.

Twenty-seven nights and twenty-six days. We were in no want of rain-water, but we had nothing else. And yet, even now, I never turned my eyes upon a waking face but it tried to brighten before mine. O, what a thing it is, in a time of danger and in the presence of death, the shining of a face upon a face! I have heard it broached that orders should be given in great new ships by electric telegraph. I admire machinery as much is any man, and am as thankful to it as any man can be for what it does for us. But it will never be a substitute for the face of a man, with his soul in it, encouraging another man to be brave and true. Never try it for that. It will break down like a straw.

I now began to remark certain changes in myself which I did not like. They caused me much disquiet. I often saw the Golden Lucy in the air above the boat. I often saw her I have spoken of before, sitting beside me. I saw the *Golden Mary* go down, as she really had gone down, twenty times in a day. And yet the sea was mostly, to my thinking, not sea neither, but moving country and extraordinary mountainous regions, the like of which have never been beheld. I felt it time to leave my last words regarding John Steadiman, in case any lips should last out to repeat them to any living ears. I said that John had told me (as he had on deck) that he had sung out "Breakers ahead!" the instant they were audible, and had tried to wear ship, but she struck before it could be done. (His cry, I dare say, had made my dream.) I said that the circumstances were altogether without warning, and out of any course that could have been guarded against; that the same loss would have happened if I had been in charge; and that John was not to blame, but from first to last had done his duty nobly, like the man he was. I tried to write it down in my pocket-book, but could make no words, though I knew what the words were that I wanted to make. When it had come to that, her hands—though she was dead so long—laid me down gently in the bottom of the boat, and she and the Golden Lucy swung me to sleep.

ALL THAT FOLLOWS, WAS WRITTEN BY
JOHN STEADIMAN, CHIEF MATE.

On the twenty-sixth day after the foundering of the *Golden Mary* at sea, I, John Steadiman, was sitting in my place in the stern-sheets of the Surf-boat, with just sense enough left in me to steer—that is to say, with my eyes strained, wide-awake, over the bows of the boat, and my brains fast asleep and dreaming—when I was roused upon a sudden by our second mate, Mr. William Rames.

"Let me take a spell in your place," says he. "And look you out for the Long-boat astern. The last time she rose on the crest of a wave, I thought I made out a signal flying aboard her."

We shifted our places, clumsily and slowly enough, for we were both of us weak and dazed with wet, cold, and hunger. I waited some time, watching the heavy rollers astern, before the Long-boat rose a-top of one of them at the same time with us. At last, she was heaved up for a moment well in view, and there, sure enough, was the signal flying aboard of her—a strip of rag of some sort, rigged to an oar, and hoisted in her bows.

"What does it mean?" says Rames to me in a quavering, trembling sort of voice. "Do they signal a sail in sight?"

"Hush, for God's sake!" says I, clapping my hand over his mouth. "Don't let the people hear you. They'll all go mad together if we mislead them about that signal. Wait a bit, till I have another look at it."

I held on by him, for he had set me all of a tremble with his notion of a sail in sight, and watched for the Long-boat again. Up she rose on the top of another roller. I made out the signal clearly, that second time, and saw that it was rigged half-mast high.

"Rames," says I, "it's a signal of distress. Pass the word forward to keep her before the sea, and no more. We must get the Long-boat within hailing distance of us, as soon as possible."

I dropped down into my old place at the tiller without another word—for the thought went through me like a knife that something had happened to Captain Ravender. I should consider myself unworthy to write another line of this statement, if I had not made up my mind to speak the truth, the whole truth, and nothing but the truth—and I must, therefore, confess plainly that now, for the first time, my heart sank within me. This weakness on my part was produced in some degree, as I take it, by the exhausting effects of previous anxiety and grief.

Our provisions—if I may give that name to what we had left—were reduced to the rind of one lemon and about a couple of handsfull of coffee-berries. Besides these great distresses, caused by the death, the danger, and the suffering among my crew and passengers, I had had a little distress of my own to shake me still more, in the death of the child whom I had got to be very fond of on the voyage out—so fond that I was secretly a little jealous of her being taken in the Long-boat instead of mine when the ship foundered. It used to be a great comfort to me, and I think to those with me also, after we had seen the last of the *Golden Mary*, to see the Golden Lucy, held up by the men in the Long-boat, when the weather allowed it, as the best and brightest sight they had to show. She looked, at the distance we saw her from, almost like a little white bird in the air. To miss her for the first time, when the weather lulled a little again, and we all looked out for our white bird and looked in vain, was a sore disappointment. To see the men's heads bowed down and the captain's hand pointing into the sea when we hailed the Long-boat, a few days after, gave me as heavy a shock and as sharp a pang of heartache to bear as ever I remember suffering in all my life. I only mention these things to show that if I did give way a little at first, under the dread that our captain was lost to us, it was not without having been a good deal shaken beforehand by more trials of one sort or another than often fall to one man's share.

I had got over the choking in my throat with the help of a drop of water, and had steadied my mind again so as to be prepared against the worst, when I heard the hail (Lord help the poor fellows, how weak it sounded!)—

"Surf-boat, ahoy!"

I looked up, and there were our companions in misfortune tossing abreast of us; not so near that we could make out the features of any of them, but near enough, with some exertion for people in our condition, to make their voices heard in the intervals when the wind was weakest.

I answered the hail, and waited a bit, and heard nothing, and then sung out the captain's name. The voice that replied did not sound like his; the words that reached us were:

"Chief-mate wanted on board!"

Every man of my crew knew what that meant as well as I did. As second officer in command, there could be but one reason for wanting me on board the Long-boat. A groan went all round us, and my men looked darkly in each other's faces, and whispered under their breaths:

"The captain is dead!"

I commanded them to be silent, and not to make too sure of bad news, at such a pass as things had now come to with us. Then, hailing the Long-boat, I signified that I was ready to go on board when the weather would let me—stopped a bit to draw a good long breath—and then called out as loud as I could the dreadful question:

"Is the captain dead?"

The black figures of three or four men in the after-part of the Long-boat all stooped down together as my voice reached them. They were lost to view for about a minute; then appeared again—one man among them was held up on his feet by the rest, and he hailed back the blessed words (a very faint hope went a very long way with people in our desperate situation): "Not yet!"

The relief felt by me, and by all with me, when we knew that our captain, though unfitted for duty, was not lost to us, it is not in words—at least, not in such words as a man like me can command—to express. I did my best to cheer the men by telling them what a good sign it was that we were not as badly off yet as we had feared; and then communicated what instructions I had to give, to William Rames, who was to be left in command in my place when I took charge of the Long-boat. After that, there was nothing to be done, but to wait for the chance of the wind dropping at sunset, and the sea going down afterwards, so as to enable our weak crews to lay the two boats alongside of each other, without undue risk—or, to put it plainer, without saddling ourselves with the necessity for any extraordinary exertion of strength or skill. Both the one and the other had now been starved out of us for days and days together.

At sunset the wind suddenly dropped, but the sea, which had

been running high for so long a time past, took hours after that before it showed any signs of getting to rest. The moon was shining, the sky was wonderfully clear, and it could not have been, according to my calculations, far off midnight, when the long, slow, regular swell of the calming ocean fairly set in, and I took the responsibility of lessening the distance between the Long-boat and ourselves.

It was, I dare say, a delusion of mine; but I thought I had never seen the moon shine so white and ghastly anywhere, either on sea or on land, as she shone that night while we were approaching our companions in misery. When there was not much more than a boat's length between us, and the white light streamed cold and clear over all our faces, both crews rested on their oars with one great shudder, and stared over the gunwale of either boat, panic-stricken at the first sight of each other.

"Any lives lost among you?" I asked, in the midst of that frightful silence.

The men in the Long-bout huddled together like sheep at the sound of my voice.

"None yet, but the child, thanks be to God!" answered one among them.

And at the sound of his voice, all my men shrank together like the men in the Long-boat. I was afraid to let the horror produced by our first meeting at close quarters after the dreadful changes that wet, cold, and famine had produced, last one moment longer than could be helped; so, without giving time for any more questions and answers, I commanded the men to lay the two boats close alongside of each other. When I rose up and committed the tiller to the hands of Rames, all my poor fellows raised their white faces imploringly to mine. "Don't leave us, sir," they said, "don't leave us." "I leave you," says I, "under the command and the guidance of Mr. William Rames, as good a sailor as I am, and as trusty and kind a man as ever stepped. Do your duty by him, as you have done it by me; and remember to the last, that while there is life there is hope. God bless and help you all!" With those words I collected what strength I had left, and caught at two arms that were held out to me, and so got from the stern-sheets of one boat into the stern-sheets of the other.

"Mind where you step, sir," whispered one of the men who had helped me into the Long-boat. I looked down as he spoke. Three figures were huddled up below me, with the moonshine falling on them in ragged streaks through the gaps between the men standing or sitting above them. The first face I made out was the face of Miss Coleshaw, her eyes were wide open and fixed on me. She seemed still to keep her senses, and, by the alternate parting and closing of her lips, to be trying to speak, but I could not hear that she uttered a single word. On her shoulder rested the head of Mrs. Atherfield. The mother of our poor little Golden Lucy must, I think, have been dreaming of the child she had lost; for there was a faint smile just ruffling the white stillness of her face, when I first saw it turned upward, with peaceful closed eyes towards the heavens. From her, I looked down a little, and there, with his head on her lap, and with one of her hands resting tenderly on his cheek—there lay the Captain, to whose help and guidance, up to this miserable time, we had never looked in vain,—there, worn out at last in our service, and for our sakes, lay the best and bravest man of all our company. I stole my hand in gently through his clothes and laid it on his heart, and felt a little feeble warmth over it, though my cold dulled touch could not detect even the faintest beating. The two men in the stern-sheets with me, noticing what I was doing—knowing I loved him like a brother—and seeing, I suppose, more distress in my face than I myself was conscious of its showing, lost command over themselves altogether, and burst into a piteous moaning, sobbing lamentation over him. One of the two drew aside a jacket from his feet, and showed me that they were bare, except where a wet, ragged strip of stocking still clung to one of them. When the ship struck the Iceberg, he had run on deck leaving his shoes in his cabin. All through the voyage in the boat his feet had been unprotected; and not a soul had discovered it until he dropped! As long as he could keep his eyes open, the very look of them had cheered the men, and comforted and upheld the women. Not one living creature in the boat, with any sense about him, but had felt the good influence of that brave man in one way or another. Not one but had heard him, over and over again, give the credit to others which was due only to himself; praising this man for patience, and thanking that man for help, when the patience and the help had really and truly, as to the best part of both, come only from him. All this, and much more, I heard pouring confusedly from the men's lips while they crouched down, sobbing and crying over their commander, and wrapping the jacket as warmly and tenderly as they could over is cold feet. It went to my heart to check them; but I knew that if this lamenting spirit spread any further, all chance of keeping alight any last sparks of hope and resolution among the boat's company would be lost for ever. Accordingly I sent them to their places, spoke a few encouraging words to the men forward, promising to serve out, when the morning came, as much as I dared, of any eatable thing left in the lockers; called to Rames, in my old boat, to keep as near us as he safely could;

drew the garments and coverings of the two poor suffering women more closely about them; and, with a secret prayer to be directed for the best in bearing the awful responsibility now laid on my shoulders, took my Captain's vacant place at the helm of the Long-boat.

This, as well as I can tell it, is the full and true account of how I came to be placed in charge of the lost passengers and crew of the *Golden Mary*, on the morning of the twenty-seventh day after the ship struck the Iceberg, and foundered at sea.

MARY E. WILKINS FREEMAN

Mary Ella Wilkins Freeman was born in 1852 in Randolph, Massachusetts. Her parents, having lost their first child in infancy ten months before, were doting yet stern, and raised her in a household built on New England Puritan values. Never a particularly healthy child or adult, Freeman lost her three-year-old brother when she was six, and her younger sister by seven years died when she was seventeen and Freeman was twenty-four. These losses haunted much of her work and formed the basis for the haunted texture to many of her stories.

After graduating high school in 1870, Freeman attended Mt. Holyoke Female Seminary, staying only one year before returning home. She worked for a while as a teacher, then tried painting, until finally settling upon writing, discovering she had a gift for story after showing her work to her father and to a Vermont clergyman, both of whom urged her to pursue her craft. Her first successes were writing for children, but in 1882, she won a fifty-dollar award from the *Boston Sunday Budget* for her first story for adults; she then sent another story to *Harper's Bazaar,* which accepted the work, thereby beginning a long and respected career with that publication. In 1887 her book A *Humble Romance and Other Stories* was published, followed by *A New England Nun and Other Stories* in 1891, and arguably her best work, *Pembroke,* in 1894.

Freedman continued to write, and in 1926 was awarded the William

Dean Howells Gold Medal for Fiction by the American Academy of Letters; later that year she and Edith Wharton became the first women inducted into the National Institute of Arts and Letters. Though hers is now a name that has faded with time, her impact upon American literature, and especially of the depiction of women of abiding faith, cannot be underestimated. She died of heart failure at her home in Metuchen, New Jersey, in March of 1930.

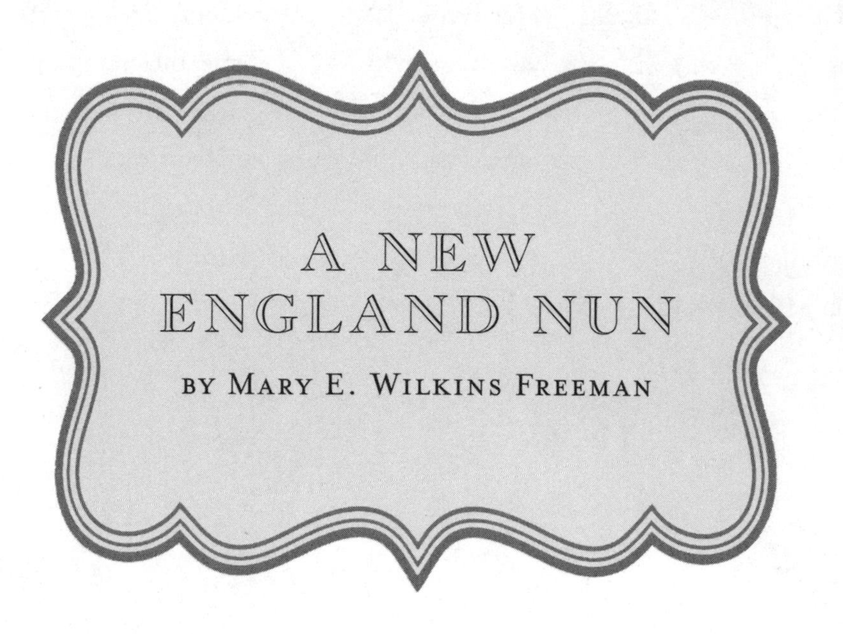

A NEW ENGLAND NUN

BY MARY E. WILKINS FREEMAN

It was late in the afternoon, and the light was waning. There was a difference in the look of the tree shadows out in the yard. Somewhere in the distance cows were lowing and a little bell was tinkling; now and then a farm-wagon tilted by, and the dust flew; some blue-shirted laborers with shovels over their shoulders plodded past; little swarms of flies were dancing up and down before the peoples' faces in the soft air. There seemed to be a gentle stir arising over everything for the mere sake of subsidence—a very premonition of rest and hush and night.

This soft diurnal commotion was over Louisa Ellis also. She had been peacefully sewing at her sitting-room window all the afternoon. Now she quilted her needle carefully into her work, which she folded precisely, and laid in a basket with her thimble and thread and scissors. Louisa Ellis could not remember that ever in her life she had mislaid one of these little feminine appurtenances, which had become, from long use and constant association, a very part of her personality.

Louisa tied a green apron round her waist, and got out a flat straw hat with a green ribbon. Then she went into the garden with a little blue crockery bowl, to pick some currants for her tea. After the currants were picked she sat on the back doorstep and stemmed them, collecting the stems carefully in her apron, and afterwards throwing them into the hen-coop. She looked sharply at the grass beside the step to see if any had fallen there.

Louisa was slow and still in her movements; it took her a long time to prepare her tea; but when ready it was set forth with as much grace as if she had been a veritable guest to her own self. The little square table stood exactly in the centre of the kitchen, and was covered with a starched linen cloth whose border pattern of flowers glistened. Louisa had a damask napkin on her tea-tray, where were arranged a cut-glass tumbler full of teaspoons, a silver cream-pitcher, a china sugar-bowl, and one pink china cup and saucer. Louisa used china every day—something which none of her neighbors did. They whispered about it among themselves. Their daily tables were laid with common crockery, their sets of best china stayed in the parlor closet, and Louisa Ellis was no richer nor better bred than they. Still she would use the china. She had for her supper a glass dish full of sugared currants, a plate of little cakes, and one of light white biscuits. Also a leaf or two of lettuce, which she cut up daintily. Louisa was very fond of lettuce, which she raised to perfection in her little garden. She ate quite heartily, though in a delicate, pecking way; it seemed almost surprising that any considerable bulk of the food should vanish.

After tea she filled a plate with nicely baked thin corn-cakes, and carried them out into the back-yard.

"Caesar!" she called. "Caesar! Caesar!"

There was a little rush, and the clank of a chain, and a large yellow-and-white dog appeared at the door of his tiny hut, which was half hidden among the tall grasses and flowers. Louisa patted him and gave him the corn-cakes. Then she returned to the house and washed the tea-things, polishing the china carefully. The twilight had deepened; the chorus of the frogs floated in at the open window wonderfully loud and shrill, and once in a while a long sharp drone from a tree-toad pierced it. Louisa took off her green gingham apron, disclosing a shorter one of pink and white print. She lighted her lamp, and sat down again with her sewing.

In about half an hour Joe Dagget came. She heard his heavy step on the walk, and rose and took off her pink-and-white apron. Under that was still another—white linen with a little cambric edging on the bottom; that was Louisa's company apron. She never wore it without her calico sewing apron over it unless she had a guest. She had barely folded the pink and white one with methodical haste and laid it in a table-drawer when the door opened and Joe Dagget entered.

He seemed to fill up the whole room. A little yellow canary that had been asleep in his green cage at the south window woke up and fluttered wildly, beating his little yellow wings against the wires. He always did so when Joe Dagget came into the room.

"Good-evening," said Louisa. She extended her hand with a kind of solemn cordiality.

"Good-evening, Louisa," returned the man, in a loud voice.

She placed a chair for him, and they sat facing each other, with the table between them. He sat bolt-upright, toeing out his heavy feet squarely, glancing with a good-humored uneasiness around the room. She sat gently erect, folding her slender hands in her white-linen lap.

"Been a pleasant day," remarked Dagget.

"Real pleasant," Louisa assented, softly. "Have you been haying?" she asked, after a little while.

"Yes, I've been haying all day, down in the ten-acre lot. Pretty hot work."

"It must be."

"Yes, it's pretty hot work in the sun."

"Is your mother well to-day?"

"Yes, mother's pretty well."

"I suppose Lily Dyer's with her now?"

Dagget colored. "Yes, she's with her," he answered, slowly.

He was not very young, but there was a boyish look about his large face. Louisa was not quite as old as he, her face was fairer and smoother, but she gave people the impression of being older.

"I suppose she's a good deal of help to your mother," she said, further.

"I guess she is; I don't know how mother'd get along without her," said Dagget, with a sort of embarrassed warmth.

"She looks like a real capable girl. She's pretty-looking too," remarked Louisa.

"Yes, she is pretty fair looking."

Presently Dagget began fingering the books on the table. There was a square red autograph album, and a Young Lady's Gift-Book which had belonged to Louisa's mother. He took them up one after the other and opened them; then laid them down again, the album on the Gift-Book.

Louisa kept eying them with mild uneasiness. Finally she rose and changed the position of the books, putting the album underneath. That was the way they had been arranged in the first place.

Dagget gave an awkward little laugh. "Now what difference did it make which book was on top?" said he.

Louisa looked at him with a deprecating smile. "I always keep them that way," murmured she.

"You do beat everything," said Dagget, trying to laugh again. His large face was flushed.

He remained about an hour longer, then rose to take leave. Going out, he stumbled over a rug, and trying to recover himself, hit Louisa's work-basket on the table, and knocked it on the floor.

He looked at Louisa, then at the rolling spools; he ducked himself awkwardly toward them, but she stopped him. "Never mind," said she; "I'll pick them up after you're gone."

She spoke with a mild stiffness. Either she was a little disturbed, or his nervousness affected her, and made her seem constrained in her effort to reassure him.

When Joe Dagget was outside he drew in the sweet evening air with a sigh, and felt much as an innocent and perfectly well-intentioned bear might after his exit from a china shop.

Louisa, on her part, felt much as the kind-hearted, long-suffering owner of the china shop might have done after the exit of the bear.

She tied on the pink, then the green apron, picked up all the scattered treasures and replaced them in her work-basket, and straightened the rug. Then she set the lamp on the floor, and began sharply examining the carpet. She even rubbed her fingers over it, and looked at them.

"He's tracked in a good deal of dust," she murmured. "I thought he must have."

Louisa got a dust-pan and brush, and swept Joe Dagget's track carefully.

If he could have known it, it would have increased his perplexity and uneasiness, although it would not have disturbed his loyalty in the least. He came twice a week to see Louisa Ellis, and every time, sitting there in her delicately sweet room, he felt as if surrounded by a hedge of lace. He was afraid to stir lest he should put a clumsy foot or hand through the fairy web, and he had always the consciousness that Louisa was watching fearfully lest he should.

Still the lace and Louisa commanded perforce his perfect respect and patience and loyalty. They were to be married in a month, after a singular courtship which had lasted for a matter of fifteen years. For fourteen out of the fifteen years the two had not once seen each other, and they had seldom exchanged letters. Joe had been all those years in Australia, where he had gone to make his fortune, and where he had stayed until he made it. He would have stayed fifty years if it had taken so long, and come home feeble and tottering, or never come home at all, to marry Louisa.

But the fortune had been made in the fourteen years, and he had come home now to marry the woman who had been patiently and unquestioningly waiting for him all that time.

Shortly after they were engaged he had announced to Louisa his determination to strike out into new fields, and secure a competency before they should be married. She had listened and assented with the sweet serenity which never failed her, not even when her lover set forth on that long and uncertain journey. Joe, buoyed up as he was by his sturdy determination, broke down a little at the last, but Louisa kissed him with a mild blush, and said good-by.

"It won't be for long," poor Joe had said, huskily; but it was for fourteen years.

In that length of time much had happened. Louisa's mother and brother had died, and she was all alone in the world. But greatest happening of all—a subtle happening which both were too simple to understand—Louisa's feet had turned into a path, smooth maybe under a calm, serene sky, but so straight and unswerving that it could only meet a check at her grave, and so narrow that there was no room for any one at her side.

Louisa's first emotion when Joe Dagget came home (he had not apprised her of his coming) was consternation, although she would not admit it to herself, and he never dreamed of it. Fifteen years ago she had been in love with him—at least she considered herself to be. Just at that time, gently acquiescing with and falling into the natural drift of girlhood, she had seen marriage ahead as a reasonable feature and a probable desirability of life. She had listened with calm docility to her mother's views upon the subject. Her mother was remarkable for her cool sense and sweet, even temperament. She talked wisely to her daughter when Joe Dagget presented himself, and Louisa accepted him with no hesitation. He was the first lover she had ever had.

She had been faithful to him all these years. She had never dreamed of the possibility of marrying any one else. Her life, especially for the last seven years, had been full of a pleasant peace, she had never felt discontented nor impatient over her lover's absence; still she had always looked forward to his return and their marriage as the inevitable conclusion of things. However, she had fallen into a way of placing it so far in the future that it was almost equal to placing it over the boundaries of another life.

When Joe came she had been expecting him, and expecting to be married for fourteen years, but she was as much surprised and taken aback as if she had never thought of it.

Joe's consternation came later. He eyed Louisa with an instant confirmation of his old admiration. She had changed but little. She still kept her pretty manner and soft grace, and was, he considered, every whit as attractive as ever. As for himself, his stent was done; he had turned his face away from fortune-seeking, and the old winds of romance whistled as loud and sweet as ever through his ears. All the song which he had been wont to hear in them was Louisa; he had for a long time a loyal belief that he heard it still, but finally it seemed to him that although the winds sang always that one song, it had another name. But for Louisa the wind had never more than murmured; now it had gone down, and everything was still. She listened for a little while with half-wistful attention; then she turned quietly away and went to work on her wedding clothes.

Joe had made some extensive and quite magnificent alterations in his house. It was the old homestead; the newly-married couple would live there, for Joe could not desert his mother, who refused to leave her old home. So Louisa must leave hers. Every morning, rising and going about among her neat maidenly possessions, she felt as one looking her last upon the faces of dear friends. It was true that in a measure she could take them with her, but, robbed of their old environments, they would appear in such new guises that they would almost cease to be themselves. Then there were some peculiar features of her happy solitary life which she would probably be obliged to relinquish altogether. Sterner tasks than these graceful but half-needless ones would probably devolve upon her. There would be a large house to care for; there would be company to entertain; there would be Joe's rigorous and feeble old mother to wait upon; and it would be contrary to all thrifty village traditions for her to keep more than one servant. Louisa had a little still, and she used to occupy herself pleasantly in summer weather with distilling the sweet and aromatic essences from roses and peppermint and spearmint. By-and-by her still must be laid away. Her store of essences was already considerable, and there would be no time for her to distil for the mere pleasure of it. Then Joe's mother would think it foolishness; she had already hinted her opinion in the matter. Louisa dearly loved to sew a linen seam, not always for use, but for the simple, mild pleasure which she took in it. She would have been loath to confess how more than once she had ripped a seam for the mere delight of sewing it together again. Sitting at her window during long sweet afternoons, drawing her needle gently through the dainty fabric, she was peace itself. But there was small chance of such foolish comfort in the future. Joe's mother, domineering, shrewd old matron that she was even in her old age, and very likely even Joe himself, with his honest masculine rudeness, would laugh and frown down all these pretty but senseless old maiden ways.

Louisa had almost the enthusiasm of an artist over the mere order and cleanliness of her solitary home. She had throbs of genuine triumph at the sight of the window-panes which she had polished until they shone like jewels. She gloated gently over her orderly bureau-drawers, with their exquisitely folded contents redolent with lavender and sweet clover and very purity. Could she be sure of the endurance of even this? She had visions, so startling that she half repudiated them as indelicate, of coarse masculine belongings strewn about in endless litter; of dust and disorder arising necessarily from a coarse masculine presence in the midst of all this delicate harmony.

Among her forebodings of disturbance, not the least was with regard to Caesar. Caesar was a veritable hermit of a dog. For the greater part of his life he had dwelt in his secluded hut, shut out from the society of his kind and all innocent canine joys. Never had Caesar since his early youth watched at a woodchuck's hole; never had he known the delights of a stray bone at a neighbor's kitchen door. And it was all on account of a sin committed when hardly out of his puppyhood. No one knew the possible depth of remorse of which this mild-visaged, altogether innocent-looking old dog might be capable; but whether or not he had encountered remorse, he had encountered a full measure of righteous retribution. Old Caesar seldom lifted up his voice in a growl or a bark; he was fat and sleepy; there were yellow rings which looked like spectacles around his dim old eyes; but there was a neighbor who bore on his hand the imprint of several of Caesar's sharp white youthful teeth, and for that he had lived at the end of a chain, all alone in a little hut, for fourteen years. The neighbor, who was choleric and smarting with the pain of his wound, had demanded either Caesar's death or complete ostracism. So Louisa's brother, to whom the dog had belonged, had built him his little kennel and tied him up. It was now fourteen years since, in a flood of youthful spirits, he had inflicted that memorable bite, and with the exception of short excursions, always at the end of the chain, under the strict guardianship of his master or Louisa, the old dog had remained a close prisoner. It is doubtful if, with his limited ambition, he took much pride in the fact, but it is certain that he was possessed of considerable cheap fame. He was regarded by all the children in the village and by many adults as a very monster of ferocity. St. George's dragon could hardly have surpassed in evil repute Louisa Ellis's old yellow dog. Mothers charged their children with solemn emphasis not to go too near to him, and the children listened and believed greedily, with a fascinated appetite for terror, and ran by Louisa's house stealthily, with many sidelong and backward glances at the terrible dog. If perchance he sounded a hoarse bark, there was a panic. Wayfarers chancing into Louisa's yard eyed him with respect, and inquired if the chain were stout. Caesar at large might have seemed a very ordinary dog, and excited no comment whatever; chained, his reputation overshadowed him, so that he lost his own proper outlines and looked darkly vague and enormous. Joe Dagget, however, with his good-humored sense and shrewdness, saw him as he was. He strode valiantly up to him and patted him on the head, in spite of Louisa's soft clamor of warning, and even attempted to set him loose. Louisa grew so alarmed that he desisted, but kept announcing his opinion in the matter quite forcibly at intervals. "There ain't a better-natured dog in town," he would say, "and it's down-right cruel to keep him tied up there. Some day I'm going to take him out."

Louisa had very little hope that he would not, one of these days, when their interests and possessions should be more completely fused in one. She pictured to herself Caesar on the rampage through the quiet and unguarded village. She saw innocent children bleeding in his path. She was herself very fond of the old dog, because he had belonged to her dead brother, and he was always very gentle with her; still she had great faith in his ferocity. She always warned people not to go too near him. She fed him on ascetic fare of corn-mush and cakes, and never fired his dangerous temper with heating and sanguinary diet of flesh and bones. Louisa looked at the old dog munching his simple fare, and thought of her approaching marriage and trembled. Still no anticipation of disorder and confusion in lieu of sweet peace and harmony, no forebodings of Caesar on the rampage, no wild fluttering of her little yellow canary, were sufficient to turn her a hair's-breadth. Joe Dagget had been fond of her and working for her all these years. It was not for her, whatever came to pass, to prove untrue and break his heart. She put the exquisite little stitches into her wedding-garments, and the time went on until it was only a week before her wedding-day. It was a Tuesday evening, and the wedding was to be a week from Wednesday.

There was a full moon that night. About nine o'clock Louisa strolled down the road a little way. There were harvest-fields on either hand, bordered by low stone walls. Luxuriant clumps of bushes grew beside the wall, and trees—wild cherry and old apple-trees—at intervals. Presently Louisa sat down on the wall and looked about her with mildly sorrowful reflectiveness. Tall shrubs of blueberry and meadow-sweet, all woven together and tangled with blackberry vines and horsebriers, shut her in on either side. She had a little clear space between them. Opposite her, on the other side of the road, was a spreading tree; the moon shone between its boughs, and the leaves twinkled like silver. The road was bespread with a beautiful shifting dapple of silver and shadow; the air was full of a mysterious sweetness. "I wonder if it's wild grapes?" murmured Louisa. She sat there some time. She was just thinking of rising, when she heard footsteps and low voices, and remained quiet. It was a lonely place, and she felt a little timid. She thought she would keep still in the shadow and let the persons, whoever they might be, pass her.

But just before they reached her the voices ceased, and the footsteps. She understood that their owners had also found seats upon the stone wall. She was wondering if she could not steal away unobserved, when the voice broke the stillness. It was Joe Dagget's. She sat still and listened.

The voice was announced by a loud sigh, which was as familiar as itself. "Well," said Dagget, "you've made up your mind, then, I suppose?"

"Yes," returned another voice; "I'm going day after to-morrow."

"That's Lily Dyer," thought Louisa to herself. The voice embodied itself in her mind. She saw a girl tall and full-figured, with a firm, fair face, looking fairer and firmer in the moonlight, her strong yellow hair braided in a close knot. A girl full of a calm rustic strength and bloom, with a masterful way which might have beseemed a princess. Lily Dyer was a favorite with the village folk; she had just the qualities to arouse the admiration. She was good and handsome and smart. Louisa had often heard her praises sounded.

"Well," said Joe Dagget, "I ain't got a word to say."

"I don't know what you could say," returned Lily Dyer.

"Not a word to say," repeated Joe, drawing out the words heavily. Then there was a silence. "I ain't sorry," he began at last, "that that happened yesterday—that we kind of let on how we felt to each other. I guess it's just as well we knew. Of course I can't do anything any different. I'm going right on an' get married next week. I ain't going back on a woman that's waited for me fourteen years, an' break her heart."

"If you should jilt her to-morrow, I wouldn't have you," spoke up the girl, with sudden vehemence.

"Well, I ain't going to give you the chance," said he; "but I don't believe you would, either."

"You'd see I wouldn't. Honor's honor, an' right's right. An' I'd never think anything of any man that went against 'em for me or any other girl; you'd find that out, Joe Dagget."

"Well, you'll find out fast enough that I ain't going against 'em for you or any other girl," returned he. Their voices sounded almost as if they were angry with each other. Louisa was listening eagerly.

"I'm sorry you feel as if you must go away," said Joe, "but I don't know but it's best."

"Of course it's best. I hope you and I have got common-sense."

"Well, I suppose you're right." Suddenly Joe's voice got an undertone of tenderness. "Say, Lily," said he, "I'll get along well enough myself, but I can't bear to think—You don't suppose you're going to fret much over it?"

"I guess you'll find out I sha'n't fret much over a married man."

"Well, I hope you won't—I hope you won't, Lily. God knows I do. And—I hope—one of these days—you'll—come across somebody else —"

"I don't see any reason why I shouldn't." Suddenly her tone changed. She spoke in a sweet, clear voice, so loud that she could have been heard across the street. "No, Joe Dagget," said she, "I'll never marry any other man as long as I live. I've got good sense, an' I ain't going to break my heart nor make a fool of myself; but I'm never going to be married, you can be sure of that. I ain't that sort of a girl to feel this way twice."

Louisa heard an exclamation and a soft commotion behind the bushes; then Lily spoke again—the voice sounded as if she had risen. "This must be put a stop to," said she. "We've stayed here long enough. I'm going home."

Louisa sat there in a daze, listening to their retreating steps. After a while she got up and slunk softly home herself. The next day she did her housework methodically; that was as much a matter of course as breathing; but she did not sew on her wedding-clothes. She sat at her window and meditated. In the evening Joe came. Louisa Ellis had never known that she had any diplomacy in her, but when she came to look for it that night she found it, although meek of its kind, among her little feminine weapons. Even now she could hardly believe that she had heard aright, and that she would not do Joe a terrible injury should she break her troth-plight. She wanted to sound him without betraying too soon her own inclinations in the matter. She did it successfully, and they finally came to an understanding; but it was a difficult thing, for he was as afraid of betraying himself as she.

She never mentioned Lily Dyer. She simply said that while she had no cause of complaint against him, she had lived so long in one way that she shrank from making a change.

"Well, I never shrank, Louisa," said Dagget. "I'm going to be honest enough to say that I think maybe it's better this way; but if you'd wanted to keep on, I'd have stuck to you till my dying day. I hope you know that."

"Yes, I do," said she.

That night she and Joe parted more tenderly than they had done for a long time. Standing in the door, holding each other's hands, a last great wave of regretful memory swept over them.

"Well, this ain't the way we've thought it was all going to end, is it, Louisa?" said Joe.

She shook her head. There was a little quiver on her placid face.

"You let me know if there's ever anything I can do for you," said he. "I ain't ever going to forget you, Louisa." Then he kissed her, and went down the path.

Louisa, all alone by herself that night, wept a little, she hardly knew why; but the next morning, on waking, she felt like a queen who, after fearing lest her domain be wrested away from her, sees it firmly insured in her possession.

Now the tall weeds and grasses might cluster around Caesar's little hermit hut, the snow might fall on its roof year in and year out, but he never would go on a rampage through the unguarded village. Now the little canary might turn itself into a peaceful yellow ball night after night, and have no need to wake and flutter with wild terror against its bars. Louisa could sew linen seams, and distil roses, and dust and polish and fold away in lavender, as long as she listed. That afternoon she sat with her needle-work at the window, and felt fairly steeped in peace. Lily Dyer, tall and erect and blooming, went past; but she felt no qualm. If Louisa Ellis had sold her birthright she did not know it, the taste of the pottage was so delicious, and had been her sole satisfaction for so long. Serenity and placid narrowness had become to her as the birthright itself. She gazed ahead through a long reach of future days strung together like pearls in a rosary, every one like the others, and all smooth and flawless and innocent, and her heart went up in thankfulness. Outside was the fervid summer afternoon; the air was filled with the sounds of the busy harvest of men and birds and bees; there were halloos, metallic clatterings, sweet calls, and long hummings. Louisa sat, prayerfully numbering her days, like an uncloistered nun.

SARAH ORNE JEWETT

BORN IN THE MAINE VILLAGE OF SOUTH BERWICK IN 1849, Sarah Orne Jewett received her formal education at Berwick Academy, though because she suffered from arthritis, she could not attend regularly. Still, she read widely and was influenced by such American authors as Ralph Waldo Emerson and Harriet Beecher Stowe, but her greatest influence remained her father, whose life as a doctor she deeply admired and hoped to emulate.

Yet her talent as a writer bloomed early, and her first published story appeared when she was nineteen; a year later a story of hers appeared in the *Atlantic Monthly,* beginning a long association with the magazine and its editor, William Dean Howells, who encouraged her to collect her short fiction and sketches to form her first book, the novel *Deephaven,* which appeared in 1877. Many books followed, including *A Country Doctor* in 1884, but her masterpiece, *The Country of Pointed Firs,* would not appear until 1896.

Though she traveled widely as one of America's most highly regarded writers during her lifetime—travels that allowed her to meet and befriend such literary luminaries as Mark Twain, Henry James, Christina Rosetti, Rudyard Kipling, Alfred Lord Tennyson, Willa Cather, and Oliver Wendell Holmes—it was to her home in Maine that she always returned, and about which she wrote most all of her work: stories of the strong willed and deeply faithful women and men there, and the beauty and mystery of the New England countryside. She died at her home in South Berwick in 1909.

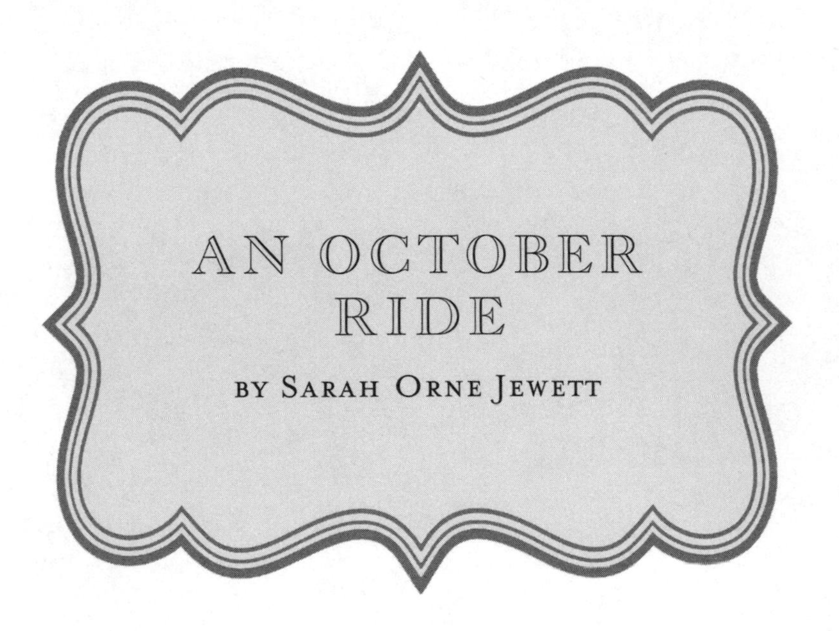

AN OCTOBER RIDE

BY SARAH ORNE JEWETT

It was a fine afternoon, just warm enough and just cool enough, and I started off alone on horseback, though I do not know why I should say alone when I find my horse such good company. She is called Sheila, and she not only gratifies one's sense of beauty, but is very interesting in her character, while her usefulness in this world is beyond question. I grow more fond of her every week; we have had so many capital good times together, and I am certain that she is as much pleased as I when we start out for a run.

I do not say to every one that I always pronounce her name in German fashion because she occasionally shies, but that is the truth. I do not mind her shying, or a certain mysterious and apparently unprovoked jump, with which she sometimes indulges herself, and no one else rides her, so I think she does no harm, but I do not like the principle of allowing her to be wicked, unrebuked and unhindered, and some day I shall give my mind to admonishing this four-footed Princess of Thule, who seems at present to consider herself at the top of royalty in this kingdom or any other. I believe I should not like her half so well if she were tamer and entirely and stupidly reliable; I glory in her good spirits and I think she has a right to be proud and willful if she chooses. I am proud myself of her quick eye and ear, her sure foot, and her slender, handsome chestnut head. I look at her points of high breeding with admiration, and I thank her heartily for all the pleasure she has given me, and for what I am sure is a steadfast friendship between us,—and a mutual understanding that rarely knows a disappointment or a mistake. She is careful when I come home late through the shadowy, twilighted woods, and I can hardly see my way; she forgets then all her little tricks and capers, and is as steady as a clock with her tramp, tramp, over the rough, dark country roads. I feel as if I had suddenly grown a pair of wings when she fairly flies over the ground and the wind whistles in my ears. There never was a time when she could not go a little faster, but she is willing to go step by step through the close woods, pushing her way through the branches, and stopping considerately when a bough that will not bend tries to pull me off the saddle. And she never goes away and leaves me when I dismount to get some flowers or a drink of spring water, though sometimes she thinks what fun it would be. I cannot speak of all her virtues for I have not learned them yet. We are still new friends, for I have only ridden her two years and I feel all the fascination of the first meeting every time I go out with her, she is so unexpected in her ways; so amusing, so sensible, so brave, and in every way so delightful a horse.

It was in October, and it was a fine day to look at, though some of the great clouds that sailed through the sky were a little too heavy-looking to promise good weather on the morrow, and over in the west (where the wind was coming from) they were packed close together and looked gray and wet. It might be cold and cloudy later, but that would not hinder my ride; it is a capital way to keep warm, to come along a smooth bit of road on the run, and I should have time at any rate to go the way I wished, so Sheila trotted quickly through the gate and out of the village. There was a flicker of color left on the oaks and maples, and though it was not Indian-summer weather it was first cousin to it. I took off my cap to let the wind blow through my hair; I had half a mind to go down to the sea, but it was too late for that; there was no moon to light me home. Sheila took the strip of smooth turf just at the side of the road for her own highway, she tossed her head again and again until I had my hand full of her thin, silky mane, and she gave quick pulls at her bit and hurried little jumps ahead as if she expected me already to pull the reins tight and steady her for a hard gallop. I patted her and whistled at her, I was so glad to see her again and to be out riding, and I gave her part of her reward to begin with, because I knew she would earn it, and then we were on better terms than ever. She has such a pretty way of turning her head to take the square lump of sugar, and she never bit my fingers or dropped the sugar in her life.

Down in the lower part of the town on the edge of York, there is a long tract of woodland, covering what is called the Rocky Hills; rough, high land, that stretches along from beyond Agamenticus, near the sea, to the upper part of Eliot, near the Piscataqua River. Standing on Agamenticus, the woods seem to cover nearly the whole of the country as far as one can see, and there is hardly a clearing to break this long reach of forest of which I speak; there must be twenty miles of it in an almost unbroken line. The roads cross it here and there, and one can sometimes see small and lonely farms hiding away in the heart of it. The trees are for the most part young growth of oak or pine, though I could show you yet many a noble company of great pines that once would have been marked with the king's arrow, and many a royal old oak which has been overlooked in the search for ships' knees and plank for the navy yard, and piles for the always shaky, up-hill and down, pleasant old Portsmouth bridge. The part of these woods which I know best lies on either side the already old new road to York on the Rocky Hills, and here I often ride, or even take perilous rough drives through the cart-paths, the wood roads which are busy thoroughfares in the winter, and are silent and shady, narrowed by green branches and carpeted with slender brakes, and seldom traveled over, except by me, all summer long.

It was a great surprise, or a succession of surprises, one summer, when I found that every one of the old uneven tracks led to or at least led by what had once been a clearing, and in old days must have been the secluded home of some of the earliest adventurous farmers of this region. It must have taken great courage, I think, to strike the first blow of one's axe here in the woods, and it must have been a brave certainty of one's perseverance that looked forward to the smooth field which was to succeed the unfruitful wilderness. The farms were far enough apart to be very lonely, and I suppose at first the cry of fierce wild creatures in the forest was an every-day sound, and the Indians stole like snakes through the bushes and crept from tree to tree about the houses watching, begging, and plundering, over and over again. There are some of these farms still occupied, where the land seems to have become thoroughly civilized, but most of them were deserted long ago; the people gave up the fight with such a persistent willfulness and wildness of nature and went away to the village, or to find more tractable soil and kindlier neighborhoods.

I do not know why it is these silent, forgotten places are so delightful to me; there is one which I always call my farm, and it was a long time after I knew it well before I could find out to whom it had once belonged. In some strange way the place has become a part of my world and to belong to my thoughts and my life.

I suppose every one can say, "I have a little kingdom where I give laws." Each of us has truly a kingdom in thought, and a certain spiritual possession. There are some gardens of mine where somebody plants the seeds and pulls the weeds for me every year without my ever taking a bit of trouble. I have trees and fields and woods and seas and houses, I own a great deal of the world to think and plan and dream about. The picture belongs most to the man who loves it best and sees entirely its meaning. We can always have just as much as we can take of things, and we can lay up as much treasure as we please in the higher world of thought that can never be spoiled or hindered by moth or rust, as lower and meaner wealth can be.

AS FOR THIS FARM OF MINE, I FOUND IT ONE DAY WHEN I WAS coming through the woods on horseback trying to strike a shorter way out into the main road. I was pushing through some thick underbrush, and looking ahead I noticed a good deal of clear sky as if there were an open place just beyond, and presently I found myself on the edge of a clearing. There was a straggling orchard of old apple-trees, the grass about them was close and short like the wide door-yard of an old farm-house and into this cleared space the little pines were growing on every side. The old pines stood a little way back watching their children march in upon their inheritance, as if they were ready to interfere and protect and defend, if any trouble came. I could see that it would not be many years, if they were left alone, before the green grass would be covered, and the old apple-trees would grow mossy and die for lack of room and sunlight in the midst of the young woods. It was a perfect acre of turf, only here and there I could already see a cushion of juniper, or a tuft of sweet fern or bayberry. I walked the horse about slowly, picking a hard little yellow apple here and there from the boughs over my head, and at last I found a cellar all grown over with grass, with not even a bit of a crumbling brick to be seen in the hollow of it. No doubt there were some underground. It was a very large cellar, twice as large as any I had ever found before in any of these deserted places, in the woods or out. And that told me at once that there had been a large house above it, an unusual house for those old days; the family was either a large one, or it had made for itself more than a merely sufficient covering and shelter, with no inch of unnecessary room. I knew I was on very high land, but the trees were so tall and close that I could not see beyond them. The wind blew over pleasantly and it was a curiously protected and hidden place, sheltered and quiet, with its one small crop of cider apples dropping ungathered to the ground, and unharvested there, except by hurrying black ants and sticky, witless little snails.

I suppose my feeling toward this place was like that about a ruin, only this seemed older than a ruin. I could not hear my horse's footfalls, and an apple startled me when it fell with a soft thud, and I watched it roll a foot or two and then stop, as if it knew it never would have anything more to do in the world. I remembered the Enchanted Palace and the Sleeping Beauty in the Wood, and it seemed as if I were on the way to it, and this was a corner of that palace garden. The horse listened and stood still, without a bit of restlessness, and when we heard the far cry of a bird she looked round at me, as if she wished me to notice that we were not alone in the world, after all. It was strange, to be sure, that people had lived there, and had had a home where they were busy, and where the fortunes of life had found them; that they had followed out the law of existence in its succession of growth and flourishing and failure and decay, within that steadily narrowing circle of trees.

The relationship of untamed nature to what is tamed and cultivated is a very curious and subtle thing to me; I do not know if every one feels it so intensely. In the darkness of an early autumn evening I sometimes find myself whistling a queer tune that chimes in with the crickets' piping and the cries of the little creatures around me in the garden. I have no thought of the rest of the world. I wonder what I am; there is a strange self-consciousness, but I am only a part of one great existence which is called nature. The life in me is a bit of all life, and where I am happiest is where I find that which is next of kin to me, in friends, or trees, or hills, or seas, or beside a flower, when I turn back more than once to look into its face.

The world goes on year after year. We can use its forces, and shape and mould them, and perfect this thing or that, but we cannot make new forces; we only use the tools we find to carve the wood we find. There is nothing new; we discover and combine and use. Here is the wild fruit,—the same fruit at heart as that with which the gardener wins his prize. The world is the same world. You find a diamond, but the diamond was there a thousand years ago; you did not make it by finding it. We grow spiritually, until we grasp some new great truth of God; but it was always true, and waited for us until we came. What is there new and strange in the world except ourselves! Our thoughts are our own; God gives our life to us moment by moment, but He gives it to be our own.

"Ye on your harps must lean to hear
A secret chord that mine will bear."

As I looked about me that day I saw the difference that men had made slowly fading out of sight. It was like a dam in a river; when it is once swept away the river goes on the same as before. The old patient, sublime forces were there at work in their appointed way, but perhaps by and by, when the apple-trees are gone and the cellar is only a rough hollow in the woods, some one will again set aside these forces that have worked unhindered, and will bring this corner of the world into a new use and shape. What if we could stop or change forever the working of these powers! But Nature repossesses herself surely of what we boldly claim. The pyramids stand yet, it happens, but where are all those cities that used also to stand in old Egypt, proud and strong, and dating back beyond men's memories or traditions,—turned into sand again and dust that is like all the rest of the desert, and blows about in the wind? Yet there cannot be such a thing as life that is lost. The tree falls and decays, in the dampness of the woods, and is part of the earth under foot, but another tree is growing out of it; perhaps it is part of its own life that is springing again from the part of it that died. God must always be putting again to some use the life that is withdrawn; it must live, because it is Life. There can be no confusion to God in this wonderful world, the new birth of the immortal, the new forms of the life that is from everlasting to everlasting, or the new way in which it comes. But it is only God who can plan and order it all,—who is a father to his children, and cares for the least of us. I thought of his unbroken promises; the people who lived and died in that lonely place knew Him, and the chain of events was fitted to their thoughts and lives, for their development and education. The world was made for them, and God keeps them yet; somewhere in his kingdom they are in their places,—they are not lost; while the trees they left grow older, and the young trees spring up, and the fields they cleared are being covered over and turned into wild land again.

I HAD VISITED THIS FARM OF MINE MANY TIMES SINCE THAT first day, but since the last time I had been there I had found out, luckily, something about its last tenant. An old lady whom I knew in the village had told me that when she was a child she remembered another very old woman, who used to live here all alone, far from any neighbors, and that one afternoon she had come with her mother to see her. She remembered the house very well; it was larger and better than most houses in the region. Its owner was the last of her family; but why she lived alone, or what became of her at last, or of her money or her goods, or who were her relatives in the town, my friend did not know. She was a thrifty, well-to-do old soul, a famous weaver and spinner, and she used to come to the meeting-house at the Old Fields every Sunday, and sit by herself in a square pew. Since I knew this, the last owner of my farm has become very real to me, and I thought of her that day a great deal, and could almost see her as she sat alone on her door-step in the twilight of a summer evening, when the thrushes were calling in the woods; or going down the hills to church, dressed in quaint fashion, with a little sadness in her face as she thought of her lost companions and how she did not use to go to church alone. And I pictured her funeral to myself, and watched her carried away at last by the narrow road that wound among the trees; and there was nobody left in the house after the neighbors from the nearest farms had put it to rights, and had looked over her treasures to their hearts' content. She must have been a fearless woman, and one could not stay in such a place as this, year in and year out, through the long days of summer and the long nights of winter, unless she found herself good company.

I do not think I could find a worse avenue than that which leads to my farm, I think sometimes there must have been an easier way out which I have yet failed to discover, but it has its advantages, for the trees are beautiful and stand close together, and I do not know such green brakes anywhere as those which grow in the shadiest places. I came into a well-trodden track after a while, which led into a small granite quarry, and then I could go faster, and at last I reached a pasture wall which was quickly left behind and I was only a little way from the main road. There were a few young cattle scattered about in the pasture, and some of them which were lying down got up in a hurry and stared at me suspiciously as I rode along. It was very uneven ground, and I passed some stiff, straight mullein stalks which stood apart together in a hollow as if they wished to be alone. They always remind me of the rigid old Scotch Covenanters, who used to gather themselves together in companies, against the law, to worship God in some secret hollow of the bleak hill-side. Even the smallest and youngest of the mulleins was a Covenanter at heart; they had all put by their yellow flowers, and they will stand there, gray and unbending, through the fall rains and winter snows, to keep their places and praise God in their own fashion, and they take great credit to themselves for doing it, I have no doubt, and think it is far better to be a stern and respectable mullein than a straying, idle clematis, that clings and wanders, and cannot bear wet weather. I saw members of the congregation scattered through the pasture and felt like telling them to hurry, for the long sermon had already begun! But one ancient worthy, very late on his way to the meeting, happened to stand in our way, and Sheila bit his dry head off, which was a great pity.

After I was once on the high road it was not long before I found myself in another part of the town altogether. It is great fun to ride about the country; one rouses a great deal of interest; there seems to be something exciting in the sight of a girl on horseback, and people who pass you in wagons turn to look after you, though they never would take the trouble if you were only walking. The country horses shy if you go by them fast, and sometimes you stop to apologize. The boys will leave anything to come and throw a stone at your horse. I think Sheila would like to bite a boy, though sometimes she goes through her best paces when she hears them hooting, as if she thought they were admiring her, which I never allow myself to doubt. It is considered a much greater compliment if you make a call on horseback than if you came afoot, but carriage people are nothing in the country to what they are in the city.

I was on a good road and Sheila was trotting steadily, and I did not look at the western sky behind me until I suddenly noticed that the air had grown colder and the sun had been for a long time behind a cloud; then I found there was going to be a shower, in a very little while, too. I was in a thinly settled part of the town, and at first I could not think of any shelter, until I remembered that not very far distant there was an old house, with a long, sloping roof, which had formerly been the parsonage of the north parish; there had once been a church near by, to which most of the people came who lived in this upper part of the town. It had been for many years the house of an old minister, of widespread fame in his day; I had always heard of him from the elderly people, and I had often thought I should like to go into his house, and had looked at it with great interest, but until within a year or two there had been people living there. I had even listened with pleasure to a story of its being haunted, and this was a capital chance to take a look at the old place, so I hurried toward it.

As I went in at the broken gate it seemed to me as if the house might have been shut up and left to itself fifty years before, when the minister died, so soon the grass grows up after men's footsteps have worn it down, and the traces are lost of the daily touch and care of their hands. The home lot was evidently part of a pasture, and the sheep had nibbled close to the door-step, while tags of their long, spring wool, washed clean by summer rains, were caught in the rose-bushes near by.

It had been a very good house in its day, and had a dignity of its own, holding its gray head high, as if it knew itself to be not merely a farm-house, but a Parsonage. The roof looked as if the next winter's weight of snow might break it in, and the window panes had been loosened so much in their shaking frames that many of them had fallen out on the north side of the house, and were lying on the long grass underneath, blurred and thin but still unbroken. That was the last letter of the house's death warrant, for now the rain could get in, and the crumbling timbers must loose their hold of each other quickly. I had found a dry corner of the old shed for the horse and left her there, looking most ruefully over her shoulder after me as I hurried away, for the rain had already begun to spatter down in earnest. I was not sorry when I found that somebody had broken a pane of glass in the sidelight of the front door, near the latch, and I was very pleased when I found that by reaching through I could unfasten a great bolt and let myself in, as perhaps some tramp in search of shelter had done before me. However, I gave the blackened brass knocker a ceremonious rap or two, and I could have told by the sound of it, if in no other way, that there was nobody at home. I looked up to see a robin's nest on the cornice overhead, and I had to push away the lilacs and a withered hop vine which were both trying to cover up the door.

It gives one a strange feeling, I think, to go into an empty house so old as this. It was so still there that the noise my footsteps made startled me, and the floor creaked and cracked as if some one followed me about. There was hardly a straw left or a bit of string or paper, but the rooms were much worn, the bricks in the fire-places were burnt out, rough and crumbling, and the doors were all worn smooth and round at the edges. The best rooms were wainscoted, but up-stairs there was a long, unfinished room with a little square window at each end, under the sloping roof, and as I listened there to the rain I remembered that I had once heard an old man say wistfully, that he had slept in just such a "linter" chamber as this when he was a boy, and that he never could sleep anywhere now so well as he used there while the rain fell on the roof just over his bed.

Down-stairs I found a room which I knew must have been the study. It was handsomely wainscoted, and the finish of it was even better than that of the parlor. It must have been a most comfortable place, and I fear the old parson was luxurious in his tastes and less ascetic, perhaps, than the more puritanical members of his congregation approved. There was a great fire-place with a broad hearth-stone, where I think he may have made a mug of flip sometimes, and there were several curious, narrow, little cupboards built into the wall at either side, and over the fire-place itself two doors opened and there were shelves inside, broader at the top as the chimney sloped back. I saw some writing on one of these doors and went nearer to read it. There was a date at the top, some time in 1802, and his reverence had had a good quill pen and ink which bravely stood the test of time; he must have been a tall man to have written so high. I thought it might be some record of a great storm or other notable event in his house or parish, but I was amused to find that he had written there on the unpainted wood some valuable recipes for the medical treatment of horses. "It is Useful for a Sprain—and For a Cough, Take of Elecampane"—and so on. I hope he was not a hunting parson, but one could hardly expect to find any reference to the early fathers or federal headship in Adam on the cupboard door. I thought of the stories I had heard of the old minister and felt very well acquainted with him, though his books had been taken down and his fire was out, and he himself had gone away. I was glad to think what a good, faithful man he was, who spoke comfortable words to his people and lived pleasantly with them in this quiet country place so many years. There are old people living who have told me that nobody preaches nowadays as he used to preach, and that he used to lift his hat to everybody; that he liked a good dinner, and always was kind to the poor.

I thought as I stood in the study, how many times he must have looked out of the small-paned western windows across the fields, and how in his later days he must have had a treasure of memories of the people who had gone out of that room the better for his advice and consolation, the people whom he had helped and taught and ruled. I could not imagine that he ever angrily took his parishioners to task for their errors of doctrine; indeed, it was not of his active youth and middle age that I thought at all, but of the last of his life, when he sat here in the sunshine of a winter afternoon, and the fire flickered and snapped on the hearth, and he sat before it in his arm-chair with a brown old book which he laid on his knee while he thought and dozed, and roused himself presently to greet somebody who came in, a little awed at first, to talk with him. It was a great thing to be a country minister in those old days, and to be such a minister as he was; truly the priest and ruler of his people. The times have changed, and the temporal power certainly is taken away. The divine right of ministers is almost as little believed in as that of kings, by many people; it is not possible for the influence to be so great, the office and the man are both looked at with less reverence. It is a pity that it should be so, but the conservative people who like old-fashioned ways cannot tell where to place all the blame. And it is very odd to think that these iconoclastic and unpleasant new times of ours will, a little later, be called old times, and that the children, when they are elderly people, will sigh to have them back again.

I was very glad to see the old house, and I told myself a great many stories there, as one cannot help doing in such a place. There must have been so many things happen in so many long lives which were lived there; people have come into the world and gone out of it again from those square rooms with their little windows, and I believe if there are ghosts who walk about in daylight I was only half deaf to their voices, and heard much of what they tried to tell me that day. The rooms which had looked empty at first were filled again with the old clergymen, who met together with important looks and complacent dignity, and eager talk about some minor point in theology that is yet unsettled; the awkward, smiling couples, who came to be married; the mistress of the house, who must have been a stately person in her day; the little children who, under all their shyness, remembered the sugar-plums in the old parson's pockets,—all these, and even the tall cane that must have stood in the entry, were visible to my mind's eye. And I even heard a sermon from the old preacher who died so long ago, on the beauty of a life well spent.

The rain fell steadily and there was no prospect of its stopping, though I could see that the clouds were thinner and that it was only a shower. In the kitchen I found an old chair which I pulled into the study, which seemed more cheerful than the rest of the house, and then I remembered that there were some bits of board in the kitchen also, and the thought struck me that it would be good fun to make a fire in the old fire-place. Everything seemed right about the chimney. I even went up into the garret to look at it there, for I had no wish to set the parsonage on fire, and I brought down a pile of old corn husks for kindlings which I found on the garret floor. I built my fire carefully, with two bricks for andirons, and when I lit it it blazed up gayly, I poked it and it crackled, and though I was very well contented there alone I wished for some friend to keep me company, it was selfish to have so much pleasure with no one to share it. The rain came faster than ever against the windows, and the room would have been dark if it had not been for my fire, which threw out a magnificent yellow light over the old brown wood-work. I leaned back and watched the dry sticks fall apart in red coals and thought I might have to spend the night there, for if it were a storm and not a shower I was several miles from home, and a late October rain is not like a warm one in June to fall upon one's shoulders. I could hear the house leaking when it rained less heavily, and the soot dropped down the chimney and great drops of water came down, too, and spluttered in the fire. I thought what a merry thing it would be if a party of young people ever had to take refuge there, and I could almost see their faces and hear them laugh, though until that minute they had been strangers to me.

But the shower was over at last, and my fire was out, and the last pale shining of the sun came into the windows, and I looked out to see the distant fields and woods all clear again in the late afternoon light. I must hurry to get home before dark, so I raked up the ashes and left my chair beside the fire-place, and shut and fastened the front door after me, and went out to see what had become of my horse, shaking the dust and cobwebs off my dress as I crossed the wet grass to the shed. The rain had come through the broken roof and poor Sheila looked anxious and hungry as if she thought I might have meant to leave her there till morning in that dismal place. I offered her my apologies, but she made even a shorter turn than usual when I had mounted, and we scurried off down the road, spattering ourselves as we went. I hope the ghosts who live in the parsonage watched me with friendly eyes, and I looked back myself, to see a thin blue whiff of smoke still coming up from the great chimney. I wondered who it was that had made the first fire there,—but I think I shall have made the last.

GEORGE MACDONALD

GEORGE MACDONALD WAS BORN IN SCOTLAND IN 1824, THE son of a farmer and his wife living in western Aberdeenshire. Educated first at local schools, in which Gaelic myths and Old Testament stories were taught side by side, he went on to study at Aberdeen University, and then to Highbury College, London, where he studied for the Congregationalist ministry. For three years he served as a pastor in West Sussex, but then resigned his position after having been harangued by his superiors for not being dogmatic enough in his sermons.

MacDonald wrote some of the most influential fantasy novels and stories in the English language, including *At the Back of the North Wind, The Princess and the Goblin, Lilith,* and his definitive work, *Phantastes.* Among those eminent writers who claimed MacDonald as integral to their careers as authors were J.R.R. Tolkien, G.K. Chesterton, and C.S. Lewis, who wrote of MacDonald, "I know hardly any other writer who seems closer, or more continually close, to the Spirit of Christ himself."

A successful author in terms of having his work published and read, MacDonald was never financially secure, and was, finally, pensioned by Queen Victoria in 1877; due to poor health, he moved to Italy, where he lived with his family—he and his wife Louisa had six sons and five daughters—from 1881 to 1902, when Louisa passed away. He then moved back to England, where he died in 1905. Though he was cremated and his ashes were interred with his beloved wife's at their home in Italy, a memorial to MacDonald was erected at the Drumblade Churchyard in his homeland of Aberdeenshire.

THE BROKEN SWORDS

BY GEORGE MACDONALD

The eyes of three, two sisters and a brother, gazed for the last time on a great pale-golden star, that followed the sun down the steep west. It went down to arise again; and the brother about to depart might return, but more than the usual doubt hung upon his future. For between the white dresses of the sisters, shone his scarlet coat and golden sword-knot, which he had put on for the first time, more to gratify their pride than his own vanity. The brightening moon, as if prophetic of a future memory, had already begun to dim the scarlet and the gold, and to give them a pale, ghostly hue. In her thoughtful light the whole group seemed more like a meeting in the land of shadows, than a parting in the substantial earth.—But which should be called the land of realities?—the region where appearance, and space, and time drive between, and stop the flowing currents of the soul's speech? or that region where heart meets heart, and appearance has become the slave to utterance, and space and time are forgotten?

Through the quiet air came the far-off rush of water, and the near cry of the land-rail. Now and then a chilly wind blew unheeded through the startled and jostling leaves that shaded the ivy-seat. Else, there was calm everywhere, rendered yet deeper and more intense by the dusky sorrow that filled their hearts. For, far away, hundreds of miles beyond the hearing of their ears, roared the great war-guns; next week their brother must sail with his regiment to join the army; and to-morrow he must leave his home.

The sisters looked on him tenderly, with vague fears about his fate. Yet little they divined it. That the face they loved might lie pale and bloody, in a heap of slain, was the worst image of it that arose before them; but this, had they seen the future, they would, in ignorance of the further future, have infinitely preferred to that which awaited him. And even while they looked on him, a dim feeling of the unsuitableness of his lot filled their minds. For, indeed, to all judgments it must have seemed unsuitable that the home-boy, the loved of his mother, the pet of his sisters, who was happy womanlike (as Coleridge says), if he possessed the signs of love, having never yet sought for its proofs—that he should be sent amongst soldiers, to command and be commanded; to kill, or perhaps to be himself crushed out of the fair earth in the uproar that brings back for the moment the reign of Night and Chaos. No wonder that to his sisters it seemed strange and sad. Yet such was their own position in the battle of life, in which their father had died with doubtful conquest, that when their old military uncle sent the boy an ensign's commission, they did not dream of refusing the only path open, as they thought, to an honourable profession, even though it might lead to the trench-grave. They heard it as the voice of destiny, wept, and yielded.

If they had possessed a deeper insight into his character, they would have discovered yet further reason to doubt the fitness of the profession chosen for him; and if they had ever seen him at school, it is possible the doubt of fitness might have strengthened into a certainty of incongruity. His comparative inactivity amongst his schoolfellows, though occasioned by no dullness of intellect, might have suggested the necessity of a quiet life, if inclination and liking had been the arbiters in the choice. Nor was this inactivity the result of defective animal spirits either, for sometimes his mirth and boyish frolic were unbounded; but it seemed to proceed from an over-activity of the inward life, absorbing, and in some measure checking, the outward manifestation. He had so much to do in his own hidden kingdom, that he had not time to take his place in the polity and strife of the commonwealth around him. Hence, while other boys were acting, he was thinking. In this point of difference, he felt keenly the superiority of many of his companions; for another boy would have the obstacle overcome, or the adversary subdued, while he was meditating on the propriety, or on the means, of effecting the desired end. He envied their promptitude, while they never saw reason to envy his wisdom; for his conscience, tender and not strong, frequently transformed slowness of determination into irresolution: while a delicacy of the sympathetic nerves tended to distract him from any predetermined course, by the diversity of their vibrations, responsive to influences from all quarters, and destructive to unity of purpose.

Of such a one, the a priori judgment would be, that he ought to be left to meditate and grow for some time, before being called upon to produce the fruits of action. But add to these mental conditions a vivid imagination, and a high sense of honour, nourished in childhood by the reading of the old knightly romances, and then put the youth in a position in which action is imperative, and you have elements of strife sufficient to reduce that fair kingdom of his to utter anarchy and madness. Yet so little do we know ourselves, and so different are the symbols with which the imagination works its algebra, from the realities which those symbols represent, that as yet the youth felt no uneasiness, but contemplated his new calling with a glad enthusiasm and some vanity; for all his prospect lay in the glow of the scarlet and the gold. Nor did this excitement receive any check till the day before his departure, on which day I have introduced him to my readers, when, accidentally taking up a newspaper of a week old, his eye fell on these words—"Already crying women are to be met in the streets." With this cloud afar on his horizon, which, though no bigger than a man's hand, yet cast a perceptible shadow over his mind, he departed next morning. The coach carried him beyond the consecrated circle of home laws and impulses, out into the great tumult, above which rises ever and anon the cry of Cain, "Am I my brother's keeper?"

Every tragedy of higher order, constructed in Christian times, will correspond more or less to the grand drama of the Bible; wherein the first act opens with a brilliant sunset vision of Paradise, in which childish sense and need are served with all the profusion of the indulgent nurse. But the glory fades off into grey and black, and night settles down upon the heart which, rightly uncontent with the childish, and not having yet learned the childlike, seeks knowledge and manhood as a thing denied by the Maker, and yet to be gained by the creature; so sets forth alone to climb the heavens, and instead of climbing, falls into the abyss. Then follows the long dismal night of feverish efforts and delirious visions, or, it may be, helpless despair; till at length a deeper stratum of the soul is heaved to the surface; and amid the first dawn of morning, the youth says within him, "I have sinned against my Maker—I will arise and go to my Father." More or less, I say, will Christian tragedy correspond to this—a fall and a rising again; not a rising only, but a victory; not a victory merely, but a triumph. Such, in its way and degree, is my story. I have shown, in one passing scene, the home paradise; now I have to show a scene of a far differing nature.

The young ensign was lying in his tent, weary, but wakeful. All day long the cannon had been bellowing against the walls of the city, which now lay with wide, gaping breach, ready for the morrow's storm, but covered yet with the friendly darkness. His regiment was ordered to be ready with the earliest dawn to march up to the breach. That day, for the first time, there had been blood on his sword—there the sword lay, a spot on the chased hilt still. He had cut down one of the enemy in a skirmish with a sally party of the besieged and the look of the man as he fell, haunted him. He felt, for the time, that he dared not pray to the Father, for the blood of a brother had rushed forth at the stroke of his arm, and there was one fewer of living souls on the earth because he lived thereon. And to-morrow he must lead a troop of men up to that poor disabled town, and turn them loose upon it, not knowing what might follow in the triumph of enraged and victorious foes, who for weeks had been subjected, by the constancy of the place, to the greatest privations. It was true the general had issued his commands against all disorder and pillage; but if the soldiers once yielded to temptation, what might not be done before the officers could reclaim them! All the wretched tales he had read of the sack of cities rushed back on his memory. He shuddered as he lay. Then his conscience began to speak, and to ask what right he had to be there.—Was the war a just one?—He could not tell; for this was a bad time for settling nice questions. But there he was, right or wrong, fighting and shedding blood on God's earth, beneath God's heaven.

Over and over he turned the question in his mind; again and again the spouting blood of his foe, and the death-look in his eye, rose before him; and the youth who at school could never fight with a companion because he was not sure that he was in the right, was alone in the midst of undoubting men of war, amongst whom he was driven helplessly along, upon the waves of a terrible necessity. What wonder that in the midst of these perplexities his courage should fail him! What wonder that the consciousness of fainting should increase the faintness! or that the dread of fear and its consequences should hasten and invigorate its attacks! To crown all, when he dropped into a troubled slumber at length, he found himself hurried, as on a storm of fire, through the streets of the captured town, from all the windows of which looked forth familiar faces, old and young, but distorted from the memory of his boyhood by fear and wild despair. On one spot lay the body of his father, with his face to the earth; and he woke at the cry of horror and rage that burst from his own lips, as he saw the rough, bloody hand of a soldier twisted in the loose hair of his elder sister, and the younger fainting in the arms of a scoundrel belonging to his own regiment. He slept no more. As the grey morning broke, the troops appointed for the attack assembled without sound of trumpet or drum, and were silently formed in fitting order. The young ensign was in his place, weary and wretched after his miserable night. Before him he saw a great, broad-shouldered lieutenant, whose brawny hand seemed almost too large for his sword-hilt, and in any one of whose limbs played more animal life than in the whole body of the pale youth. The firm-set lips of this officer, and the fire of his eye, showed a concentrated resolution, which, by the contrast, increased the misery of the ensign, and seemed, as if the stronger absorbed the weaker, to draw out from him the last fibres of self-possession: the sight of unattainable determination, while it increased the feeling of the arduousness of that which required such determination, threw him into the great gulf which lay between him and it. In this disorder of his nervous and mental condition, with a doubting conscience and a shrinking heart, is it any wonder that the terrors which lay before him at the gap in those bristling walls, should draw near, and, making sudden inroad upon his soul, overwhelm the government of a will worn out by the tortures of an unassured spirit? What share fear contributed to unman him, it was impossible for him, in the dark, confused conflict of differing emotions, to determine; but doubtless a natural shrinking from danger, there being no excitement to deaden its influence, and no hope of victory to encourage to the struggle, seeing victory was dreadful to him as defeat, had its part in the sad result. Many men who have courage, are dependent on ignorance and a low state of the moral feeling for that courage; and a further progress towards the development of the higher nature would, for a time at least, entirely overthrow it. Nor could such loss of courage be rightly designated by the name of cowardice. But, alas! the colonel happened to fix his eyes upon him as he passed along the file; and this completed his confusion. He betrayed such evident symptoms of perturbation, that that officer ordered him under arrest; and the result was, that, chiefly for the sake of example to the army, he was, upon trial by court-martial, expelled from the service, and had his sword broken over his head. Alas for the delicate minded youth! Alas for the home-darling!

Long after, he found at the bottom of his chest the pieces of the broken sword, and remembered that, at the time, he had lifted them from the ground and carried them away. But he could not recall under what impulse he had done so. Perhaps the agony he suffered, passing the bounds of mortal endurance, had opened for him a vista into the eternal, and had shown him, if not the injustice of the sentence passed upon him, yet his freedom from blame, or, endowing him with dim prophetic vision, had given him the assurance that some day the stain would be wiped from his soul, and leave him standing clear before the tribunal of his own honour. Some feeling like this, I say, may have caused him, with a passing gleam of indignant protest, to lift the fragments from the earth, and carry them away; even as the friends of a so-called traitor may bear away his mutilated body from the wheel. But if such was the case, the vision was soon overwhelmed and forgotten in the succeeding anguish. He could not see that, in mercy to his doubting spirit, the question which had agitated his mind almost to madness, and which no results of the impending conflict could have settled for him, was thus quietly set aside for the time; nor that, painful as was the dark, dreadful existence that he was now to pass in self-torment and moaning, it would go by, and leave his spirit clearer far, than if, in his apprehension, it had been stained with further blood-guiltiness, instead of the loss of honour. Years after, when he accidentally learned that on that very morning the whole of his company, with parts of several more, had, or ever they began to mount the breach, been blown to pieces by the explosion of a mine, he cried aloud in bitterness, "Would God that my fear had not been discovered before I reached that spot!" But surely it is better to pass into the next region of life having reaped some assurance, some firmness of character, determination of effort, and consciousness of the worth of life, in the present world; so approaching the future steadily and faithfully, and if in much darkness and ignorance, yet not in the oscillations of moral uncertainty.

Close upon the catastrophe followed a torpor, which lasted he did not know how long, and which wrapped in a thick fog all the succeeding events. For some time he can hardly be said to have had any conscious history. He awoke to life and torture when half-way across the sea towards his native country, where was no home any longer for him. To this point, and no farther, could his thoughts return in after years. But the misery which he then endured is hardly to be understood, save by those of like delicate temperament with himself. All day long he sat silent in his cabin; nor could any effort of the captain, or others on board, induce him to go on deck till night came on, when, under the starlight, he ventured into the open air. The sky soothed him then, he knew not how. For the face of nature is the face of God, and must bear expressions that can influence, though unconsciously to them, the most ignorant and hopeless of His children. Often did he watch the clouds in hope of a storm, his spirit rising and falling as the sky darkened or cleared; he longed, in the necessary selfishness of such suffering, for a tumult of waters to swallow the vessel; and only the recollection of how many lives were involved in its safety besides his own, prevented him from praying to God for lightning and tempest, borne on which he might dash into the haven of the other world. One night, following a sultry calm day, he thought that Mercy had heard his unuttered prayer. The air and sea were intense darkness, till a light as intense for one moment annihilated it, and the succeeding darkness seemed shattered with the sharp reports of the thunder that cracked without reverberation. He who had shrunk from battle with his fellow-men, rushed to the mainmast, threw himself on his knees, and stretched forth his arms in speechless energy of supplication; but the storm passed away overhead, and left him kneeling still by the uninjured mast. At length the vessel reached her port. He hurried on shore to bury himself in the most secret place he could find. Out of sight was his first, his only thought. Return to his mother he would not, he could not; and, indeed, his friends never learned his fate, until it had carried him far beyond their reach.

For several weeks he lurked about like a malefactor, in low lodging-houses in narrow streets of the seaport to which the vessel had borne him, heeding no one, and but little shocked at the strange society and conversation with which, though only in bodily presence, he had to mingle. These formed the subjects of reflection in after times; and he came to the conclusion that, though much evil and much misery exist, sufficient to move prayers and tears in those who love their kind, yet there is less of both than those looking down from a more elevated social position upon the weltering heap of humanity, are ready to imagine; especially if they regard it likewise from the pedestal of self-congratulation on which a meagre type of religion has elevated them. But at length his little stock of money was nearly expended, and there was nothing that he could do, or learn to do, in this seaport. He felt impelled to seek manual labour, partly because he thought it more likely he could obtain that sort of employment, without a request for reference as to his character, which would lead to inquiry about his previous history; and partly, perhaps, from an instinctive feeling that hard bodily labour would tend to lessen his inward suffering.

He left the town, therefore, at nightfall of a July day, carrying a little bundle of linen, and the remains of his money, somewhat augmented by the sale of various articles of clothing and convenience, which his change of life rendered superfluous and unsuitable. He directed his course northwards, travelling principally by night—so painfully did he shrink from the gaze even of foot-farers like himself; and sleeping during the day in some hidden nook of wood or thicket, or under the shadow of a great tree in a solitary field. So fine was the season, that for three successive weeks he was able to travel thus without inconvenience, lying down when the sun grew hot in the forenoon, and generally waking when the first faint stars were hesitating in the great darkening heavens that covered and shielded him. For above every cloud, above every storm, rise up, calm, clear, divine, the deep infinite skies; they embrace the tempest even as the sunshine; by their permission it exists within their boundless peace: therefore it cannot hurt, and must pass away, while there they stand as ever, domed up eternally, lasting, strong, and pure.

Several times he attempted to get agricultural employment; but the whiteness of his hands and the tone of his voice not merely suggested unfitness for labour, but generated suspicion as to the character of one who had evidently dropped from a rank so much higher, and was seeking admittance within the natural masonic boundaries and secrets and privileges of another. Disheartened somewhat, but hopeful, he journeyed on. I say hopeful; for the blessed power of life in the universe in fresh air and sunshine absorbed by active exercise, in winds, yea in rain, though it fell but seldom, had begun to work its natural healing, soothing effect, upon his perturbed spirit. And there was room for hope in his new endeavour. As his bodily strength increased, and his health, considerably impaired by inward suffering, improved, the trouble of his soul became more endurable—and in some measure to endure is to conquer and destroy. In proportion as the mind grows in the strength of patience, the disturber of its peace sickens and fades away. At length, one day, a widow lady in a village through which his road led him, gave him a day's work in her garden. He laboured hard and well, notwithstanding his soon-blistered hands, received his wages thankfully, and found a resting-place for the night on the low part of a hay-stack from which the upper portion had been cut away. Here he ate his supper of bread and cheese, pleased to have found such comfortable quarters, and soon fell fast asleep.

When he awoke, the whole heavens and earth seemed to give a

full denial to sin and sorrow. The sun was just mounting over the horizon, looking up the clear cloud-mottled sky. From millions of water-drops hanging on the bending stalks of grass, sparkled his rays in varied refraction, transformed here to a gorgeous burning ruby, there to an emerald, green as the grass, and yonder to a flashing, sunny topaz. The chanting priest-lark had gone up from the low earth, as soon as the heavenly light had begun to enwrap and illumine the folds of its tabernacle; and had entered the high heavens with his offering, whence, unseen, he now dropped on the earth the sprinkled sounds of his overflowing blessedness. The poor youth rose but to kneel, and cry, from a bursting heart, "Hast Thou not, O Father, some care for me? Canst Thou not restore my lost honour? Can anything befall Thy children for which Thou hast no help? Surely, if the face of Thy world lie not, joy and not grief is at the heart of the universe. Is there none for me?"

The highest poetic feeling of which we are now conscious, springs not from the beholding of perfected beauty, but from the mute sympathy which the creation with all its children manifests with us in the groaning and travailing which look for the sonship. Because of our need and aspiration, the snowdrop gives birth in our hearts to a loftier spiritual and poetic feeling, than the rose most complete in form, colour, and odour. The rose is of Paradise—the snowdrop is of the striving, hoping, longing Earth. Perhaps our highest poetry is the expression of our aspirations in the sympathetic forms of visible nature. Nor is this merely a longing for a restored Paradise; for even in the ordinary history of men, no man or woman that has fallen, can be restored to the position formerly held. Such must rise to a yet higher place, whence they can behold their former standing far beneath their feet. They must be restored by the attainment of something better than they ever possessed before, or not at all. If the law be a weariness, we must escape it by taking refuge with the spirit, for not otherwise can we fulfill the law than by being above the law. To escape the overhanging rocks of Sinai, we must climb to its secret top.

"Is thy strait horizon dreary?
Is thy foolish fancy chill?
Change the feet that have grown weary
For the wings that never will."

Thus, like one of the wandering knights searching the wide earth for the Sangreal, did he wander on, searching for his lost honour, or rather (for that he counted gone for ever) seeking unconsciously for the peace of mind which had departed from him, and taken with it, not the joy merely, but almost the possibility, of existence.

At last, when his little store was all but exhausted, he was employed by a market gardener, in the neighbourhood of a large country town, to work in his garden, and sometimes take his vegetables to market. With him he continued for a few weeks, and wished for no change; until, one day driving his cart through the town, he saw approaching him an elderly gentleman, whom he knew at once, by his gait and carriage, to be a military man. Now he had never seen his uncle the retired officer, but it struck him that this might be he; and under the tyranny of his passion for concealment, he fancied that, if it were he, he might recognise him by some family likeness—not considering the improbability of his looking at him. This fancy, with the painful effect which the sight of an officer, even in plain clothes, had upon him, recalling the torture of that frightful day, so overcame him, that he found himself at the other end of an alley before he recollected that he had the horse and cart in charge. This increased his difficulty; for now he dared not return, lest his inquiries after the vehicle, if the horse had strayed from the direct line, should attract attention, and cause interrogations which he would be unable to answer. The fatal want of self-possession seemed again to ruin him. He forsook the town by the nearest way, struck across the country to another line of road, and before he was missed, was miles away, still in a northerly direction.

But although he thus shunned the face of man, especially of any one who reminded him of the past, the loss of his reputation in their eyes was not the cause of his inward grief. That would have been comparatively powerless to disturb him, had he not lost his own respect. He quailed before his own thoughts; he was dishonoured in his own eyes. His perplexity had not yet sufficiently cleared away to allow him to see the extenuating circumstances of the case; not to say the fact that the peculiar mental condition in which he was at the time, removed the case quite out of the class of ordinary instances of cowardice. He condemned himself more severely than any of his judges would have dared; remembering that portion of his mental sensations which had savoured of fear, and forgetting the causes which had produced it. He judged himself a man stained with the foulest blot that could cleave to a soldier's name, a blot which nothing but death, not even death, could efface. But, inwardly condemned and outwardly degraded, his dread of recognition was intense; and feeling that he was in more danger of being discovered where the population was sparser, he resolved to hide himself once more in the midst of poverty; and, with this view, found his way to one of the largest of the manufacturing towns.

He reached it during the strike of a great part of the workmen; so that, though he found some difficulty in procuring employment, as might be expected from his ignorance of machine-labour, he yet was sooner successful than he would otherwise have been. Possessed of a natural aptitude for mechanical operations, he soon became a tolerable workman; and he found that his previous education assisted to the fitting execution of those operations even which were most purely mechanical.

He found also, at first, that the unrelaxing attention requisite for the mastering of the many niceties of his work, of necessity drew his mind somewhat from its brooding over his misfortune, hitherto almost ceaseless. Every now and then, however, a pang would shoot suddenly to his heart, and turn his face pale, even before his consciousness had time to inquire what was the matter. So by degrees, as attention became less necessary, and the nervo-mechanical action of his system increased with use, his thoughts again returned to their old misery. He would wake at night in his poor room, with the feeling that a ghostly nightmare sat on his soul; that a want—a loss—miserable, fearful—was present; that something of his heart was gone from him; and through the darkness he would hear the snap of the breaking sword, and lie for a moment overwhelmed beneath the assurance of the incredible fact. Could it be true that he was a coward? that his honour was gone, and in its place a stain? that he was a thing for men—and worse, for women—to point the finger at, laughing bitter laughter? Never lover or husband could have mourned with the same desolation over the departure of the loved; the girl alone, weeping scorching tears over her degradation, could resemble him in his agony, as he lay on his bed, and wept and moaned.

His sufferings had returned with the greater weight, that he was no longer upheld by the "divine air" and the open heavens, whose sunlight now only reached him late in an afternoon, as he stood at his loom, through windows so coated with dust that they looked like frosted glass; showing, as it passed through the air to fall on the dirty floor, how the breath of life was thick with dust of iron and wood, and films of cotton; amidst which his senses were now too much dulled by custom to detect the exhalations from greasy wheels and over-tasked human-kind. Nor could he find comfort in the society of his fellow-labourers. True, it was a kind of comfort to have those near him who could not know of his grief; but there was so little in common between them, that any interchange of thought was impossible. At least, so it seemed to him. Yet sometimes his longing for human companionship would drive him out of his dreary room at night, and send him wandering through the lower part of the town, where he would gaze wistfully on the miserable faces that passed him, as if looking for some one—some angel, even there—to speak goodwill to his hungry heart.

Once he entered one of those gin-palaces, which, like the golden gates of hell, entice the miserable to worse misery, and seated himself close to a half-tipsy, good-natured wretch, who made room for him on a bench by the wall. He was comforted even by this proximity to one who would not repel him. But soon the paintings of warlike action—of knights, and horses, and mighty deeds done with battle-axe, and broad-sword, which adorned the panels all round, drove him forth even from this heaven of the damned; yet not before the impious thought had arisen in his heart, that the brilliantly painted and sculptural roof, with the gilded vine-leaves and bunches of grapes trained up the windows, all lighted with the great shining chandeliers, was only a microcosmic repetition of the bright heavens and the glowing earth, that overhung and surrounded the misery of man. But the memory of how kindly they had comforted and elevated him, at one period of his painful history, not only banished the wicked thought, but brought him more quiet, in the resurrection of a past blessing, than he had known for some time. The period, however, was now at hand when a new grief, followed by a new and more elevated activity, was to do its part towards the closing up of the fountain of bitterness.

Amongst his fellow-labourers, he had for a short time taken some interest in observing a young woman, who had lately joined them. There was nothing remarkable about her, except what at first sight seemed a remarkable plainness. A slight scar over one of her rather prominent eyebrows, increased this impression of plainness. But the first day had not passed, before he began to see that there was something not altogether common in those deep eyes; and the plain look vanished before a closer observation, which also discovered, in the forehead and the lines of the mouth, traces of sorrow or other suffering. There was an expression, too, in the whole face, of fixedness of purpose, without any hardness of determination. Her countenance altogether seemed the index to an interesting mental history. Signs of mental trouble were always an attraction to him; in this case so great, that he overcame his shyness, and spoke to her one evening as they left the works. He often walked home with her after that; as, indeed, was natural, seeing that she occupied an attic in the same poor lodging-house in which he lived himself. The street did not bear the best character; nor, indeed, would the occupations of all the inmates of the house have stood investigation; but so retiring and quiet was this girl, and so seldom did she go abroad after work hours, that he had not discovered till then that she lived in the same street, not to say the same house with himself.

He soon learned her history—a very common one as outward events, but not surely insignificant because common. Her father and mother were both dead, and hence she had to find her livelihood alone, and amidst associations which were always disagreeable, and sometimes painful. Her quick womanly instinct must have discovered that he too had a history; for though, his mental prostration favouring the operation of outward influences, he had greatly approximated in appearance to those amongst whom he laboured, there were yet signs, besides the educated accent of his speech, which would have distinguished him to an observer; but she put no questions to him, nor made any approach towards seeking a return of the confidence she reposed in him. It was a sensible alleviation to his sufferings to hear her kind voice, and look in her gentle face, as they walked home together; and at length the expectation of this pleasure began to present itself, in the midst of the busy, dreary work-hours, as the shadow of a heaven to close up the dismal, uninteresting day.

But one morning he missed her from her place, and a keener pain passed through him than he had felt of late; for he knew that the Plague was abroad, feeding in the low stagnant places of human abode; and he had but too much reason to dread that she might be now struggling in its grasp. He seized the first opportunity of slipping out and hurrying home. He sprang upstairs to her room. He found the door locked, but heard a faint moaning within. To avoid disturbing her, while determined to gain an entrance, he went down for the key of his own door, with which he succeeded in unlocking hers, and so crossed her threshold for the first time. There she lay on her bed, tossing in pain, and beginning to be delirious. Careless of his own life, and feeling that he could not die better than in helping the only friend he had; certain, likewise, of the difficulty of finding a nurse for one in this disease and of her station in life; and sure, likewise, that there could be no question of propriety, either in the circumstances with which they were surrounded, nor in this case of terrible fever almost as hopeless for her as dangerous to him, he instantly began the duties of a nurse, and returned no more to his employment. He had a little money in his possession, for he could not, in the way in which he lived, spend all his wages; so he proceeded to make her as comfortable as he could, with all the pent-up tenderness of a loving heart finding an outlet at length. When a boy at home, he had often taken the place of nurse, and he felt quite capable of performing its duties. Nor was his boyhood far behind yet, although the trials he had come through made it appear an age since he had lost his light heart. So he never left her bedside, except to procure what was necessary for her. She was too ill to oppose any of his measures, or to seek to prohibit his presence. Indeed, by the time he had returned with the first medicine, she was insensible; and she continued so through the whole of the following week, during which time he was constantly with her.

That action produces feeling is as often true as its converse; and it is not surprising that, while he smoothed the pillow for her head, he should have made a nest in his heart for the helpless girl. Slowly and unconsciously he learned to love her. The chasm between his early associations and the circumstances in which he found her, vanished as he drew near to the simple, essential womanhood. His heart saw hers and loved it; and he knew that, the centre once gained, he could, as from the fountain of life, as from the innermost secret of the holy place, the hidden germ of power and possibility, transform the outer intellect and outermost manners as he pleased. With what a thrill of joy, a feeling for a long time unknown to him, and till now never known in this form or with this intensity, the thought arose in his heart that here lay one who some day would love him; that he should have a place of refuge and rest; one to lie in his bosom and not despise him! "For," said he to himself, "I will call forth her soul from where it sleeps, like an unawakened echo, in an unknown cave; and like a child, of whom I once dreamed, that was mine, and to my delight turned in fear from all besides, and clung to me, this soul of hers will run with bewildered, half-sleeping eyes, and tottering steps, but with a cry of joy on its lips, to me as the life-giver. She will cling to me and worship me. Then will I tell her, for she must know all, that I am low and contemptible; that I am an outcast from the world, and that if she receive me, she will be to me as God. And I will fall down at her feet and pray her for comfort, for life, for restoration to myself; and she will throw herself beside me, and weep and love me, I know. And we will go through life together, working hard, but for each other; and when we die, she shall lead me into paradise as the prize her angel-hand found cast on a desert shore, from the storm of winds and waves which I was too weak to resist—and raised, and tended, and saved." Often did such thoughts as these pass through his mind while watching by her bed; alternated, checked, and sometimes destroyed, by the fears which attended her precarious condition, but returning with every apparent betterment or hopeful symptom.

I will not stop to decide the nice question, how far the intention was right, of causing her to love him before she knew his story. If in the whole matter there was too much thought of self, my only apology is the sequel. One day, the ninth from the commencement of her illness, a letter arrived, addressed to her; which he, thinking he might prevent some inconvenience thereby, opened and read, in the confidence of that love which already made her and all belonging to her appear his own. It was from a soldier—her lover. It was plain that they had been betrothed before he left for the continent a year ago; but this was the first letter which he had written to her. It breathed changeless love, and hope, and confidence in her. He was so fascinated that he read it through without pause.

Laying it down, he sat pale, motionless, almost inanimate. From the hard-won sunny heights, he was once more cast down into the shadow of death. The second storm of his life began, howling and raging, with yet more awful lulls between. "Is she not mine?" he said, in agony. "Do I not feel that she is mine? Who will watch over her as I? Who will kiss her soul to life as I? Shall she be torn away from me, when my soul seems to have dwelt with hers for ever in an eternal house? But have I not a right to her? Have I not given my life for hers? Is he not a soldier, and are there not many chances that he may never return? And it may be that, although they were engaged in word, soul has never touched soul with them; their love has never reached that point where it passes from the mortal to the immortal, the indissoluble: and so, in a sense, she may be yet free. Will he do for her what I will do? Shall this precious heart of hers, in which I see the buds of so many beauties, be left to wither and die?"

But here the voice within him cried out, "Art thou the disposer of destinies? Wilt thou, in a universe where the visible God hath died for the Truth's sake, do evil that a good, which He might neglect or overlook, may be gained? Leave thou her to Him, and do thou right." And he said within himself, "Now is the real trial for my life! Shall I conquer or no?" And his heart awoke and cried, "I will. God forgive me for wronging the poor soldier! A brave man, brave at least, is better for her than I."

A great strength arose within him, and lifted him up to depart. "Surely I may kiss her once," he said. For the crisis was over, and she slept. He stooped towards her face, but before he had reached her lips he saw her eyelids tremble; and he who had longed for the opening of those eyes, as of the gates of heaven, that she might love him, stricken now with fear lest she should love him, fled from her, before the eyelids that hid such strife and such victory from the unconscious maiden had time to unclose. But it was agony—quietly to pack up his bundle of linen in the room below, when he knew she was lying awake above, with her dear, pale face, and living eyes! What remained of his money, except a few shillings, he put up in a scrap of paper, and went out with his bundle in his hand, first to seek a nurse for his friend, and then to go he knew not whither. He met the factory people with whom he had worked, going to dinner, and amongst them a girl who had herself but lately recovered from the fever, and was yet hardly able for work. She was the only friend the sick girl had seemed to have amongst the women at the factory, and she was easily persuaded to go and take charge of her. He put the money in her hand, begging her to use it for the invalid, and promising to send the equivalent of her wages for the time he thought she would have to wait on her. This he easily did by the sale of a ring, which, besides his mother's watch, was the only article of value he had retained. He begged her likewise not to mention his name in the matter; and was foolish enough to expect that she would entirely keep the promise she had made him.

Wandering along the street, purposeless now and bereft, he spied a recruiting party at the door of a public-house; and on coming nearer, found, by one of those strange coincidences which do occur in life, and which have possibly their root in a hidden and wondrous law, that it was a party, perhaps a remnant, of the very regiment in which he had himself served, and in which his misfortune had befallen him. Almost simultaneously with the shock which the sight of the well-known number on the soldiers' knapsacks gave him, arose in his mind the romantic, ideal thought, of enlisting in the ranks of this same regiment, and recovering, as a private soldier and unknown, that honour which as officer he had lost. To this determination, the new necessity in which he now stood for action and change of life, doubtless contributed, though unconsciously. He offered himself to the sergeant; and, notwithstanding that his dress indicated a mode of life unsuitable as the antecedent to a soldier's, his appearance, and the necessity for recruits combined, led to his easy acceptance.

The English armies were employed in expelling the enemy from an invaded and helpless country. Whatever might be the political motives which had induced the Government to this measure, the young man was now able to feel that he could go and fight, individually and for his part, in the cause of liberty. He was free to possess his own motives for joining in the execution of the schemes of those who commanded his commanders.

With a heavy heart, but with more of inward hope and strength than he had ever known before, he marched with his comrades to the seaport and embarked. It seemed to him that because he had done right in his last trial, here was a new glorious chance held out to his hand. True, it was a terrible change to pass from a woman in whom he had hoped to find healing, into the society of rough men, to march with them, "*mit gleichem Tritt und Schritt*,"[1] up to the bristling bayonets or the horrid vacancy of the cannon mouth. But it was the only cure for the evil that consumed his life.

He reached the army in safety, and gave himself, with religious assiduity, to the smallest duties of his new position. No one had a brighter polish on his arms, or whiter belts than he. In the necessary movements, he soon became precise to a degree that attracted the attention of his officers; while his character was remarkable for all the virtues belonging to a perfect soldier.

One day, as he stood sentry, he saw the eyes of his colonel intently fixed on him. He felt his lip quiver, but he compressed and stilled it, and tried to look as unconscious as he could; which effort was assisted by the formal bearing required by his position. Now the colonel, such had been the losses of the regiment, had been promoted from a lieutenancy in the same, and had belonged to it at the time of the ensign's degradation. Indeed, had not the changes in the regiment been so great, he could hardly have escaped so long without discovery. But the poor fellow would have felt that his name was already free of reproach, if he had seen what followed on the close inspection which had awakened his apprehensions, and which, in fact, had convinced the colonel of his identity with the disgraced ensign. With a hasty and less soldierly step than usual the colonel entered his tent, threw himself on his

1. with the same footstep and step

bed and wept like a child. When he rose he was overheard to say these words—and these only escaped his lips: "He is nobler than I."

But this officer showed himself worthy of commanding such men as this private; for right nobly did he understand and meet his feelings. He uttered no word of the discovery he had made, till years afterwards; but it soon began to be remarked that whenever anything arduous, or in any manner distinguished, had to be done, this man was sure to be of the party appointed. In short, as often as he could, the colonel "set him in the forefront of the battle." Passing through all with wonderful escape, he was soon as much noticed for his reckless bravery, as hitherto for his precision in the discharge of duties bringing only commendation and not honour. But his final lustration was at hand.

A great part of the army was hastening, by forced marches, to raise the siege of a town which was already on the point of falling into the hands of the enemy. Forming one of a reconnoitering party, which preceded the main body at some considerable distance, he and his companions came suddenly upon one of the enemy's outposts, occupying a high, and on one side precipitous rock, a short way from the town, which it commanded. Retreat was impossible, for they were already discovered, and the bullets were falling amongst them like the first of a hail-storm. The only possibility of escape remaining for them was a nearly hopeless improbability. It lay in forcing the post on this steep rock; which if they could do before assistance came to the enemy, they might, perhaps, be able to hold out, by means of its defences, till the arrival of the army. Their position was at once understood by all; and, by a sudden, simultaneous impulse, they found themselves half-way up the steep ascent, and in the struggle of a close conflict, without being aware of any order to that effect from their officer. But their courage was of no avail; the advantages of the place were too great; and in a few minutes the whole party was cut to pieces, or stretched helpless on the rock. Our youth had fallen amongst the foremost; for a musket ball had grazed his skull, and laid him insensible.

But consciousness slowly returned, and he succeeded at last in raising himself and looking around him. The place was deserted. A few of his friends, alive, but grievously wounded, lay near him. The rest were dead. It appeared that, learning the proximity of the English forces from this rencontre with part of their advanced guard, and dreading lest the town, which was on the point of surrendering, should after all be snatched from their grasp, the commander of the enemy's forces had ordered an immediate and general assault; and had for this purpose recalled from their outposts the whole of his troops thus stationed, that he might make the attempt with the utmost strength he could accumulate.

As the youth's power of vision returned, he perceived, from the height where he lay, that the town was already in the hands of the enemy. But looking down into the level space immediately below him, he started to his feet at once; for a girl, bare-headed, was fleeing towards the rock, pursued by several soldiers. "Aha!" said he, divining her purpose—the soldiers behind and the rock before her— "I will help you to die!" And he stooped and wrenched from the dead fingers of a sergeant the sword which they clenched by the bloody hilt. A new throb of life pulsed through him to his very finger-tips; and on the brink of the unseen world he stood, with the blood rushing through his veins in a wild dance of excitement. One who lay near him wounded, but recovered afterwards, said that he looked like one inspired. With a keen eye he watched the chase. The girl drew nigh; and rushed up the path near which he was standing. Close on her footsteps came the soldiers, the distance gradually lessening between them.

Not many paces higher up, was a narrower part of the ascent, where the path was confined by great stones, or pieces of rock. Here had been the chief defence in the preceding assault, and in it lay many bodies of his friends. Thither he went and took his stand.

On the girl came, over the dead, with rigid hands and flying feet, the bloodless skin drawn tight on her features, and her eyes awfully large and wild. She did not see him though she bounded past so near that her hair flew in his eyes. "Never mind!" said he, "we shall meet soon." And he stepped into the narrow path just in time to face her pursuers—between her and them. Like the red lightning the bloody sword fell, and a man beneath it. Cling! clang! went the echoes in the rocks—and another man was down; for, in his excitement, he was a destroying angel to the breathless pursuers. His stature rose, his chest dilated; and as the third foe fell dead, the girl was safe; for her body lay a broken, empty, but undesecrated temple, at the foot of the rock. That moment his sword flew in shivers from his grasp. The next instant he fell, pierced to the heart; and his spirit rose triumphant, free, strong, and calm, above the stormy world, which at length lay vanquished beneath him.

FLANNERY O'CONNOR

THE ONLY CHILD OF A MIDDLE-CLASS CATHOLIC FAMILY, Flannery O'Connor was born in Savannah, Georgia, in 1925. At age six she was already interested in drawing and writing, and her literary endeavors were encouraged by her father early on. In 1938 the family moved to O'Connor's mother's hometown of Milledgeville, Georgia, as her father's lupus no longer allowed him to work; he died in 1940. At age 16, she enrolled at Georgia State College for Women there in Milledgeville, studying sociology, and after graduating in 1945 after only three years, she attended the University of Iowa's Writers Workshop. There she began what became a literary career that saw the awarding of three O. Henry awards, grants from the *Kenyon Review*, the National Institute of Arts and Letters, and the Ford Foundation, and residencies at Yaddo, an important artists' colony in New York.

But in 1950 she began to develop the first signs of lupus, and she was forced to move home to Milledgeville, where her mother took care of her for the rest of her life. It was here she wrote her most important stories, and here that her Catholic worldview played its greatest role in honing her tough and funny and fiercely Christian fiction. Her books include the novels *Wise Blood* and *The Violent Bear It Away*, though she is best known for her two story collections, *A Good Man Is Hard to Find* and the posthumously published *Everything That Rises Must Converge*. Her collection of essays on faith, art, and writing, *Mystery and Manners,* remains a classic meditation on what it means to be a Christian and to practice the habit of art. She died on August 3, 1964, at home in Milledgeville.

A CIRCLE IN THE FIRE

BY FLANNERY O'CONNOR

Sometimes the last line of trees was a solid gray-blue wall a little darker than the sky but this afternoon it was almost black and behind it the sky was a livid glaring white. "You know that woman that had that baby in that iron lung?" Mrs. Pritchard said. She and the child's mother were underneath the window the child was looking down from. Mrs. Pritchard was leaning against the chimney, her arms folded on a shelf of a stomach, one foot crossed and the toe pointed into the ground. She was a large woman with a small pointed face and steady ferreting eyes. Mrs. Cope was the opposite, very small and trim, with a large round face and black eyes that seemed to be enlarging all the time behind her glasses as if she were continually being astonished. She was squatting down pulling grass out of the border beds around the house. Both women had on sunhats that had once been identical but now Mrs. Pritchard's was faded and out of shape while Mrs. Cope's was still stiff and bright green.

"I read about her," she said.

"She was a Pritchard that married a Brookins and so's kin to me—about my seventh or eighth cousin by marriage."

"Well, well," Mrs. Cope muttered and threw a large clump of nut grass behind her. She worked at the weeds and nut grass as if they were an evil sent directly by the devil to destroy the place.

"Beinst she was kin to us, we gone to see the body," Mrs. Pritchard said. "Seen the little baby too."

Mrs. Cope didn't say anything. She was used to these calamitous stories; she said they wore her to a frazzle. Mrs. Pritchard would go thirty miles for the satisfaction of seeing anybody laid away. Mrs. Cope always changed the subject to something cheerful but the child had observed that this only put Mrs. Pritchard in a bad humor.

The child thought the blank sky looked as if it were pushing against the fortress wall, trying to break through. The trees across the near field were a patchwork of gray and yellow greens. Mrs. Cope was always worrying about fires in her woods. When the nights were very windy, she would say to the child, "Oh Lord, do pray there won't be any fires, it's so windy," and the child would grunt from behind her book or not answer at all because she heard it so often. In the evenings in the summer when they sat on the porch, Mrs. Cope would say to the child who was reading fast to catch the last light, "Get up and look at the sunset, it's gorgeous. You ought to get up and look at it," and the child would scowl and not answer or glare up once across the lawn and two front pastures to the gray-blue sentinel line of trees and then begin to read again with no change of expression, sometimes muttering for meanness, "It looks like a fire. You better get up and smell around and see if the woods ain't on fire."

"She had her arm around it in the coffin," Mrs. Pritchard went on, but her voice was drowned out by the sound of the tractor that the Negro, Culver, was driving up the road from the barn. The wagon was attached and another Negro was sitting in the back, bouncing, his feet jogging about a foot from the ground. The one on the tractor drove it past the gate that led into the field on the left.

Mrs. Cope turned her head and saw that he had not gone through the gate because he was too lazy to get off and open it. He was going the long way around at her expense. "Tell him to stop and come here!" she shouted.

Mrs. Pritchard heaved herself from the chimney and waved her arm in a fierce circle but he pretended not to hear. She stalked to the edge of the lawn and screamed, "Get off, I toljer! She wants you!"

He got off and started toward the chimney, pushing his head and shoulders forward at each step to give the appearance of hurrying. His head was thrust up to the top in a white cloth hat streaked with different shades of sweat. The brim was down and hid all but the lower parts of his reddish eyes.

Mrs. Cope was on her knees, pointing the trowel into the ground. "Why aren't you going through the gate there?" she asked and waited, her eyes shut and her mouth stretched flat as if she were prepared for any ridiculous answer.

"Got to raise the blade on the mower if we do," he said and his gaze bore just to the left of her. Her Negroes were as destructive and impersonal as the nut grass.

Her eyes, as she opened them, looked as if they would keep on enlarging until they turned her wrongsideout. "Raise it," she said and pointed across the road with the trowel.

He moved off.

"It's nothing to them," she said. "They don't have the responsibility. I thank the Lord all these things don't come at once. They'd destroy me."

"Yeah, they would," Mrs. Pritchard shouted against the sound of the tractor. He opened the gate and raised the blade and drove through and down into the field; the noise diminished as the wagon disappeared. "I don't see myself how she had it *in* it," she went on in her normal voice.

Mrs. Cope was bent over, digging fiercely at the nut grass again. "We have a lot to be thankful for," she said. "Every day you should say a prayer of thanksgiving. Do you do that?"

"Yes'm," Mrs. Pritchard said. "See she was in it four months before she even got thataway. Look like to me if I was in one of them, I would leave off . . . how you reckon they . . . ?"

"Every day I say a prayer of thanksgiving," Mrs. Cope said. "Think of all we have. Lord," she said and sighed, "we have everything," and she looked around her rich pastures and hills heavy with timber and shook her head as if it might all be a burden she was trying to shake off her back.

Mrs. Pritchard studied the woods. "All I got is four abscess teeth," she remarked.

"Well, be thankful you don't have five," Mrs. Cope snapped and threw back a clump of grass. "We might all be destroyed by a hurricane. I can always find something to be thankful for."

Mrs. Pritchard took up a hoe resting against the side of the house and struck lightly at a weed that had come up between two bricks in the chimney. "I reckon *you* can," she said, her voice a little more nasal than usual with contempt.

"Why, think of all those poor Europeans," Mrs. Cope went on, "that they put in boxcars like cattle and rode them to Siberia. Lord," she said, "we ought to spend half our time on our knees."

"I know if I was in an iron lung there would be some things I wouldn't do," Mrs. Pritchard said, scratching her bare ankle with the end of the hoe.

"Even that poor woman had plenty to be thankful for," Mrs. Cope said.

"She could be thankful she wasn't dead."

"Certainly," Mrs. Cope said, and then she pointed the trowel up at Mrs. Pritchard and said, "I have the best kept place in the county and do you know why? Because I work. I've had to work to save this place and work to keep it." She emphasized each word with the trowel. "I don't let anything get ahead of me and I'm not always looking for trouble. I take it as it comes."

"If it all come at oncet sometime," Mrs. Pritchard began.

"It doesn't all come at once," Mrs. Cope said sharply.

The child could see over to where the dirt road joined the highway. She saw a pick-up truck stop at the gate and let off three boys who started walking up the pink dirt road. They walked single file, the middle one bent to the side carrying a black pig-shaped valise.

"Well, if it ever did," Mrs. Pritchard said, "it wouldn't be nothing you could do but fling up your hands."

Mrs. Cope didn't even answer this. Mrs. Pritchard folded her arms and gazed down the road as if she could easily enough see all these fine hills flattened to nothing. She saw the three boys who had almost reached the front walk by now. "Lookit yonder," she said. "Who you reckon they are?"

Mrs. Cope leaned back and supported herself with one hand behind her and looked. The three came toward them but as if they were going to walk on through the side of the house. The one with the suitcase was in front now. Finally about four feet from her, he stopped and set it down. The three boys looked something alike except that the middle-sized one wore silver-rimmed spectacles and carried the suitcase. One of his eyes had a slight cast to it so that his gaze seemed to be coming from two directions at once as if it had them surrounded. He had on a sweat shirt with a faded destroyer printed on it but his chest was so hollow that the destroyer was broken in the middle and seemed on the point of going under. His hair was stuck to his forehead with sweat. He looked to be about thirteen.

All three boys had white penetrating stares. "I don't reckon you remember me, Mrs. Cope," he said.

"Your face is certainly familiar," she murmured, scrutinizing him. "Now let's see . . ."

"My daddy used to work here," he hinted.

"Boyd?" she said. "Your father was Mr. Boyd and you're J.C.?"

"Nome, I'm Powell, the secont one, only I've growed some since then and my daddy he's daid now. Done died."

"Dead. Well I declare," Mrs. Cope said as if death were always an unusual thing. "What was Mr. Boyd's trouble?"

One of Powell's eyes seemed to be making a circle of the place, examining the house and the white water tower behind it and the chicken houses and the pastures that rolled away on either side until they met the first line of woods. The other eye looked at her. "Died in Florda," he said and began kicking the valise.

"Well I declare," she murmured. After a second she said, "And how is your mother?"

"Mah'd again." He kept watching his foot kick the suitcase. The other two boys stared at her impatiently.

"And where do you all live now?" she asked.

"Atlanta," he said. "You know, out to one of them developments."

"Well I see," she said, "I see." After a second she said it again. Finally she asked, "And who are these other boys?" and smiled at them.

"Garfield Smith him, and W. T. Harper him," he said, nodding his head backward first in the direction of the large boy and then the small one.

"How do you boys do?" Mrs. Cope said. "This is Mrs. Pritchard. Mr. and Mrs. Pritchard work here now."

They ignored Mrs. Pritchard who watched them with steady beady eyes. The three seemed to hang there, waiting, watching Mrs. Cope.

"Well well," she said, glancing at the suitcase, "it's nice of you to stop and see me. I think that was real sweet of you."

Powell's stare seemed to pinch her like a pair of tongs. "Come back to see how you was doing," he said hoarsely.

"Listen here," the smallest boy said, "all the time we been knowing him he's been telling us about this here place. Said it was everything here. Said it was horses here. Said he had the best time of his entire life right here on this here place. Talks about it all the time."

"Never shuts his trap about this place," the big boy grunted, drawing his arms across his nose as if to muffle his words.

"Always talking about them horses he rid here," the small one continued, "and said he would let us ride them too. Said it was one named Gene."

Mrs. Cope was always afraid someone would get hurt on her place and sue her for everything she had. "They aren't shod," she said quickly. "There was one named Gene but he's dead now but I'm afraid you boys can't ride the horses because you might get hurt. They're dangerous," she said, speaking very fast.

The large boy sat down on the ground with a noise of disgust and began to finger rocks out of his tennis shoe. The small one darted looks here and there and Powell fixed her with his stare and didn't say anything.

After a minute the little boy said, "Say, lady, you know what he said one time? He said when he died he wanted to come here!"

For a second Mrs. Cope looked blank; then she blushed; then a peculiar look of pain came over her face as she realized that these children were hungry. They were staring because they were hungry! She almost gasped in their faces and then she asked them quickly if they would have something to eat. They said they would but their expressions, composed and unsatisfied, didn't lighten any. They looked as if they were used to being hungry and it was no business of hers.

The child upstairs had grown red in the face with excitement. She was kneeling down by the window so that only her eyes and forehead showed over the sill. Mrs. Cope told the boys to come around on the other side of the house where the lawn chairs were and she led the way and Mrs. Pritchard followed. The child moved from the right bedroom across the hall and over into the left bedroom and looked down on the other side of the house where there were three white lawn chairs and red hammock strung between two hazelnut trees. She was a pale fat girl of twelve with a frowning squint and a large mouth full of silver bands. She knelt down at the window.

The three boys came around the corner of the house and the large one threw himself into the hammock and lit a stub of cigarette. The small boy tumbled down on the grass next to the black suitcase and rested his head on it and Powell sat down on the edge of one of the chairs and looked as if he were trying to enclose the whole place in one encircling stare. The child heard her mother and Mrs. Pritchard in a muted conference in the kitchen. She got up and went out into the hall and leaned over the banisters.

Mrs. Cope's and Mrs. Pritchard's legs were facing each other in the back hall. "Those poor children are hungry," Mrs. Cope said in a dead voice.

"You seen that suitcase?" Mrs. Pritchard asked. "What if they intend to spend the night with you?"

Mrs. Cope gave a slight shriek. "I can't have three boys in here with only me and Sally Virginia," she said. "I'm sure they'll go when I feed them."

"I only know they got a suitcase," Mrs. Pritchard said.

The child hurried back to the window. The large boy was stretched out in the hammock with his wrists crossed under his head and the cigarette stub in the center of his mouth. He spit it out in an arc just as Mrs. Cope came around the corner of the house with a plate of crackers. She stopped instantly as if a snake had been slung in her path. "Ashfield!" she said. "Please pick that up. I'm afraid of fires."

"Gawfield!" the little boy shouted indignantly. "Gawfield!"

The large boy raised himself without a word and lumbered for the butt. He picked it up and put it in his pocket and stood with his back to her, examining a tattooed heart on his forearm. Mrs. Pritchard came up holding three Coca-Colas by the necks in one hand and gave one to each of them.

"I remember everything about this place," Powell said, looking down the opening of his bottle.

"Where did you all go when you left here?" Mrs. Cope asked and put the plate of crackers on the arm of his chair.

He looked at it but didn't take one. He said, "I remember it was one name Gene and it was one name George. We gone to Florda and my daddy he, you know, died, and then we gone to my sister's and then my mother she, you know, mah'd, and we been there ever since."

"There are some crackers," Mrs. Cope said and sat down in the chair across from him.

"He don't like it in Atlanta," the little boy said, sitting up and reaching indifferently for a cracker. "He ain't ever satisfied with where he's at except this place here. Lemme tell you what he'll do, lady. We'll be playing ball, see, on this here place in this development we got to play ball on, see, and he'll quit playing and say, 'Goddam, it was a horse down there name Gene and if I had him here I'd bust this concrete to hell riding him!'"

"I'm sure Powell doesn't use words like that, do you, Powell?" Mrs. Cope said.

"No, mam," Powell said. His head was turned completely to the side as if he were listening for the horses in the field.

"I don't like them kind of crackers," the little boy said and returned his to the plate and got up.

Mrs. Cope shifted in her chair. "So you boys live in one of those nice new developments," she said.

"The only way you can tell your own is by smell," the small boy volunteered. "They're four stories high and there's ten of them, one behind the other. Let's go see them horses," he said.

Powell turned his pinching look on Mrs. Cope. "We thought we would just spend the night in your barn," he said. "My uncle brought us this far on his pick-up truck and he's going to stop for us again in the morning."

There was a moment in which she didn't say a thing and the child in the window thought: she's going to fly out of that chair and hit the tree.

"Well, I'm afraid you can't do that," she said, getting up suddenly. "The barn's full of hay and I'm afraid of fire from your cigarettes."

"We won't smoke," he said.

"I'm afraid you can't spend the night in there just the same," she repeated as if she were talking politely to a gangster.

"Well, we can camp out in the woods then," the little boy said. "We brought our own blankets anyways. That's what we got in theter suitcase. Come on."

"In the woods!" she said. "Oh no! The woods are very dry now, I can't have people smoking in my woods. You'll have to camp out in the field, in this field here next to the house, where there aren't any trees."

"Where she can keep her eye on you," the child said under her breath.

"Her woods," the large boy muttered and got out of the hammock.

"We'll sleep in the field," Powell said but not particularly as if he were talking to her. "This afternoon I'm going to show them about this place." The other two were already walking away and he got up and bounded after them and the two women sat with the black suitcase between them.

"Not no thank you, not no nothing," Mrs. Pritchard remarked.

"They only played with what we gave them to eat," Mrs. Cope said in a hurt voice.

Mrs. Pritchard suggested that they might not like *soft* drinks.

"They certainly *looked* hungry," Mrs. Cope said.

About sunset they appeared out of the woods, dirty and sweating, and came to the back porch and asked for water. They did not ask for food but Mrs. Cope could tell that they wanted it. "All I have is some cold guinea," she said. "Would you boys like some guinea and some sandwiches?"

"I wouldn't eat nothing bald-headed like a guinea," the little boy said. "I would eat a chicken or a turkey but not no guinea."

"Dog wouldn't eat one of them," the large boy said. He had taken off his shirt and stuck it in the back of his trousers like a tail. Mrs.

Cope carefully avoided looking at him. The little boy had a cut on his arm.

"You boys haven't been riding the horses when I asked you not to, have you?" she asked suspiciously and they all said, "No mam!" at once in loud enthusiastic voices like the Amens are said in country churches.

She went into the house and made them sandwiches and, while she did it, she held a conversation with them from inside the kitchen, asking what their fathers did and how many brothers and sisters they had and where they went to school. They answered in short explosive sentences, pushing each other's shoulders and doubling up with laughter as if the questions had meanings she didn't know about. "And do you have men teachers or lady teachers at your school?" she asked.

"Some of both and some you can't tell which," the big boy hooted.

"And does your mother work, Powell?" she asked quickly.

"She ast you does your mother work!" the little boy yelled. "His mind's affected by them horses he only looked at," he said. "His mother she works at a factory and leaves him to mind the rest of them only he don't mind them much. Lemme tell you, lady, one time he locked his little brother in a box and set it on fire."

"I'm sure Powell wouldn't do a thing like that," she said, coming out with the plate of sandwiches and setting it down on the step. They emptied the plate at once and she picked it up and stood holding it, looking at the sun which was going down in front of them, almost on top of the tree line. It was swollen and flame-colored and hung in a net of ragged cloud as if it might burn through any second and fall into the woods. From the upstairs window the child saw her shiver and catch both arms to her sides. "We have so much to be thankful for," she said suddenly in a mournful marveling tone. "Do you boys thank God every night for all He's done for you? Do you thank Him for everything?"

This put an instant hush over them. They bit into the sandwiches as if they had lost all taste for food.

"Do you?" she persisted.

They were as silent as thieves hiding. They chewed without a sound.

"Well, I know I do," she said at length and turned and went back to the house and the child watched their shoulders drop. The large one stretched his legs out as if he were releasing himself from a trap. The sun burned so fast that it seemed to be trying to set everything in sight on fire. The white water tower was glazed pink and the grass was an unnatural green as if it were turning to glass. The child suddenly stuck her head far out the window and said, "Ugggghhrhh," in a loud voice, crossing her eyes and hanging her tongue out as far as possible as if she were going to vomit.

The large boy looked up and stared at her. "Jesus," he growled, "another woman."

She dropped back from the window and stood with her back against the wall, squinting fiercely as if she had been slapped in the face and couldn't see who had done it. As soon as they left the steps, she came down into the kitchen where Mrs. Cope was washing the dishes. "If I had that big boy down I'd beat the daylight out of him," she said.

"You keep away from those boys," Mrs. Cope said, turning sharply. "Ladies don't beat the daylight out of people. You keep out of their way. They'll be gone in the morning."

But in the morning they were not gone.

When she went out on the porch after breakfast, they were standing around the back door, kicking the steps. They were smelling the bacon she had had for her breakfast. "Why boys!" she said. "I thought you were going to meet your uncle." They had the same look of hardened hunger that had pained her yesterday but today she felt faintly provoked.

The big boy turned his back at once and the small one squatted down and began to scratch in the sand. "We ain't, though," Powell said.

The big boy turned his head just enough to take in a small section of her and said, "We ain't bothering nothing of yours."

He couldn't see the way her eyes enlarged but he could take note of the significant silence. After a minute she said in an altered voice, "Would you boys care for some breakfast?"

"We got plenty of our own food," the big boy said. "We don't want nothing of yours."

She kept her eyes on Powell. His thin white face seemed to confront but not actually to see her. "You boys know that I'm glad to have you," she said, "but I expect you to behave. I expect you to act like gentlemen."

They stood there, each looking in a different direction, as if they were waiting for her to leave. "After all," she said in a suddenly high voice, "this is my place."

The big boy made some ambiguous noise and they turned and walked off toward the barn, leaving her there with a shocked look as if she had had a searchlight thrown on her in the middle of the night.

In a little while Mrs. Pritchard came over and stood in the kitchen door with her cheek against the edge of it. "I reckon you know they rode them horses all yesterday afternoon," she said. "Stole a bridle out of the saddleroom and rode bareback because Hollis seen them. He runnum out the barn at nine o'clock last night and then he runnum out the milk room this morning and there was milk all over their mouths like they had been drinking out the cans."

"I cannot have this," Mrs. Cope said and stood at the sink with both fists knotted at her sides. "I cannot have this," and her expression was the same as when she tore at the nut grass.

"There ain't a thing you can do about it," Mrs. Pritchard said. "What I expect is you'll have them for a week or so until school begins. They just figure to have themselves a vacation in the country and there ain't nothing you can do but fold your hands."

"I do not fold my hands," Mrs. Cope said. "Tell Mr. Pritchard to put the horses up in the stalls."

"He's already did that. You take a boy thirteen year old is equal in meanness to a man twict his age. It's no telling what he'll think up to do. You never know where he'll strike next. This morning Hollis seen them behind the bull pen and that big one ast if it wasn't some place they could wash at and Hollis said no it wasn't and that you didn't want no boys dropping cigarette butts in your woods and he said, 'She don't own them woods,' and Hollis said, 'Shes does too,' and that there little one he said, 'Man, Gawd owns them woods and her too,' and that there one with the glasses said, 'I reckon she owns the sky over this place too,' and that there littlest one says, 'Owns the sky and can't no airplane go over here without she says so,' and then the big one says, 'I never seen a place with so many damn women on it, how do you stand it here?' and Hollis said he had done had enough of their big talk by then and he turned and walked off without giving no reply one way or the other."

"I'm going out there and tell those boys they can get a ride away from here on the milk truck," Mrs. Cope said and she went out the back door, leaving Mrs. Pritchard and the child together in the kitchen.

"Listen," the child said. "I could handle them quicker than that."

"Yeah?" Mrs. Pritchard murmured, giving her a long leering look. "How'd you handle them?"

The child gripped both hands together and made a contorted face as if she were strangling someone.

"They'd handle you," Mrs. Pritchard said with satisfaction.

The child retired to the upstairs window to get out of her way and looked down where her mother was walking off from the three boys who were squatting under the water tower, eating something out of a cracker box. She heard her come in the kitchen door and say, "They say they'll go on the milk truck, and no wonder they aren't hungry—they have that suitcase half full of food."

"Likely stole every bit of it too," Mrs. Pritchard said.

When the milk truck came, the three boys were nowhere in sight, but as soon as it left without them their three faces appeared, looking out of the opening in the top of the calf barn. "Can you beat this?" Mrs. Cope said, standing at one of the upstairs windows with her hands at her hips. "It's not that I wouldn't be glad to have them—it's their attitude."

"You never like nobody's attitude," the child said. "I'll go tell them they got five minutes to leave here in."

"You are not to go anywhere near those boys, do you hear me?" Mrs. Cope said.

"Why?" the child asked.

"I'm going out there and give them a piece of my mind," Mrs. Cope said.

The child took over the position in the window and in a few minutes she saw the stiff green hat catching the glint of the sun as her mother crossed the road toward the calf barn. The three faces immediately disappeared from the opening, and in a second the large boy dashed across the lot, followed an instant later by the other two. Mrs. Pritchard came out and the two women started for the grove of trees the boys had vanished into. Presently the two sunhats disappeared in the woods and the three boys came out at the left side of it and ambled across the field and into another patch of woods. By the time Mrs. Cope and Mrs. Pritchard reached the field, it was empty and there was nothing for them to do but come home again.

Mrs. Cope had not been inside long before Mrs. Pritchard came running toward the house, shouting something. "They've let out the bull!" she hollered. "Let out the bull!" And in a second she was followed by the bull himself, ambling, black and leisurely, with four geese hissing at his heels. He was not mean until hurried and it took Mr. Pritchard and the two Negroes a half-hour to ease him back to his pen. While the men were engaged in this, the boys let the oil out of the three tractors and then disappeared again into the woods.

Two blue veins had come out on either side of Mrs. Cope's forehead and Mrs. Pritchard observed them with satisfaction. "Like I toljer," she said, "there ain't a thing you can do about it."

Mrs. Cope ate her dinner hastily, not conscious that she had her sunhat on. Every time she heard a noise, she jumped up. Mrs. Pritchard came over immediately after dinner and said, "Well, you want to know where they are now?" and smiled in an omniscient rewarded way.

"I want to know at once," Mrs. Cope said, coming to an almost military attention.

"Down to the road, throwing rocks at your mailbox," Mrs. Pritchard said, leaning comfortably in the door. "Done already about knocked it off its stand."

"Get in the car," Mrs. Cope said.

The child got in too and the three of them drove down the road to the gate. The boys were sitting on the embankment on the other side of the highway, aiming rocks across the road at the mailbox. Mrs. Cope stopped the car almost directly beneath them and looked up out of her window. The three of them stared at her as if they had never seen her before, the large boy with the sullen glare, the small one glint-eyed and unsmiling, and Powell with his two-sided glassed gaze hanging vacantly over the crippled destroyer on his shirt.

"Powell," she said, "I'm sure your mother would be ashamed of you," and she stopped and waited for this to make its effect. His face seemed to twist slightly but he continued to look through her at nothing in particular.

"Now I've put up with this as long as I can," she said. "I've tried to be nice to you boys. Haven't I been nice to you boys?"

They might have been three statues except that big one, barely opening his mouth, said, "We're not even on your side the road, lady."

"There ain't a thing you can do about it," Mrs. Pritchard hissed loudly. The child was sitting on the back seat close to the side. She had a furious outraged look on her face but she kept her head drawn back from the window so that they couldn't see her.

Mrs. Cope spoke slowly, emphasizing every word. "I think I have been very nice to you boys. I've fed you twice. Now I'm going into town and if you're still here when I come back, I'll call the sheriff," and with this, she drove off. The child, turning quickly so that she could see out the back window, observed that they had not moved; they had not even turned their heads.

"You done angered them now," Mrs. Pritchard said, "and it ain't any telling what they'll do."

"They'll be gone when we get back," Mrs. Cope said.

Mrs. Pritchard could not stand an anticlimax. She required the taste of blood from time to time to keep her equilibrium. "I known a man oncet that his wife was poisoned by a child she had adopted out of pure kindness," she said. When they returned from town, the boys were not on the embankment and she said, "I would rather to see them than not to see them. When you see them you know what they're doing."

"Ridiculous," Mrs. Cope muttered. "I've scared them and they've gone and now we can forget them."

"I ain't forgetting them," Mrs. Pritchard said. "I wouldn't be none surprised if they didn't have a gun in that there suitcase."

Mrs. Cope prided herself on the way she handled the type of mind that Mrs. Pritchard had. When Mrs. Pritchard saw signs and omens, she exposed them calmly for the figments of imagination that they were, but this afternoon her nerves were taut and she said, "Now I've had about enough of this. Those boys are gone and that's that."

"Well, we'll wait and see," Mrs. Pritchard said.

Everything was quiet for the rest of the afternoon but at supper time, Mrs. Pritchard came over to say that she had heard a high vicious laugh pierce out of the bushes near the hog pen. It was an evil laugh, full of calculated meanness, and she had heard it come three times, herself, distinctly.

"I haven't heard a thing," Mrs. Cope said.

"I look for them to strike just after dark," Mrs. Pritchard said.

That night Mrs. Cope and the child sat on the porch until nearly ten o'clock and nothing happened. The only sounds came from tree frogs and from one whippoorwill who called faster and faster from the same spot of darkness. "They've gone," Mrs. Cope said, "poor things," and she began to tell the child how much they had to be thankful for, for she said they might have had to live in a development themselves or they might have been Negroes or they might have been in iron lungs or they might have been Europeans ridden in boxcars like cattle, and she began a litany of her blessings, in a stricken voice, that the child, straining her attention for a sudden shriek in the dark, didn't listen to.

There was no sign of them the next morning either. The fortress line of trees was a hard granite blue, the wind had risen overnight and the sun had come up a pale gold. The season was changing. Even a small change in the weather made Mrs. Cope thankful, but when the seasons changed she seemed almost frightened at her good fortune in escaping whatever it was that pursued her. As she sometimes did when one thing was finished and another about to begin, she turned her attention to the child who had put on a pair of overalls over her dress and had pulled a man's old felt hat down as far as it would go on her head and was arming herself with two pistols in a decorated holster that she had fastened around her waist. The hat was very tight and seemed to be squeezing the redness into her face. It came down almost to the tops of her glasses. Mrs. Cope watched her with a tragic look. "Why do you have to look like an idiot?" she asked. "Suppose company were to come? When are you going to grow up? What's going to become of you? I look at you and I want to cry! Sometimes you look like you might belong to Mrs. Pritchard!"

"Leave me be," the child said in a high irritated voice. "Leave me be. Just leave me be. I ain't you," and she went off to the woods as if she were stalking out an enemy, her head thrust forward and each hand gripped on a gun.

Mrs. Pritchard came over, sour-humored, because she didn't have anything calamitous to report. "I got the misery in my face today," she said, holding on to what she could salvage. "Theseyer teeth. They each one feel like an individual boil."

THE CHILD CRASHED THROUGH THE WOODS, MAKING THE FALLEN leaves sound ominous under her feet. The sun had risen a little and was only a white hole like an opening for the wind to escape through in a sky a little darker than itself, and the tops of the trees were black against the glare. "I'm going to get you one by one and beat you black and blue. Line up. LINE UP!" she said and waved one of the pistols at a cluster of long bare-trunked pines, four times her height, as she passed them. She kept moving, muttering and growling to herself and occasionally hitting out with one of the guns at a branch that got in her way. From time to time she stopped to remove the thorn vine that caught in her shirt and she would say,

"Leave me be, I told you. Leave me be," and give it a crack with the pistol and then stalk on.

Presently she sat down on a stump to cool off but she planted both feet carefully and firmly on the ground. She lifted them and put them down several times, grinding them fiercely into the dirt as if she were crushing something under her heels. Suddenly she heard a laugh.

She sat up, prickle-skinned. It came again. She heard the sound of splashing and she stood up, uncertain which way to run. She was not far from where this patch of woods ended and the back pasture began. She eased toward the pasture, careful not to make a sound, and coming suddenly to the edge of it, she saw the three boys, not twenty feet away, washing in the cow trough. Their clothes were piled against the black valise out of reach of the water that flowed over the side of the tank. The large boy was standing up and the small one was trying to climb onto his shoulders. Powell was sitting down looking straight ahead through glasses that were splashed with water. He was not paying any attention to the other two. The trees must have looked like green waterfalls through his wet glasses. The child stood partly hidden behind a pine trunk, the side of her face pressed into the bark.

"I wish I lived here!" the little boy shouted, balancing with his knees clutched around the big one's head.

"I'm goddam glad I don't," the big boy panted, and jumped up to dislodge him.

Powell sat without moving, without seeming to know that the other two were behind him, and looked straight ahead like a ghost sprung right up in his coffin. "If this place was not here any more," he said, "you would never have to think of it again."

"Listen," the big boy said, sitting down quietly in the water with the little one still moored to his shoulders, "it don't belong to nobody."

"It's ours," the little boy said.

The child behind the tree did not move.

Powell jumped out of the trough and began to run. He ran all the way around the field as if something were after him and as he passed the tank again, the other two jumped out and raced with him, the sun glinting on their long wet bodies. The big one ran the fastest and was the leader. They dashed around the field twice and finally dropped down by their clothes and lay there with their ribs moving up and down. After a while, the big one said hoarsely, "Do you know what I would do with this place if I had the chance?"

"No, what?" the little boy said and sat up to give him his full attention.

"I'd build a big parking lot on it, or something," he muttered.

They began to dress. The sun made two white spots on Powell's glasses and blotted out his eyes. "I know what let's do," he said. He took something small from his pocket and showed it to them. For almost a minute they sat looking at what he had in his hand. Then without any more discussion, Powell picked up the suitcase and they got up and moved past the child and entered the woods not ten feet from where she was standing, slightly away from the tree now, with the imprint of the bark embossed red and white on the side of her face.

She watched with a dazed stare as they stopped and collected all the matches they had between them and began to set the brush on fire. They began to whoop and holler and beat their hands over their mouths and in a few seconds there was a narrow line of fire widening between her and them. While she watched, it reached up from the brush, snatching and biting at the lowest branches of the trees. The wind carried rags of it higher and the boys disappeared shrieking behind it.

She turned and tried to run across the field but her legs were too heavy and she stood there, weighted down with some new unplaced misery that she had never felt before. But finally she began to run.

Mrs. Cope and Mrs. Pritchard were in the field behind the barn when Mrs. Cope saw smoke rising from the woods across the pasture. She shrieked and Mrs. Pritchard pointed up the road to where the child came loping heavily, screaming, "Mama, Mama, they're going to build a parking lot here!"

Mrs. Cope began to scream for the Negroes while Mrs. Pritchard, charged now, ran down the road shouting. Mr. Pritchard came out of the open end of the barn and the two Negroes stopped filling the manure spreader in the lot and started toward Mrs. Cope with their shovels. "Hurry, hurry!" she shouted. "Start throwing dirt on it!" They passed her almost without looking at her and headed off slowly across the field toward the smoke. She ran after them a little way, shrilling, "Hurry, hurry, don't you see it! Don't you see it!"

"It'll be there when we git there," Culver said and they thrust their shoulders forward a little and went on at the same pace.

The child came to a stop beside her mother and stared up at her face as if she had never seen it before. It was the face of the new misery she felt, but on her mother it looked old and it looked as if it might have belonged to anybody, a Negro or a European or to Powell himself. The child turned her head quickly, and past the Negroes' ambling figures she could see the column of smoke rising and widening unchecked inside the granite line of trees. She stood taut, listening, and could just catch in the distance a few wild high shrieks of joy as if the prophets were dancing in the fiery furnace, in the circle the angel had cleared for them.

GINA OCHSNER

BORN IN 1970 IN SALEM, OREGON, GINA OCHSNER ATTENDED George Fox University, a small Quaker college in western Oregon. Upon graduation in 1992, she enrolled in the graduate English program at Iowa State University, where she received her master's degree in 1994. She then moved back to Oregon, where she began writing and publishing her first short stories.

A contemporary master of magical realism, Ochsner's first collection of stories, *The Necessary Grace to Fall,* was named the 2002 winner of the Flannery O'Connor Award for Short Fiction, an annual prize that National Public Radio has called "one of the most prestigious series in university press publishing"; the book went on to win the Oregon Book Award for Short Fiction and the Pacific Northwest Booksellers Association Book Award. Her second book, the collection *People I Wanted to Be,* was published in 2005. Her stories have been widely acclaimed and have appeared in many of the country's best and most influential journals, among them the *New Yorker,* the *Kenyon Review,* and *Prairie Schooner*. In addition, her work has received the Raymond Carver Prize and the Chelsea Award for Short Fiction, and in 2006 she received a fellowship in literature from the National Endowment for the Arts.

The mother of four children, she is married to a carpenter and spends her days, as one might well imagine, with her hands full. She teaches in the MFA program at Seattle Pacific University, and is presently working on a novel, tentatively titled *Russian Dreambook of Color and Flight,* scheduled to release in 2009.

A DARKNESS HELD

BY GINA OCHSNER

"In God's wildness lies the hope of the world."

—John Muir

Imogene McCrary fingers her rosary and waits patiently while Father Dismus mumbles a prayer for Sister Clement, whose legs are rigged in traction. It has been thirty-six hours since her fall down a metal staircase outside Saint Mary's Star of the Sea, and Father Dismus has roped Imogene, a former student of Sister Clement's, into this visit.

When Father Dismus finishes his prayer, Imogene makes to touch Sister Clement, but she slaps her hand away hard. With a crooked finger, Father Dismus lifts a slat of the blinds and winces at the daylight unfiltered and sharpened by the glass. Outside the traffic moves along the North Oregon coastal highway, all the logging trucks and campers and buses pushing into the wind. Everyone is just passing through Gearheart toward someplace else.

"We're all so sorry about that spill down the stairs. I hope you don't fault the children," Father Dismus speaks to the glass, to the flat table of sea beyond the spit of land outside.

"I didn't fall. I was pushed," Sister Clement says through clenched teeth. Her voice shakes with fury or pain, Imogene can't tell. She's too busy watching the transparent bag clipped to the bed rail soundlessly fill with urine. It's been over three years since Imogene has last seen Sister Clement at mass and now she's having a hard time getting used to this new image of the nun. Instead of her black woolen habit, she's wearing a pale green hospital gown with immodest slits in the side. With her legs hiked unceremoniously in the air, Sister Clement appears small and ordinary and diminished. Not at all like the fierce woman of superhuman size and strength she remembered from her days in school, a woman whose unswerving sense of Christian duty and firm grip on the ruler fractured knuckles and gave middling students like her brother, Frank, small ulcers.

"Just watch yourself around those kids." Sister Clement turns toward Imogene. "They're not right." A fleck of spittle clings to her lower lip. "And don't turn your back on them—not even for a second!"

The woman is a nun, a bride, Imogene reminds herself. The spotless bride of Christ.

"Ha!" Father Dismus laughs. "They can't be that bad!"

Imogene rises from her chair, grabs a hospital pamphlet warning against the dangers of deep vein thrombosis, and follows Father Dismus out the door and down the hall of St. Michael's. The shadows they cast are crisp and their tread is soundless over the shiny waxed floor. He holds open the heavy glass door for Imogene and points to the parish station wagon in the parking lot. "She loves these children, she really does. It's just the pain talking." He draws his breath through his teeth. "It could have been so much worse. At least she has her arms."

Imogene nods, makes a clucking sound and rubs the spot on her hand that is already rising to a bruise.

IT'S A SHORT DRIVE FROM THE HOSPITAL TO ST. MARY'S STAR of the Sea, where the upper floors of the church serve as the dormitory and school for the boarders, all children in grades K-12. Behind the church is the playground, an uncovered parking lot of hard packed gravel spray-painted with hopscotch squares. The gravel crunches and pops under the tires as the station wagon labors over the lot. It's high tide and the wind off the water a few blocks away sends the monkey bars clacking, the canary yellow tetherball on the chain bobbing. The children—all fifty of them—are shrieking. Two girls shower a smaller, red-haired girl with gravel. The teacher's aide, Judy Johns, grimaces fiercely and wrings her hands.

Father Dismus switches off the engine. Together they squint at the children. The light is like that here, sharp enough to force a grimace, but never strong enough to break her out in a sweat. "I know it's short notice, but we need a sub and I heard you needed the work." Father Dismus turns to Imogene. "Besides, Sister Clement asked for you specifically."

"Why me?" Imogene is beyond bewildered. If anyone knows how unfit she is for a sub job these days, it's Sister Clement and Father Dismus, who have recently spotted her leaving the AA meetings held in the basement of the church and heading directly to the bar across the street.

With his thumb Father Dismus pushes his glasses higher onto the bridge of his nose. "You're one of her old students. You'd remember how she'd want things run."

Imogene swallows hard. She remembers well her days in Sister's Clement's classroom. Remembers Frank sitting at the desk in front of hers. It was Sister Clement's habit to assault him with the catechism, a series of questions regarding man's purpose and relationship to God, while it was Frank's habit to stand there trembling, a stream of urine speeding down his leg. Imogene shakes her head. "Give me a day to think about it," she says, shoving open the door and sliding from the seat.

BEFORE SHE LOST HER TEACHING LICENSE ON ACCOUNT OF HER drinking, when she was still working in the Clatsop County and

North Plains sub pool, she'd get calls from schools as far north as Astoria and as far south as Manzanita. And because of the money she'd go. Because of the money she'd endure that awful moment of stepping through the door of the classroom and being sized up by the students. In Warrenton, she could always smell the contempt of the sixth grade girls—sixth graders!—who already knew how to wear make-up and high heels, their slim hips rolling with the lazy walk of people who knew things Imogene never would. Those were the days she wished for the refuge of a uniform as full as a habit. Growing up poor and with a horsy face, Imogene had as a high school student contemplated life in a convent, a life balanced between service to others and solitude, a comfortable prospect. If nothing else, she could hide her bulging body behind the thick folds of the habit, that floor-length costume that made even the fat nuns look as if they floated on air when they walked.

As graduation approached and everyone else in her class, Judy Johns included, settled on a mate or a job or more education, or all three, Imogene settled on nothing. And though she had never been one for visions, one day the answer seemed to present itself this way as she was standing beside Sister Clement. A shaft of light illuminated the nun's face and neck, and she tipped her chin toward the sun. The lenses of her glasses reflected such a piercing brightness that Imogene had to shield her eyes. Feeling in her rudderless, girlish heart a roiling mixture of fear of Sister Clement and a terrible desire for her approval, Imogene decided right then that she would in fact be a nun, an Ursuline like her, and Imogene made the mistake of saying so.

"Some girls aren't built for it. It's a lonely life," Sister Clement said, gripping the railing and Imogene noticed for the first time how chapped her knuckles were, how red the meat of her fingers. "A nun never stops being a nun. We don't have off hours or breaks," she explained. "We can drink a little, but never ever do we smoke." Sister Clement turned and gave her a thorough look. Imogene and her brother Frank were known for their halos of smoke and their trail of cigarette butts.

"I could quit smoking," Imogene said.

"You mean for Lent, like."

"No, for good."

Sister Clement snorted. "Too late. If God is the air we breathe then our lungs must be pure." She turned to Imogene and poked her in the chest with a finger. "I'll bet with your bad ticker and your tarred up pipes, you couldn't run these steps without keeling over."

The steps were narrow and steep and one look told Imogene that Sister Clement was right. The next day Imogene filled out the loan applications for a series of teacher training courses at the community college and stopped talking about being a nun.

IMOGENE LIGHTS ANOTHER CIGARETTE AND STEPS OUT ONTO the cinder block porch of her single wide. Overhead the wind pushes the clouds to the horizon, where the sky is rare-steak red. The kind of sky the fishers and crabbers like and if the water doesn't go to chop, she might soon see the lights of their boats. She inhales deep, draws the smoke into her lungs, thinks she's burning, on fire, and smiles.

When she considers the reliable ingredients that make up her life—the misery of being routinely dumped, the comfort of boxed wine—she can't overlook her many sub jobs in the lower grades. And she suddenly feels generous. They may give her a headache, but nothing seems as right or true as children. And though they may make demands, may disappoint, rarely do they break her heart. From her pocket Imogene retrieves her vial of Digitek and taps out two pills, holds the bottle to her ear and gives it a shake. Kids do not expect as much. You could screw up and they'd forgive you. At least the young ones were like that. For all these reasons and a few more, Imogene genuinely likes children more than she had thought she would, and she gets pangs some days, wanting a few of her own. This is the clencher, the deciding vote. Imogene leans against the glass slider, gummy in the tracks with sand, then makes her way to the kitchenette to call Father Dismus.

THE ENTIRE ROOM BURSTS WITH HANDS ON IMOGENE'S FIRST day at St. Mary's: orange palm prints bordering the wall are turkeys, the thumbs forming the heads and wattles. Green hands are shamrocks, blue prints are peacocks, purple ones fat starfish. Hands are the sun, the finger the rays. Ten fists are ten moons. Ten fists pressed knuckle-side down are owls perched on the thick branches of thumbs.

A weary fleet of ancient microscopes are stationed on the desks and behind each microscope sits a third-grade child, staring at her, measuring her, reading the lines on her face. In their school-issue uniforms of starched shirts and jumpers for the girls, trousers for the boys, they look too clean-cut, too subdued to have pushed a nun as substantial as Sister Clement down a staircase.

Imogene clears her throat. "My name is Miss McCrary, or Miss M, if you like. I know we are all keeping Sister Clement in our prayers and she wanted me to thank you and tell you that she misses you all." She can feel her smile going stale. It's sneaky to speak for someone else.

In the front row a boy lifts his fat, grimy hand high in the air. "You're not a nun, are you?" he asks. His hair is so blond it threatens an instant headache.

"No," Imogene says, fingering her white lace collar. The collar is attached to the most conservative blouse Imogene owns, the closest she'll ever get to passing for a reformed nun, but even in this, she realizes, she's failed.

"I can tell because of your shoes. Sister Clement's don't make any noise on the floor," says a dark-skinned boy with a large bandage over his arm.

"And you don't have any kids either, do you?" a freckle-faced girl with thick glasses says, her hand trailing up into the air as an afterthought. In Imogene's day, such a tardy hand raising would have earned this girl a whack from Sister Clement's ruler.

"No. But now I have all of you," Imogene says with a wink so that they will think of themselves as small gifts, the way she is reminding herself right now to think of them.

The children continue to stare. They don't even blink, Imogene notes as she lowers herself carefully into Sister Clement's chair and discovers the secret of the woman's mysterious height: stashed at the back of the knee-hole are platform rubber-soled shoes and on the seat of the chair, extra cushions. Imogene glances at the lesson book Sister Clement keeps for herself: five empty squares are headed with five different subject titles. The first square is for science, a subject she flunked twice under Sister Clement's tutelage, and Imogene feels her heart stutter stepping.

"Let's play a game." Her voice hits the far wall and bounces back.

"I'll call out your name and you tell me one interesting science fact you've learned this week." Imogene runs her finger across the top of the roster. "Anders, David."

"When a horse is sick, it crosses its legs," says the blinding towhead in the front row. Beside his name Sister Clement has written a reminder to herself: introduce to hygiene.

"Diegas, Rudy."

The boy in the back stands and adjusts his clip-on tie. "A shark throws up its stomach once a month to clean it. Afterward it swallows it back down." Next to his name Sister Clement has written: Dark skin. Sneaky; watch him.

"The universe has spots," says the girl named Graciella Fiero, her eyes trained on Imogene's throat. Graciella—the name is like water and Imogene is surprised to see a big-chested girl stuffed into a too-small uniform raising a forearm over her head as if shielding a blow. Imogene glances at Sister Clement's note: Always a bruise on her arm. Pray for her; she probably needs it.

"Not spots. Freckles," adds the red-haired Findlay girl. Sister Clement's note reads: first name Eilis, pronounced A-lish. One of those weird Irish names.

"A river has two sides: where it came from and where it is going." This from the tiny Morgan girl whose voice melts like the pure notes of a bell. If Sister Clement has a favorite, she'd probably be it. Even though she's swimming in a starched blouse three sizes too large for her, Imogene can see that she sits with perfect posture, her body like the letter L behind her desk. Imogene is not too surprised to see Sister Clement's comment: Shows promise. The closest the nun probably ever gets to doling out high praise.

Imogene closes the ledger. She bites her lip and tries to remember something, anything from her teacher training classes that will help her fill up the remaining minutes of science hour. "Does anybody have any questions?" she asks, her voice as buoyant as she knows how to make it.

The Anders boy looks to the windows and for the first time Imogene notices his funny shaped head, dished in at the rear. She notices, too, that the windows, which had all been closed—she's sure of that—are open now and sand flies are buzzing into the room.

Lilly produces a times table worksheet and holds it aloft. "Do we have to fill in all these squares?"

The words bring an instant rush of gratitude. Yes, Lilly is the perfect student, rescuing a foundering sub. "Yes," Imogene improvises. "I'll collect them at the end of the hour." And the children bend over their worksheets, counting their fingers quietly against their desks and thighs, the sight so reassuring Imogene thinks of saying a prayer of thanks as she pulls each of the windows closed and locks them one by one.

WHEN THE BELL RINGS, THE CHILDREN FILE QUIETLY THROUGH the door and merge with the other children in the school. They head down the hall to another door that leads to the metal steps. Imogene walks slowly beside them. No one speaks. But Catholic kids are like that, having been herded about all their lives with whistles and claps, or under Sister Clement's watch, a hand-held clicker. One click from Sister Clement and the ordinary chaos of movement settled to a full stop, which Imogene knew signaled to Sister Clement perfection in parochial training. But Imogene had never believed in clicking or whistling. A child is not a dog, she thinks as she walks to the head of her small rank of students.

Imogene opens the door and the children push past her, jostling against her body, jogging her arms, nearly lifting her off her feet. She grabs for the railing, thinks again of Sister Clement, her broken legs, the spittle on her lower lip, her rage. Imogene can see now how easily it happened—one misstep on a fatigued flight of stairs, or a well-placed shove at just the right moment. It probably never occurred to Sister Clement that such elemental fixtures in her routine—these stairs, her students—could ever fail her.

Imogene sits on the topmost step, pops a Digitek to settle her jittery heart. At the far edge of an overgrown field, where the dune grass and scotch broom grow tall and sharp, the older boys take turns lashing one another. It's an old game her brother Frank used to play called Crown of Thorns. Whoever looks the most like Jesus, forehead scored and palms reddened, wins. The girls on the gravel lot don't play so much as huddle and some of the younger girls play a game called Faith. They stand on a raised log, cross their arms over their chests, close their eyes, and fall backward, trusting that the three girls standing below will catch them. Mercy is a more active game that favors girls with long fingernails and strong wrists. Imogene watches two girls press the heels of their palms together and lace their fingers. With a whip of their wrists, they roll their hands under. Imogene winces, remembering this game, the rows of crescent shaped cuts on her own hands and the quick cries of *mercy,* what you said when you couldn't stand the biting of the fingernails anymore.

Judy Johns climbs the shaky stairs. "Hey," Judy says, easing her wiry body a step below Imogene's feet. She is like Imogene, thirty-eight, a survivor of Sister Clement's class. Even worse, Judy has lost a husband at sea and a child, still-born. Most women would have gone barking mad. But not Judy Johns, who possesses a persistence to keep on keeping on that both amazes and frightens Imogene.

"Hey," Imogene says, tucking her pack of cigarettes inside her purse.

Together they watch the fifth and sixth grade girls surround the Findlay girl, the only third grader available. The Findlay girl tucks her chin to her chest and holds her arms at her sides as the other girls gather handfuls of crushed razor shells and gravel. The older girls let loose with a volley of shells and rocks and the Findley girl, mouth clamped, stands there taking it. Purgatory is the name of this game. If you ducked, you had to stand there for double the time. If you kept your eyes open and asked for more, you were let go early.

"'There's nothing like old school," Judy says.

"Nothing like nostalgia," Imogene replies.

"Nothing hurts like pain." Judy clicks her tongue, her gaze steady on the girl bearing up under heavy fire.

This is, Imogene knows, the closest the two of them will ever come to holding a real conversation: parroting the pet phrases of Sister Clement.

Imogene rubs the backs of her arms, remembering how she and Judy could stand there longer than anybody, stand there with Sister Clement looking on, her whistle held between her lips. Not until she saw blood did Sister Clement blow that whistle and break things up. For even then it was Sister Clement's conviction that suffering was an essential prerequisite for any true character formation. But the Findlay girl—she doesn't even flinch! And these stones the girls throw!—are so much larger than the ones Imogene remembers throwing. These games, she's sure of it now, have grown much more vicious. What it is about suffering these kids are actually learning, Imogene wonders.

A bell rings and the children file up the steps and back into their respective classrooms. Imogene is just about to sit on Sister Clement's stacked chair when she sees the windows have been thrown open again. The flies swoop into the room and buzz around the desk and the soured heel wells of Sister Clement's shoes. "Why are these windows open?" Imogene asks, but no one answers. She walks to the windows and, one by one, pulls them closed.

"It stinks in here," Lilly Morgan sings out. Then Graciella pinches her nose and Rudy, the boy in the back, does the same. Imogene notices that his wound has spread past either side of his bandage. Imogene sniffs, thinks she can smell it.

And she notices again David's funny shaped head and Lilly's eyes that are too big for her small face. As Imogene backs into the blackboard, an oily sense that something is not right rises in her stomach. *Knock it off*, she chides herself, feeling silly and foolish for so quickly losing her internal composure. But as she straightens and distributes oversize pieces of white paper and boxes of crayons to each of the children, she can't help looking at their hands, their strong wrists, can't help wondering.

"We like drawing," David says, tapping his feet. "There aren't any test questions or quizzes and we always draw the same thing."

Imogene blinks at his shock-white hair. In her day they drew what Sister Clement told them to. Lazarus' sloppy resurrection or Jesus' oozing heart if Easter were approaching. The thought that Sister

Clement was loosening up in her later years or at least letting them draw happier pictures makes Imogene glad for the children; they will have fewer reasons to hate the woman later. But it saddens her to know that people do change in ways they can't help, even if it's for the better, and suddenly Imogene feels sorry for Sister Clement.

"Maybe we could let Sister Clement know we miss her." Imogene's words tumble out as the ideas come upon her. "We could draw get-well pictures to cheer her up. And then tomorrow I can deliver them to her."

Rudy has already rolled his paper into a tight scroll and is swatting at a fly. But the other students stare intently at Imogene.

"What if she doesn't get well?" David picks at a scab on his knee.

"A picture can't help you get better," the Findlay girl says quietly, wrinkling her nose so that her freckles gather. Imogene looks at her, at those freckles spattered in dark confusion over her face, and suddenly thinks she needs a drink, or three, maybe four.

For twenty minutes the children work in silence as Imogene makes the rounds. They pick their noses and without shame! It's enough to make her smile, though she's careful about that. When she took the training courses, she'd been told to try and be inconspicuous, especially around the making of art. Being inconspicuous was not a technique employed by Sister Clement. But then, it would be hard, Imogene decides as she stands behind David, to be inconspicuous if you were the only ruler-wielding Ursuline nun still wearing a full habit when every other nun in the country had long ago adopted more casual dress.

In the center of his empty paper, David draws a black dot. He grinds the crayon in a tight circle, following the contour of the dot so that it grows into a three-dimensional layer of wax. At the desk next to his, Lilly draws an oval, the crayon squeaking over the wax with each pass. The Findlay girl (Imogene will never get that first name, she knows—no use trying) grips a black crayon and draws something larger, something with a hump or a head, an elephant or a camel. Imogene can't tell which and rather than ask and embarrass both of them, she presses her lips together and moves on to Rudy's desk. His picture is a tangle of black scribbles.

Imogene can't help herself. "What's that supposed to be?"

"The dark middle. It moves real fast, see?" Rudy taps at the tangles.

"Nice," Imogene says and hopes Rudy doesn't notice the too-bright tone of her voice.

Graciella is the real artist—even through the scrim of her hair hanging over her drawing, Imogene can detect an animal's bristled coat, teeth, claws.

"That's really wonderful." Imogene touches her elbow. Graciella winces, hunkers low.

"It's God. Wild," Graciella's voice frays to a whisper, "but good." She turns her drawing face down.

Imogene blinks and steps away. She stations a Scotch-tape dispenser on an empty desk and observes the children, one by one, slip to the back of the room to tape their drawings to the wall. When Imogene sees their pictures side by side, she has to sit down. They read like a series of animated panels, a sure story emerging from square to square. David's dot grows to Lilly's oval, which becomes the Findlay girl's animal with legs. Rudy's picture of darkness and the speed with which it flies through the air becomes Graciella's image of a dog, mouth open, eyes glinting, lunging out of the boundaries of the white square and into the classroom. Of course Sister Clement taught her class to draw the same thing so many years ago, how a dot becomes a dog, how it pleases God, inscrutable in his ways, to assume such shapes so that we might better see and understand him. But the quickness of their hands, the sureness of their strokes, it shakes her up. Two minutes later, Imogene's heart is still locked in a stutter. She knows already that she will spend the rest of the afternoon and evening in her trailer, emptying a box of Franzia.

WHAT SHE CAN'T TELL ANYONE IS THAT SHE'S DOING THE world a favor when she drinks. The first drink relaxes the muscles in her jaw. The second keeps them relaxed. The third makes her benevolent—spacious in her heart and mind and lungs. Alcohol sands down her complicated grief for all things lost—her parents and Frank and even those things and people she'd never had and dare not hope for. But days like these, when she's increasingly long on recall, she thinks it isn't fair that her memory pains her the way it does. And this she can't quite understand: why God would make life hurt if it were meant to last so long. This, she decides, is further proof that God not only winks at a full-blown drinking problem, but is actually egging her on.

It's the kind of thinking that only confirms what Imogene has suspected all along. Sister Clement had been right; Imogene would have been a terrible nun. Forget the fact that she's lost her teaching license on account of the drinking. Forget the fact that she had never been the best of Sister Clement's students, had been held back on account of her mind that wandered, though where to it was hard to say. She supposes it drifted to playground games. To shapes in the sky, muscled forms that made her think she could see faith and hope in the substantiality of cloud.

Half a pack of cigarettes and one-third of the way through the box of Franzia, Graciella's words churn inside her: "wild, but good." It reminds her of something Sister Clement once said all those years ago when Imogene was a third grader, sitting, perhaps in the very same seat as Graciella. Imogene never forgot it. Sister Clement had been explaining a poem, "The Hound of Heaven." That Imogene can remember the lesson, drunk as she is, is a tribute to Sister Clement's matchless teaching technique: fear + shame + humiliation = total memory recall. Yes, Imogene got that poem memorized and can even remember with a caustic clarity Sister Clement's explanation of the poem's meaning. God is a dog, untamed and wild, who comes, in his grace, to overtake us in spite of ourselves, to save us from ourselves when we don't even know we need it. Imogene remembers gripping the sides of her desk so hard, her hands cramped, for these were terrible words corroborating everything she'd suspected about God: he was mean and toothy and long on punishment, just like Sister Clement.

"It's hard grace, and it might even hurt a little," Imogene remembers Sister Clement explaining.

"Why?" Imogene had asked and Frank groaned quietly in the desk in front of Imogene's.

"Well a dog does have teeth, doesn't it?" Imogene is sure she remembers a thin smile drifting across the woman's face and just as quickly disappearing.

Frank's hand slipped up. "Is this going to be on a test?" And Sister

Clement pressed her lips together tight, the way she always did just before her ruler came whistling down.

Imogene pours another drink, four fingers thick. God may be wild, but good? She's not so sure. At this very moment she decides that tomorrow she'll look those kids straight in the eye and tell them a thing or two about the God she knows, who takes away every good thing she's ever had or known simply to remind her that He can.

The phone jolts her. She senses before she answers that it will be Judy, out of breath, calling from the hospital.

"Imogene," Judy rasps. "It's Sister Clement. She's taken a turn and she's asked for you—specifically. Bless her, she's such a saint. So close to God, lying there, smiling."

"She's probably higher than a kite." Imogene squints at the clouds outside.

"She's a good woman. You shouldn't say things like that. She's had a hard life."

Haven't we all, Imogene wants to say. So what if Sister Clement joined up with the Ursulines by default, having almost been married, and having lost her fiance just days before the wedding. It was an old joke with Frank: the man probably died at the thought of waking up alongside of her for the rest of his life. But nobody made her join, nobody made her teach children. Sister Clement chose those things for herself.

Imogene downs the rest of her drink. "Frank wet the bed because of her," she says to Judy at last, sliding the phone back into its cradle. And after being turned down by the army on account of their family history of bad hearts, he enrolled in seminary to prove to people like Sister Clement that he was still worth something. And a year later, after being dismissed from the Jesuit priesthood—failed and ashamed—he climbed into their bathtub, cut his wrists along the leaders, and quietly died.

BANKS OF MACHINES BLINKING AND DRIPPING AND BEEPING transform Sister Clement's room into a metered cacophony. An oxygen tube snakes down her throat, and Father Dismus explains to Imogene how a blood clot in Sister Clement's leg is threatening to break off at any moment and lodge in her lungs. And now, the ordinary air in the room, being a mere twelve percent oxygen, is not enough for the woman. But even with this purer air, Imogene can see that Sister Clement is leaving them all behind; she is shrinking and her hands, unmoored without a ruler or a clicker to hold, rove over the vast canvas of white bedsheet.

Imogene carefully sidesteps a brown paper bag which holds Sister Clement's habit, neatly folded. She nods hello to Judy. Only then does she notice the pictures tacked up around the room, the five pictures her students drew earlier that day of the black dot becoming a dog. At the bottom corners the children have pressed their signature palm prints.

Judy pats Sister Clement's hand, but the woman's gaze is locked on the drawings.

"Who hung these pictures up?" Imogene asks.

"Why the children, of course." Judy looks to Father Dismus who looks to Sister Clement.

"They came here?" Imogene can hear alarm rising in her voice.

"And they recited a poem for her, you know the one about the dog Sister Clement teaches every year during Lent."

"I remember it." Imogene swallows, tastes something bitter in her mouth.

Judy approaches the drawings, and stands just inches from the black crayon wax. "Those kids are really smart. They got that entire poem up by heart—every bit of it without so much as a stumble or a stutter."

"It was incredible," Father Dismus says softly.

"Well, suffer the children," Judy says.

Imogene steps beside Sister Clement, leans into her line of vision and sees that her pupils are dilated, large black dots. Sister Clement's eyes begin to water slightly and she reaches for Imogene's hand. She grips her hand, pats it, even. Imogene blinks. It's the closest, she knows, the woman will ever get to expressing true affection. Sister Clement's brows suddenly join in a frown. She moves her head slightly and fixes her gaze again on the drawings. Imogene turns her head and studies the pictures, thinking if she stares at them long enough she will glimpse what it is Sister Clement sees.

THE WALK HOME FROM THE HOSPITAL TAKES IMOGENE PAST A long line of trailers, each of them ugly, but no two ugly in exactly the same way. As she passes the neighbor's property, their hound lifts his snout and bays. His voice rises and falls in the wind. It's the saddest most baleful sound she's ever heard and as Imogene skirts past her abandoned StairMaster, the handles of which she now uses to hang out her wet laundry, she actually considers praying for the dog.

In her bedroom, she can hear a slant rain beginning to fall, tapping on her corrugated roof. She pours a tall glass of Jim Beam and considers Sister Clement. No one would accuse the woman of being beautiful, but neither could Imogene deny that there in the hospital room, her face soft, her eyes wet and focused on those drawings, one hand on hers, Sister Clement had become lovely in a way that defied explanation. Gone was her trademark rage and bitterness, and in its place was something almost like calm or even tenderness. It was a sight so unfamiliar, Imogene still doesn't quite know what to think.

The phone rings.

"It's Sister Clement," Father Dismus says, his voice thin and spectral. "She's gone on. We'll say prayers for her at the church tomorrow afternoon and hold a memorial mass this Saturday. Do you want me to tell the children?"

"No," Imogene says after a long pause. "I'll do it."

With the rain teletyping messages over her roof and the neighbor's hound yodeling it's a long time before Imogene can sleep. Her thoughts are roiling. And while she hoped she might drink her way toward an epiphany, it's clear to her now that the bottle's empty that she's just as bewildered as ever. It's not that she ever thought any one of them were invincible. Frank was built of timid constitution and too good for this world anyway. But a woman like Sister Clement was far too sturdy to die the way she did and Imogene thinks again of the children, taking it upon themselves to visit the woman. What did they tell her, she wonders, when they bent over her bed to offer their comfort? What else do they know about that they've not told Imogene?

SHE TAKES HER TIME GETTING TO SCHOOL THE NEXT MORNING. The wind off the water blasts so fiercely, it drives the tears from her eyes across her temples and into her hair. She is surprised by her sorrow. She is astonished to discover that she will actually miss Sister Clement, whom she has somehow learned to appreciate like one appreciates the growling of an old generator. The noise and fury just becomes so familiar over time it actually brings comfort. After all, Sister Clement is—was—one of the few people left who remembered her and Frank as children, and without her, Imogene feels suddenly very alone.

When she gets to the school, she smokes three cigarettes before she feels bucked up enough for the classroom.

Graciella is the first to stop by Sister Clement's desk. "Do you know what happens to you when you die?" she asks her.

The question sounds odd, considering the grim message Imogene has to give the class. "You don't have to be afraid of that," Imogene says. The wound on the girl's elbow is darker and Imogene stifles the urge to touch the girl.

"I know." Graciella's gaze settles on Imogene's open purse and the empty pack of cigarettes, her near-empty vial of heart meds. "But I'm scared for you."

The bell rings and Graciella drifts back to her desk where she huddles with David, Rudy, Lilly, and the Findlay girl, their gazes trained on Imogene. The flies loop in lazy arcs through the windows and Imogene doesn't even bother closing them. Instead, she faces the children, takes a breath. "I have sad news, class. Sister Clement has passed away."

The children look at her calmly, completely unsurprised. David rubs the back of his funny shaped head.

Imogene swallows. "That means we won't see her here anymore, but someday we'll see her in heaven."

"Is this going to be on a test?" Rudy scratches at his scab. "Because that's not an essential mystery and today is Wednesday, and we always talk about essential mysteries on Wednesdays."

Imogene frantically thumbs through the book of lesson plans. Silly, she knows, because they are blank and open as a wide-brimmed day. Except for that fuzzy notion that God might be a dog, she can't remember the essential mysteries, and realizes that perhaps she never knew them in the first place. Again, she wishes she had been a better student, or at least had the foresight to bring another pack of cigarettes today. "OK," she says at last. "You call out the essential mysteries and I'll list them on the board."

"Bread is life. That's why you aren't supposed to cut it with a knife." This from Lilly in a sing-song patter and Imogene struggles to keep up at the board. The flies are starting to get to her. Her lungs ache a little at the edges, and she realizes that she's forgotten to take her meds.

Then from Rudy, swatting flies in the back of the room: "A guitar is fitted with its own coffin. So is a turtle, a violin and a pair of shoes."

"Sacrifice comes from shelter," Graciella says, her finger trailing an entry in an enormous dictionary balanced on her knees. "That's why those on the threshold need the biggest push."

David, sitting beside Graciella, flips through the pages and taps a dirty finger in the margin beside another entry. "Danger comes from the Lord."

"A blessing is a thrashing at a wound which explains why scar tissue has to be broken to be beaten," the Findlay girl says, adjusting her glasses.

Imogene squints at the girl. Her face isn't covered with freckles but with hundreds of gravel-shaped scars.

The buzzing in her ears and in the classroom begins to echo. How could such young people have the look in their eyes of such old men and women? How could they know as much as they do? She and Frank had never been in possession of such prescience or even mere insight. They'd been dutiful, obedient students, but never this wise. Imogene sinks into Sister Clement's chair and reaches for her meds. Her heart squeezes and she feels her body going limp. "I—I'm not well." In her own ears her voice sounds foreign and astonished.

The Findlay girl slides out of her chair and stands beside Imogene. "It happens to everyone," she says. "And it doesn't hurt much."

Then Rudy and Graciella pipe up: "Just because a dog has teeth doesn't mean it will bite."

"What?" Imogene asks.

"Because it pleases him sometimes to assume such shapes." Lilly's voice sails across the room. Rudy and Graciella lift Imogene by the elbows and usher her through the door, down the hallway, and to the lip of the metal staircase. They all have their hands on her now guiding her down the steps. If her feet had faltered, the gentle, steady pressure of their hands would have caught and carried her. Sister Clement had misunderstood. These were not pushes, but nudges, and there was kindness, not malice, behind these hands. She sees now why they are here, these children, these physical embodiments of God's grace, schooling her in all she'd misconstrued, with a check to the hip, lift to the elbow, propelling her across the playground.

Imogene glances at her feet which glide over the gravel—the children are that strong, that steady. Then she sees Frank. He's sitting in a swing and wearing a work flannel sleeved at the shoulders. He grips the chains and she sees his bare arms unblemished, the skin unbroken. He gives her a thumbs up and a shaky smile and then he is gone.

At the edge of the field the children hesitate. Behind them the hard packed gravel is gray and wet. Before them the weeds are long and sharp.

"I like you best." Rudy gives her a piece of Bazooka Joe bubble gum encrusted with lint and sand.

"You listened to us," says the Findlay girl. She presses a sand dollar against Imogene's palm and Imogene knows without even shaking it that the girl has given her the seven teeth, the seven lucky turtledoves. Lilly kisses her on the cheek and presses a twig of moonbrake into her hand, and David does the same, leaving her with a gull's feather. Graciella brushes her mouth against Imogene's ear. "Don't be scared," she says. And then they are gone. She can hear them behind her, skipping over the gravel and shrieking and swinging on the monkey bars. But it's the wind that's got her attention, tugging at the hem of her skirt, pulling her by the hips to the center of the field where the fog has lowered and the salt chokes the air. Her stomach spirals to a pinpoint somewhere down her left leg and with it her blood, her breath. Her heart falls rib by rib. She reaches for her pills, but in her pockets it's the gifts from the children she finds.

In a blink everything clarifies to its elements: the fog lowers and the sky becomes water and salt. She feels the salt grainy on her face, and she thinks of Sister Clement's face transformed. Thinks of revisions and remedies. Thinks of teeth. Air pure as gin rises up around her. But her heart is not hale enough, her lungs not strong enough for it. Every breath rasps sharp in her ear. Her body is stock still but her thoughts whirl, light and furious. She wonders if this was how Sister Clement felt—uncalibrated but calm.

From across the field a dark shape emerges and grows larger as it moves through the grass. *Wild, but good.* It's that dog, barreling toward her, coming to carry her off, to deliver her. She knows this now. Knows this is what Sister Clement had seen while lying in her bed. Not coming to punish. Not racing through the razor weed to deepen her wounds or tear her to bits. But even as Imogene reconciles herself to this revision, she feels for a split second afraid. So much is happening. And then she is relieved. Her jaw relaxes. *All right,* Imogene sighs. It's just one more thing on a long list of things she's miscalculated. The dog—which looks more like a wolf than a dog and is much bigger than she imagined—is almost upon her. Its ears are laid back, eyes sharp and breath trails in long clouds from its open mouth. Her heart makes a final lurch. Imogene closes her eyes, imagining the feel of the animal's hot breath on her face, her hand. She opens her eyes, leans forward and stretches her hand out to touch it.

LEO TOLSTOY

LEO TOLSTOY WAS BORN IN 1828 IN TULA PROVINCE, RUSSIA. His parents died when he was a child, and he was brought up by relatives, later studying law and oriental languages at Kazan University. He grew disappointed with the quality of the education he was receiving there and returned to his hometown of Yasnaya Polyana, spending much of his time there and in Moscow and St. Petersburg. In 1851 he and his older brother left for the Caucasus, where they enlisted with an artillery regiment. This was when he began his writing career, publishing the autobiographical trilogy *Childhood, Boyhood,* and *Youth.*

In 1857 he visited France, Switzerland, and Germany, and it was during these trips that he came to a spiritual crisis that turned him from being an author of books on privileged society to a deeply held belief in the teaching of Christ. His epic novel *War and Peace* appeared between 1865 and 1869, and his other masterpiece, *Anna Karenina,* was published from 1873 to 1877. Later, his books on the Christian life, *A Confession* and *What I Believe* (which was banned in 1884), resulted in his being excommunicated from the Russian Orthodox Church in 1901 for his writing's radical stance on the importance of a personal relationship with Christ and the perceived anarchist stance "turning the other cheek" was believed to embrace. He died of pneumonia on November 7, 1910, at a railway station far from home after choosing to live his life as an ascetic.

A LOST OPPORTUNITY

BY LEO TOLSTOY

TRANSLATED BY BENJAMIN R. TUCKER

"Then came Peter to him, and said, Lord, how oft shall my brother sin against me, and I forgive him? till seven times?" . . .

"So likewise shall my heavenly Father do also unto you, if ye from your hearts forgive not every one his brother their trespasses."

—MATTHEW 18: 21-35

In a certain village there lived a peasant by the name of Ivan Scherbakoff. He was prosperous, strong, and vigorous, and was considered the hardest worker in the whole village. He had three sons, who supported themselves by their own labor. The eldest was married, the second about to be married, and the youngest took care of the horses and occasionally attended to the plowing.

The peasant's wife, Ivanovna, was intelligent and industrious, while her daughter-in-law was a simple, quiet soul, but a hard worker.

There was only one idle person in the household, and that was Ivan's father, a very old man who for seven years had suffered from asthma, and who spent the greater part of his time lying on the brick oven.

Ivan had plenty of everything—three horses, with one colt, a cow with calf, and fifteen sheep. The women made the men's clothes, and in addition to performing all the necessary household labor, also worked in the field; while the men's industry was confined altogether to the farm.

What was left of the previous year's supply of provisions was ample for their needs, and they sold a quantity of oats sufficient to pay their taxes and other expenses.

Thus life went smoothly for Ivan.

The peasant's next-door neighbor was a son of Gordey Ivanoff, called "Gavryl the Lame." It once happened that Ivan had a quarrel with him; but while old man Gordey was yet alive, and Ivan's father was the head of the household, the two peasants lived as good neighbors should. If the women of one house required the use of a sieve or pail, they borrowed it from the inmates of the other house. The same condition of affairs existed between the men. They lived more like one family, the one dividing his possessions with the other, and perfect harmony reigned between the two families.

If a stray calf or cow invaded the garden of one of the farmers, the other willingly drove it away, saying: "Be careful, neighbor, that your stock does not again stray into my garden; we should put a fence up." In the same way they had no secrets from each other. The doors of their houses and barns had neither bolts nor locks, so sure were they of each other's honesty. Not a shadow of suspicion darkened their daily intercourse.

Thus lived the old people.

In time the younger members of the two households started farming. It soon became apparent that they would not get along as peacefully as the old people had done, for they began quarrelling without the slightest provocation.

A hen belonging to Ivan's daughter-in-law commenced laying eggs, which the young woman collected each morning, intending to keep them for the Easter holidays. She made daily visits to the barn, where, under an old wagon, she was sure to find the precious egg.

One day the children frightened the hen and she flew over their neighbor's fence and laid her egg in their garden.

Ivan's daughter-in-law heard the hen cackling, but said: "I am very busy just at present, for this is the eve of a holy day, and I must clean and arrange this room. I will go for the egg later on."

When evening came, and she had finished her task, she went to the barn, and as usual looked under the old wagon, expecting to find an egg. But, alas! no egg was visible in the accustomed place.

Greatly disappointed, she returned to the house and inquired of her mother-in-law and the other members of the family if they had taken it. "No," they said, "we know nothing of it."

Taraska, the youngest brother-in-law, coming in soon after, she also inquired of him if he knew anything about the missing egg. "Yes," he replied; "your pretty, crested hen laid her egg in our neighbors' garden, and after she had finished cackling she flew back again over the fence."

The young woman, greatly surprised on hearing this, turned and looked long and seriously at the hen, which was sitting with closed eyes beside the rooster in the chimney-corner. She asked the hen where it laid the egg. At the sound of her voice it simply opened and closed its eyes, but could make no answer.

She then went to the neighbors' house, where she was met by an old woman, who said: "What do you want, young woman?"

Ivan's daughter-in-law replied: "You see, grandmother, my hen flew into your yard this morning. Did she not lay an egg there?"

"We did not see any," the old woman replied; "we have our own hens—God be praised!—and they have been laying for this long time. We hunt only for the eggs our own hens lay, and have no use for the eggs other people's hens lay. Another thing I want to tell you, young woman: we do not go into other people's yards to look for eggs."

Now this speech greatly angered the young woman, and she replied in the same spirit in which she had been spoken to, only using much stronger language and speaking at greater length.

The neighbor replied in the same angry manner, and finally the women began to abuse each other and call vile names. It happened that old Ivan's wife, on her way to the well for water, heard the dispute, and joined the others, taking her daughter-in-law's part.

Gavryl's housekeeper, hearing the noise, could not resist the temptation to join the rest and to make her voice heard. As soon as she appeared on the scene, she, too, began to abuse her neighbor, reminding her of many disagreeable things which had happened (and many which had not happened) between them. She became so infuriated during her denunciations that she lost all control of herself, and ran around like some mad creature.

Then all the women began to shout at the same time, each trying to say two words to another's one, and using the vilest language in the quarreller's vocabulary.

"You are such and such," shouted one of the women. "You are a thief, a schlukha; your father-in-law is even now starving, and you have no shame. You beggar, you borrowed my sieve and broke it. You made a large hole in it, and did not buy me another."

"You have our scale-beam," cried another woman, "and must give it back to me;" whereupon she seized the scale-beam and tried to remove it from the shoulders of Ivan's wife.

In the melee which followed they upset the pails of water. They tore the covering from each other's head, and a general fight ensued.

Gavryl's wife had by this time joined in the fracas, and he, crossing the field and seeing the trouble, came to her rescue.

Ivan and his son, seeing that their womenfolk were being badly used, jumped into the midst of the fray, and a fearful fight followed.

Ivan was the most powerful peasant in all the country round, and it did not take him long to disperse the crowd, for they flew in all directions. During the progress of the fight Ivan tore out a large quantity of Gavryl's beard.

By this time a large crowd of peasants had collected, and it was with the greatest difficulty that they persuaded the two families to stop quarrelling.

This was the beginning.

Gavryl took the portion of his beard which Ivan had torn out, and, wrapping it in a paper, went to the moujiks' court and entered a complaint against Ivan.

Holding up the hair, he said, "I did not grow this for that bear Ivan to tear out!"

Gavryl's wife went round among the neighbors, telling them that they must not repeat what she told them, but that she and her husband were going to get the best of Ivan, and that he was to be sent to Siberia.

And so the quarrelling went on.

The poor old grandfather, sick with asthma and lying on the brick oven all the time, tried from the first to dissuade them from quarrelling, and begged of them to live in peace; but they would not listen to his good advice. He said to them: "You children are making a great fuss and much trouble about nothing. I beg of you to stop and think of what a little thing has caused all this trouble. It has arisen from only one egg. If our neighbors' children picked it up, it is all right. God bless them! One egg is of but little value, and without it God will supply sufficient for all our needs."

Ivan's daughter-in-law here interposed and said, "But they called us vile names."

The old grandfather again spoke, saying: "Well, even if they did call you bad names, it would have been better to return good for evil, and by your example show them how to speak better. Such conduct on your part would have been best for all concerned." He continued: "Well, you had a fight, you wicked people. Such things sometimes happen, but it would be better if you went afterward and asked forgiveness and buried your grievances out of sight. Scatter them to the four winds of heaven, for if you do not do so it will be the worse for you in the end."

The younger members of the family, still obstinate, refused to profit by the old man's advice, and declared he was not right, and that he only liked to grumble in his old-fashioned way.

Ivan refused to go to his neighbor, as the grandfather wished, saying: "I did not tear out Gavryl's beard. He did it himself, and his son tore my shirt and trousers into shreds."

Ivan entered suit against Gavryl. He first went to the village justice, and not getting satisfaction from him he carried his case to the village court.

While the neighbors were wrangling over the affair, each suing the other, it happened that a perch-bolt from Gavryl's wagon was lost; and the women of Gavryl's household accused Ivan's son of stealing it.

They said: "We saw him in the night-time pass by our window, on his way to where the wagon was standing." "And my sponsor," said one of them, "told me that Ivan's son had offered it for sale at the tavern."

This accusation caused them again to go into court for a settlement of their grievances.

While the heads of the families were trying to have their troubles settled in court, their home quarrels were constant, and frequently resulted in hand-to-hand encounters. Even the little children followed the example of their elders and quarrelled incessantly.

The women, when they met on the riverbank to do the family washing, instead of attending to their work passed the time in abusing each other, and not infrequently they came to blows.

At first the male members of the families were content with

accusing each other of various crimes, such as stealing and like meannesses. But the trouble in this mild form did not last long.

They soon resorted to other measures. They began to appropriate one another's things without asking permission, while various articles disappeared from both houses and could not be found. This was done out of revenge.

This example being set by the men, the women and children also followed, and life soon became a burden to all who took part in the strife.

Ivan Scherbakoff and "Gavryl the Lame" at last laid their trouble before the village meeting, in addition to having been in court and calling on the justice of the peace. Both of the latter had grown tired of them and their incessant wrangling. One time Gavryl would succeed in having Ivan fined, and if he was not able to pay it he would be locked up in the cold dreary prison for days. Then it would be Ivan's turn to get Gavryl punished in like manner, and the greater the injury the one could do the other the more delight he took in it.

The success of either in having the other punished only served to increase their rage against each other, until they were like mad dogs in their warfare.

If anything went wrong with one of them he immediately accused his adversary of conspiring to ruin him, and sought revenge without stopping to inquire into the rights of the case.

When the peasants went into court, and had each other fined and imprisoned, it did not soften their hearts in the least. They would only taunt one another on such occasions, saying: "Never mind; I will repay you for all this."

This state of affairs lasted for six years.

Ivan's father, the sick old man, constantly repeated his good advice. He would try to arouse their conscience by saying: "What are you doing, my children? Can you not throw off all these troubles, pay more attention to your business, and suppress your anger against your neighbors? There is no use in your continuing to live in this way, for the more enraged you become against each other the worse it is for you."

Again was the wise advice of the old man rejected.

At the beginning of the seventh year of the existence of the feud it happened that a daughter-in-law of Ivan's was present at a marriage. At the wedding feast she openly accused Gavryl of stealing a horse. Gavryl was intoxicated at the time and was in no mood to stand the insult, so in retaliation he struck the woman a terrific blow, which confined her to her bed for more than a week. The woman being in delicate health, the worst results were feared.

Ivan, glad of a fresh opportunity to harass his neighbor, lodged a formal complaint before the district-attorney, hoping to rid himself forever of Gavryl by having him sent to Siberia.

On examining the complaint the district-attorney would not consider it, as by that time the injured woman was walking about and as well as ever.

Thus again Ivan was disappointed in obtaining his revenge, and, not being satisfied with the district-attorney's decision, had the case transferred to the court, where he used all possible means to push his suit. To secure the favor of the village mayor he made him a present of half a gallon of sweet vodki; and to the mayor's secretary also he gave presents. By this means he succeeded in securing a verdict against Gavryl. The sentence was that Gavryl was to receive twenty lashes on his bare back, and the punishment was to be administered in the yard which surrounded the court-house.

When Ivan heard the sentence read he looked triumphantly at Gavryl to see what effect it would produce on him. Gavryl turned very white on hearing that he was to be treated with such indignity, and turning his back on the assembly left the room without uttering a word.

Ivan followed him out, and as he reached his horse he heard Gavryl saying: "Very well; my spine will burn from the lashes, but something will burn with greater fierceness in Ivan's household before long."

Ivan, on hearing these words, instantly returned to the court, and going up to the judges said: "Oh! just judges, he threatens to burn my house and all it contains."

A messenger was immediately sent in search of Gavryl, who was soon found and again brought into the presence of the judges.

"Is it true," they asked, "that you said you would burn Ivan's house and all it contained?"

Gavryl replied: "I did not say anything of the kind. You may give me as many lashes as you please—that is, if you have the power to do so. It seems to me that I alone have to suffer for the truth, while he," pointing to Ivan, "is allowed to do and say what he pleases." Gavryl wished to say something more, but his lips trembled, and the words refused to come; so in silence he turned his face toward the wall.

The sight of so much suffering moved even the judges to pity, and, becoming alarmed at Gavryl's continued silence, they said, "He may do both his neighbor and himself some frightful injury."

"See here, my brothers," said one feeble old judge, looking at Ivan and Gavryl as he spoke, "I think you had better try to arrange this matter peaceably. You, brother Gavryl, did wrong to strike a woman who was in delicate health. It was a lucky thing for you that God had mercy on you and that the woman did not die, for if she had I know not what dire misfortune might have overtaken you! It will not do either of you any good to go on living as you are at present. Go, Gavryl, and make friends with Ivan; I am sure he will forgive you, and we will set aside the verdict just given."

The secretary on hearing this said: "It is impossible to do this on the present case. According to Article 117 this matter has gone too far to be settled peaceably now, as the verdict has been rendered and must be enforced."

But the judges would not listen to the secretary, saying to him: "You talk altogether too much. You must remember that the first thing is to fulfill God's command to 'Love thy neighbor as thyself,' and all will be well with you."

Thus with kind words the judges tried to reconcile the two peasants. Their words fell on stony ground, however, for Gavryl would not listen to them.

"I am fifty years old," said Gavryl, "and have a son married, and never from my birth has the lash been applied to my back; but now this bear Ivan has secured a verdict against me which condemns me to receive twenty lashes, and I am forced to bow to this decision and suffer the shame of a public beating. Well, he will have cause to remember this."

At this Gavryl's voice trembled and he stopped speaking, and turning his back on the judges took his departure.

It was about ten versts' distance from the court to the homes of the neighbors, and this Ivan travelled late. The women had already gone out for the cattle. He unharnessed his horse and put everything in its place, and then went into the room, but found no one there.

The men had not yet returned from their work in the field and the women had gone to look for the cattle, so that all about the place was quiet. Going into the room, Ivan seated himself on a wooden bench and soon became lost in thought. He remembered how, when Gavryl first heard the sentence which had been passed upon him, he grew very pale, and turned his face to the wall, all the while remaining silent.

Ivan's heart ached when he thought of the disgrace which he had been the means of bringing upon Gavryl, and he wondered how he would feel if the same sentence had been passed upon him. His thoughts were interrupted by the coughing of his father, who was lying on the oven.

The old man, on seeing Ivan, came down off the oven, and slowly approaching his son seated himself on the bench beside him, looking at him as though ashamed. He continued to cough as he leaned on the table and said, "Well, did they sentence him?"

"Yes, they sentenced him to receive twenty lashes," replied Ivan.

On hearing this the old man sorrowfully shook his head, and said: "This is very bad, Ivan, and what is the meaning of it all? It is indeed very bad, but not so bad for Gavryl as for yourself. Well, suppose his sentence IS carried out, and he gets the twenty lashes, what will it benefit you?"

"He will not again strike a woman," Ivan replied.

"What is it he will not do? He does not do anything worse than what you are constantly doing!"

This conversation enraged Ivan, and he shouted: "Well, what did he do? He beat a woman nearly to death, and even now he threatens to burn my house! Must I bow to him for all this?"

The old man sighed deeply as he said: "You, Ivan, are strong and free to go wherever you please, while I have been lying for years on the oven. You think that you know everything and that I do not know anything. No! you are still a child, and as such you cannot see that a kind of madness controls your actions and blinds your sight. The sins of others are ever before you, while you resolutely keep your own behind your back. I know that what Gavryl did was wrong, but if he alone should do wrong there would be no evil in the world. Do you think that all the evil in the world is the work of one man alone? No! it requires two persons to work much evil in the world. You see only the bad in Gavryl's character, but you are blind to the evil that is in your own nature. If he alone were bad and you good, then there would be no wrong."

The old man, after a pause, continued: "Who tore Gavryl's beard? Who destroyed his heaps of rye? Who dragged him into court?—and yet you try to put all the blame on his shoulders. You are behaving very badly yourself, and for that reason you are wrong. I did not act in such a manner, and certainly I never taught you to do so. I lived in peace with Gavryl's father all the time we were neighbors. We were always the best of friends. If he was without flour his wife would come to me and say, 'Grandfather, we need flour.' I would then say: 'My good woman, go to the warehouse and take as much as you want.' If he had no one to care for his horses I would say, 'Go, Ivanushka, and help him to care for them.' If I required anything I would go to him and say, 'Grandfather Gordey, I need this or that,' and he would always reply, 'Take just whatever you want.' By this means we passed an easy and peaceful life. But what is your life compared with it? As the soldiers fought at Plevna, so are you and Gavryl fighting all the time, only that your battles are far more disgraceful than that fought at Plevna."

The old man went on: "And you call this living! and what a sin it all is! You are a peasant, and the head of the house; therefore, the responsibility of the trouble rests with you. What an example you set your wife and children by constantly quarrelling with your neighbor! Only a short time since your little boy, Taraska, was cursing his aunt Arina, and his mother only laughed at it, saying, 'What a bright child he is!' Is that right? You are to blame for all this. You should think of the salvation of your soul. Is that the way to do it? You say one unkind word to me and I will reply with two. You will give me one slap in the face, and I will retaliate with two slaps. No, my son; Christ did not teach us foolish people to act in such a way. If any one should say an unkind word to you it is better not to answer at all; but if you do reply do it kindly, and his conscience will accuse him, and he will regret his unkindness to you. This is the way Christ taught us to live. He tells us that if a person smite us on the one cheek we should offer unto him the other. That is Christ's command to us, and we should follow it. You should therefore subdue your pride. Am I not right?"

Ivan remained silent, but his father's words had sunk deep into his heart.

The old man coughed and continued: "Do you think Christ thought us wicked? Did he not die that we might be saved? Now you think only of this earthly life. Are you better or worse for thinking alone of it? Are you better or worse for having begun that Plevna battle? Think of your expense at court and the time lost in going back and forth, and what have you gained? Your sons have reached manhood, and are able now to work for you. You are therefore at liberty to enjoy life and be happy. With the assistance of your children you could reach a high state of prosperity. But now your property instead of increasing is gradually growing less, and why? It is the result of your pride. When it becomes necessary for you and your boys to go to the field to work, your enemy instead summons you to appear at court or before some kind of judicial person. If you do not plow at the proper time and sow at the proper time mother earth will not yield up her products, and you and your children will be left destitute. Why did your oats fail this year? When did you sow them? Were you not quarrelling with your neighbor instead of attending to your work? You have just now returned from the town, where you have been the means of having your neighbor humiliated. You have succeeded in getting him sentenced, but in the end the punishment will fall on your own shoulders. Oh! my child, it would be better for you to attend to your work on the farm and train your boys to become good farmers and honest men. If any one offend you forgive him for Christ's sake, and then prosperity will smile on your work and a light and happy feeling will fill your heart."

Ivan still remained silent.

The old father in a pleading voice continued: "Take an old man's advice. Go and harness your horse, drive back to the court, and withdraw all these complaints against your neighbor. To-morrow go to him, offer to make peace in Christ's name, and invite him to your house. It will be a holy day (the birth of the Virgin Mary). Get out the samovar and have some vodki, and over both forgive and forget each other's sins, promising not to transgress in the future, and advise your women and children to do the same."

Ivan heaved a deep sigh but felt easier in his heart, as he thought: "The old man speaks the truth;" yet he was in doubt as to how he would put his father's advice into practice.

The old man, surmising his uncertainty, said to Ivan: "Go, Ivanushka; do not delay. Extinguish the fire in the beginning, before it grows large, for then it may be impossible."

Ivan's father wished to say more to him, but was prevented by the arrival of the women, who came into the room chattering like so many magpies. They had already heard of Gavryl's sentence, and of how he threatened to set fire to Ivan's house. They found out all about it, and in telling it to their neighbors added their own versions of the story, with the usual exaggeration. Meeting in the pasture-ground, they proceeded to quarrel with Gavryl's women. They related how the latter's daughter-in-law had threatened to secure the influence of the manager of a certain noble's estate in behalf of his friend Gavryl; also that the school-teacher was writing a petition to the Czar himself against Ivan, explaining in detail his theft of the perchbolt and partial destruction of Gavryl's garden—declaring that half of Ivan's land was to be given to them.

Ivan listened calmly to their stories, but his anger was soon aroused once more, when he abandoned his intention of making peace with Gavryl.

As Ivan was always busy about the household, he did not stop to speak to the wrangling women, but immediately left the room, directing his steps toward the barn. Before getting through with his work the sun had set and the boys had returned from their plowing. Ivan met them and asked about their work, helping them to put things in order and leaving the broken horse-collar aside to be repaired. He intended to perform some other duties, but it became too dark and he was obliged to leave them till the next day. He fed the cattle, however, and opened the gate that Taraska might take his horses to pasture for the night, after which he closed it again and went into the house for his supper.

By this time he had forgotten all about Gavryl and what his father had said to him. Yet, just as he touched the door-knob, he heard sounds of quarrelling proceeding from his neighbor's house.

"What do I want with that devil?" shouted Gavryl to some one. "He deserves to be killed!"

Ivan stopped and listened for a moment, when he shook his head threateningly and entered the room. When he came in, the apartment was already lighted. His daughter-in-law was working with her loom, while the old woman was preparing the supper. The eldest son was twining strings for his peasant's shoes. The other son was sitting by the table reading a book. The room presented a pleasant appearance, everything being in order and the inmates apparently gay and happy—the only dark shadow being that cast over the household by Ivan's trouble with his neighbor.

Ivan came in very cross, and, angrily throwing aside a cat which lay sleeping on the bench, cursed the women for having misplaced a pail. He looked very sad and serious, and, seating himself in a corner of the room, proceeded to repair the horse-collar. He could not forget Gavryl, however—the threatening words he had used in the courtroom and those which Ivan had just heard.

Presently Taraska came in, and after having his supper, put on his sheepskin coat, and, taking some bread with him, returned to watch over his horses for the night. His eldest brother wished to accompany him, but Ivan himself arose and went with him as far as the porch. The night was dark and cloudy and a strong wind was blowing, which produced a peculiar whistling sound that was most unpleasant to the ear. Ivan helped his son to mount his horse, which, followed by a colt, started off on a gallop.

Ivan stood for a few moments looking around him and listening to the clatter of the horse's hoofs as Taraska rode down the village street. He heard him meet other boys on horseback, who rode quite as well as Taraska, and soon all were lost in the darkness.

Ivan remained standing by the gate in a gloomy mood, as he was unable to banish from his mind the harassing thoughts of Gavryl, which the latter's menacing words had inspired: "Something will burn with greater fierceness in Ivan's household before long."

"He is so desperate," thought Ivan, "that he may set fire to my house regardless of the danger to his own. At present everything is dry, and as the wind is so high he may sneak from the back of his own building, start a fire, and get away unseen by any of us.

"He may burn and steal without being found out, and thus go unpunished. I wish I could catch him."

This thought so worried Ivan that he decided not to return to his house, but went out and stood on the street-corner.

"I guess," thought Ivan to himself, "I will take a walk around the premises and examine everything carefully, for who knows what he may be tempted to do?"

Ivan moved very cautiously round to the back of his buildings, not making the slightest noise, and scarcely daring to breathe. Just as he reached a corner of the house he looked toward the fence, and it seemed to him that he saw something moving, and that it was slowly creeping toward the corner of the house opposite to where he was standing. He stepped back quickly and hid himself in the shadow of the building. Ivan stood and listened, but all was quiet. Not a sound could be heard but the moaning of the wind through the branches of the trees, and the rustling of the leaves as it caught them up and whirled them in all directions. So dense was the darkness that it was at first impossible for Ivan to see more than a few feet beyond where he stood.

After a time, however, his sight becoming accustomed to the gloom, he was enabled to see for a considerable distance. The plow and his other farming implements stood just where he had placed them. He could see also the opposite corner of the house.

He looked in every direction, but no one was in sight, and he thought to himself that his imagination must have played him some trick, leading him to believe that some one was moving when there really was no one there.

Still, Ivan was not satisfied, and decided to make a further examination of the premises. As on the previous occasion, he moved so very cautiously that he could not hear even the sound of his own footsteps. He had taken the precaution to remove his shoes, that he might step the more noiselessly. When he reached the corner of the barn it again seemed to him that he saw something moving, this time near the plow; but it quickly disappeared. By this time Ivan's heart was beating very fast, and he was standing in a listening attitude when a sudden flash of light illumined the spot, and he could distinctly see the figure of a man seated on his haunches with his back turned toward him, and in the act of lighting a bunch of straw which he held in his hand! Ivan's heart began to beat yet faster, and he became terribly excited, walking up and down with rapid strides, but without making a noise.

Ivan said: "Well, now, he cannot get away, for he will be caught in the very act."

Ivan had taken a few more steps when suddenly a bright light flamed up, but not in the same spot in which he had seen the figure of the man sitting. Gavryl had lighted the straw, and running to the barn held it under the edge of the roof, which began to burn fiercely; and by the light of the fire he could distinctly see his neighbor standing.

As an eagle springs at a skylark, so sprang Ivan at Gavryl, saying: "I will tear you into pieces! You shall not get away from me this time!"

But "Gavryl the Lame," hearing footsteps, wrenched himself free from Ivan's grasp and ran like a hare past the buildings.

Ivan, now terribly excited, shouted, "You shall not escape me!" and started in pursuit; but just as he reached him and was about to grasp the collar of his coat, Gavryl succeeded in jumping to one side, and Ivan's coat became entangled in something and he was thrown violently to the ground. Jumping quickly to his feet he shouted, "Watch! Catch!"

While Ivan was regaining his feet Gavryl succeeded in reaching his house, but Ivan followed so quickly that he caught up with him before he could enter. Just as he was about to grasp him he was struck on the head with some hard substance. He had been hit on the temple as with a stone. The blow was struck by Gavryl, who had picked up an oaken stave, and with it gave Ivan a terrible blow on the head.

Ivan was stunned, and bright sparks danced before his eyes, while he swayed from side to side like a drunken man, until finally all became dark and he sank to the ground unconscious.

When he recovered his senses, Gavryl was nowhere to be seen, but all around him was as light as day. Strange sounds proceeded from the direction of his house, and turning his face that way he saw that his barns were on fire. The rear parts of both were already destroyed, and the flames were leaping toward the front. Fire, smoke, and bits of burning straw were being rapidly whirled by the high wind over to where his house stood, and he expected every moment to see it burst into flames.

"What is this, brother?" Ivan cried out, as he beat his thighs with his hands. "I should have stopped to snatch the bunch of burning straw, and, throwing it on the ground, should have extinguished it with my feet!"

Ivan tried to cry out and arouse his people, but his lips refused to utter a word. He next tried to run, but he could not move his feet, and his legs seemed to twist themselves around each other. After several attempts he succeeded in taking one or two steps, when he again began to stagger and gasp for breath. It was some moments before he made another attempt to move, but after considerable exertion he finally reached the barn, the rear of which was by this time entirely consumed; and the corner of his house had already caught fire. Dense volumes of smoke began to pour out of the room, which made it difficult to approach.

A crowd of peasants had by this time gathered, but they found it impossible to save their homes, so they carried everything which they could to a place of safety. The cattle they drove into neighboring pastures and left some one to care for them.

The wind carried the sparks from Ivan's house to Gavryl's, and it, too, took fire and was consumed. The wind continued to increase with great fury, and the flames spread to both sides of the street, until in a very short time more than half the village was burned.

The members of Ivan's household had great difficulty in getting out of the burning building, but the neighbors rescued the old man and carried him to a place of safety, while the women escaped in only their night-clothes. Everything was burned, including the cattle and all the farm implements. The women lost their trunks, which were filled with quantities of clothing, the accumulation of years. The storehouse and all the provisions perished in the flames, not even the chickens being saved.

Gavryl, however, more fortunate than Ivan, saved his cattle and a few other things.

The village was burning all night.

Ivan stood near his home, gazing sadly at the burning building, and he kept constantly repeating to himself: "I should have taken away the bunch of burning straw, and have stamped out the fire with my feet."

But when he saw his home fall in a smouldering heap, in spite of the terrible heat he sprang into the midst of it and carried out a charred log. The women seeing him, and fearing that he would lose his life, called to him to come back, but he would not pay any attention to them and went a second time to get a log. Still weak from the terrible blow which Gavryl had given him, he was overcome by the heat, and fell into the midst of the burning mass. Fortunately, his eldest son saw him fall, and rushing into the fire succeeded in getting hold of him and carrying him out of it. Ivan's hair, beard, and clothing were burned entirely off. His hands were also frightfully injured, but he seemed indifferent to pain.

"Grief drove him crazy," the people said.

The fire was growing less, but Ivan still stood where he could see it, and kept repeating to himself, "I should have taken," etc.

The morning after the fire the village elder sent his son to Ivan to tell him that the old man, his father, was dying, and wanted to see him to bid him good-bye.

In his grief Ivan had forgotten all about his father, and could not understand what was being said to him. In a dazed way he asked: "What father? Whom does he want?"

The elder's son again repeated his father's message to Ivan. "Your aged parent is at our house dying, and he wants to see you and bid you good-bye. Won't you go now, uncle Ivan?" the boy said.

Finally Ivan understood, and followed the elder's son.

When Ivan's father was carried from the oven, he was slightly injured by a big bunch of burning straw falling on him just as he reached the street. To insure his safety he was removed to the elder's house, which stood a considerable distance from his late home, and where it was not likely that the fire would reach it.

When Ivan arrived at the elder's home he found only the latter's wife and children, who were all seated on the brick oven. The old man was lying on a bench holding a lighted candle in his hand (a Russian custom when a person is dying). Hearing a noise, he turned his face toward the door, and when he saw it was his son he tried to move. He motioned for Ivan to come nearer, and when he did so he whispered in a trembling voice: "Well, Ivanushka, did I not tell you before what would be the result of this sad affair? Who set the village on fire?"

"He, he, little father; he did it. I caught him. He placed the bunch of burning straw to the barn in my presence. Instead of running after him, I should have snatched the bunch of burning straw and throwing it on the ground have stamped it out with my feet; and then there would have been no fire."

"Ivan," said the old man, "death is fast approaching me, and remember that you also will have to die. Who did this dreadful thing? Whose is the sin?"

Ivan gazed at the noble face of his dying father and was silent. His heart was too full for utterance.

"In the presence of God," the old man continued, "whose is the sin?"

It was only now that the truth began to dawn upon Ivan's mind, and that he realized how foolish he had acted. He sobbed bitterly, and fell on his knees before his father, and, crying like a child, said:

"My dear father, forgive me, for Christ's sake, for I am guilty before God and before you!"

The old man transferred the lighted candle from his right hand to the left, and, raising the former to his forehead, tried to make the sign of the cross, but owing to weakness was unable to do so.

"Glory to Thee, O Lord! Glory to Thee!" he exclaimed; and turning his dim eyes toward his son, he said: "See here, Ivanushka! Ivanushka, my dear son!"

"What, my dear father?" Ivan asked.

"What are you going to do," replied the old man, "now that you have no home?"

Ivan cried and said: "I do not know how we shall live now."

The old man closed his eyes and made a movement with his lips, as if gathering his feeble strength for a final effort. Slowly opening his eyes, he whispered:

"Should you live according to God's commands you will be happy and prosperous again."

The old man was now silent for awhile and then, smiling sadly, he continued:

"See here, Ivanushka, keep silent concerning this trouble, and do not tell who set the village on fire. Forgive one sin of your neighbor's, and God will forgive two of yours."

Grasping the candle with both hands, Ivan's father heaved a deep sigh, and, stretching himself out on his back, yielded up the ghost.

IVAN FOR ONCE ACCEPTED HIS FATHER'S ADVICE. HE DID NOT betray Gavryl, and no one ever learned the origin of the fire.

Ivan's heart became more kindly disposed toward his old enemy, feeling that much of the fault in connection with this sad affair rested with himself.

Gavryl was greatly surprised that Ivan did not denounce him before all the villagers, and at first he stood in much fear of him, but he soon afterward overcame this feeling.

The two peasants ceased to quarrel, and their families followed their example. While they were building new houses, both families lived beneath the same roof, and when they moved into their respective homes, Ivan and Gavryl lived on as good terms as their fathers had done before them.

Ivan remembered his dying father's command, and took deeply to heart the evident warning of God that A FIRE SHOULD BE

EXTINGUISHED IN THE BEGINNING. If any one wronged him he did not seek revenge, but instead made every effort to settle the matter peaceably. If any one spoke to him unkindly, he did not answer in the same way, but replied softly, and tried to persuade the person not to speak evil. He taught the women and children of his household to do the same.

Ivan Scherbakoff was now a reformed man.

He lived well and peacefully, and again became prosperous.

Let us, therefore, have peace, live in brotherly love and kindness, and we will be happy.

JOHN UPDIKE

PERHAPS THE MOST IMPORTANT AMERICAN WRITER OF THE second half of the twentieth century, John Updike was born in Reading, Pennsylvania, in 1932, and grew up reading voraciously. An only child—his mother was an aspiring writer, his father a high school science teacher—Updike attended Harvard, where he majored in English and worked summers as a copy boy at the *Reading Eagle*, his hometown's local newspaper. Before graduating *cum laude* in 1954, he sold his first poem and short story to the *New Yorker*, beginning what has been a lifelong relationship with the premier journal publishing fiction in America.

The author of more than sixty books, including his perennially best-selling novels, his short story collections, poetry volumes, plays, essays, memoirs, and literary criticism, he is one of only three Americans ever to have twice won the Pulitzer Prize for fiction, first for *Rabbit Is Rich* in 1981, and again in 1991 for *Rabbit at Rest*; he also won the National Book Award for his novel *The Centaur*. In addition, he has been awarded both the National Medal for the Humanities and the National Medal for the Arts, and in 1964, at age thirty-two, he became the youngest person ever elected to the National Institute of Arts and Letters.

In his popular works, Updike is a writer who looks fearlessly at the inner lives of characters who wrestle with questions of mortality, of eternity, of God and Christ and sin and the temptations modern man faces in a world that has lost any sense of God's presence. He has all his life been a student of Christian theology and a dedicated churchgoer, and in 1997 the Jesuit magazine *America* awarded him its Campion Award, citing him as a "distinguished Christian person of letters."

PIGEON
FEATHERS
BY JOHN UPDIKE

When they moved to Firetown, things were upset, displaced, rearranged. A red cane-back sofa that had been the chief piece in the living room at Olinger was here banished, too big for the narrow country parlor, to the barn, and shrouded under a tarpaulin. Never again would David lie on its length all afternoon eating raisins and reading mystery novels and science fiction and P. G. Wodehouse. The blue wing chair that had stood for years in the ghostly, immaculate guest bedroom, gazing through the windows curtained with dotted swiss toward the telephone wires and horse-chestnut trees and opposite houses, was here established importantly in front of the smutty little fireplace that supplied, in those first cold April days, their only heat. As a child, David had been afraid of the guest bedroom—it was there that he, lying sick with the measles, had seen a black rod the size of a yardstick jog along at a slight slant beside the edge of the bed and vanish when he screamed—and it was disquieting to have one of the elements of its haunted atmosphere basking by the fire, in the center of the family, growing sooty with use. The books that at home had gathered dust in the case beside the piano were here hastily stacked, all out of order, in the shelves that the carpenters had built along one wall below the deep-silled windows. David, at fourteen, had been more moved than a mover; like the furniture, he had to find a new place, and on the Saturday of the second week he tried to work off some of his disorientation by arranging the books.

It was a collection obscurely depressing to him, mostly books his mother had acquired when she was young: college anthologies of Greek plays and Romantic poetry, Will Durant's *Story of Philosophy*, a softleather set of Shakespeare with string bookmarks sewed to the bindings, *Green Mansions* boxed and illustrated with woodcuts, *I, the*

Tiger, by Manuel Komroff, novels by names like Galsworthy and Ellen Glasgow and Irvin S. Cobb and Sinclair Lewis and "Elizabeth." The odor of faded taste made him feel the ominous gap between himself and his parents, the insulting gulf of time that existed before he was born. Suddenly he was tempted to dip into this time. From the heaps of books piled around him on the worn old floorboards, he picked up Volume II of a four-volume set of *The Outline of History,* by H. G. Wells. Once David had read *The Time Machine* in an anthology; this gave him a small grip on the author. The book's red binding had faded to orange-pink on the spine. When he lifted the cover, there was a sweetish, attic-like smell, and his mother's maiden name written in unfamiliar handwriting on the flyleaf—an upright, bold, yet careful signature, bearing a faint relation to the quick scrunched backslant that flowed with marvelous consistency across her shopping lists and budget accounts and Christmas cards to college friends from this same, vaguely menacing long ago.

He leafed through, pausing at drawings, done in an old-fashioned stippled style, of bas-reliefs, masks, Romans without pupils in their eyes, articles of ancient costume, fragments of pottery found in unearthed homes. He knew it would be interesting in a magazine, sandwiched between ads and jokes, but in this undiluted form history was somehow sour. The print was determinedly legible, and smug, like a lesson book. As he bent over the pages, yellow at the edges, they seemed rectangles of dusty glass through which he looked down into unreal and irrelevant worlds. He could see things sluggishly move, and an unpleasant fullness came into his throat. His mother and grandmother fussed in the kitchen; the puppy, which they had just acquired, for "protection in the country," was cowering, with a sporadic panicked scrabble of claws, under the dining table that in their old home had been reserved for special days but that here was used for every meal.

Then, before he could halt his eyes, David slipped into Wells's account of Jesus. He had been an obscure political agitator, a kind of hobo, in a minor colony of the Roman Empire. By an accident impossible to construct, he (the small *h* horrified David) survived his own crucifixion and presumably died a few weeks later. A religion was founded on the freakish incident. The credulous imagination of the times retrospectively assigned miracles and supernatural pretensions to Jesus; a myth grew, and then a church, whose theology at most points was in direct contradiction of the simple, rather communistic teachings of the Galilean.

It was as if a stone that for weeks and even years had been gathering weight in the web of David's nerves snapped them and plunged through the page and a hundred layers of paper underneath. These fantastic falsehoods—plainly untrue; churches stood everywhere, the entire nation was founded "under God"—did not at first frighten him; it was the fact that they had been permitted to exist in an actual human brain. This was the initial impact—that at a definite spot in time and space a brain black with the denial of Christ's divinity had been suffered to exist; that the universe had not spit out this ball of tar but allowed it to continue in its blasphemy, to grow old, win honors, wear a hat, write books that, if true, collapsed everything into a jumble of horror. The world outside the deep-silled windows—a rutted lawn, a whitewashed barn, a walnut tree frothy with fresh green—seemed a haven from which he was forever sealed off. Hot washrags seemed pressed against his cheeks.

He read the account again. He tried to supply out of his ignorance objections that would defeat the complacent march of these black words, and found none. Survivals and misunderstandings more far-fetched were reported daily in the papers. But none of them caused churches to be built in every town. He tried to work backwards through the churches, from their brave high fronts through their shabby, ill attended interiors back into the events at Jerusalem, and felt himself surrounded by shifting gray shadows, centuries of history, where he knew nothing. The thread dissolved in his hands. Had Christ ever come to him, David Kern, and said, "Here. Feel the wound in My side"? No; but prayers had been answered. What prayers? He had prayed that Rudy Mohn, whom he had purposely tripped so he cracked his head on their radiator, not die, and he had not died. But for all the blood, it was just a cut; Rudy came back the same day, wearing a bandage and repeating the same teasing words. He could never have died. Again, David had prayed for two separate war-effort posters he had sent away for to arrive tomorrow, and though they did not, they did arrive, some days later, together, popping through the clacking letter slot like a rebuke from God's mouth: *I answer your prayers in My way, in My time.* After that, he had made his prayers less definite, less susceptible of being twisted into a scolding. But what a tiny, ridiculous coincidence this was, after all, to throw into battle against H. G. Wells's engines of knowledge! Indeed, it proved the enemy's point: Hope bases vast premises on foolish accidents, and reads a word where in fact only a scribble exists.

HIS FATHER CAME HOME. THOUGH SATURDAY WAS A FREE DAY for him, he had been working. He taught school in Olinger and spent all his days performing, with a curious air of panic, needless errands. Also, a city boy by birth, he was frightened of the farm and seized any excuse to get away. The farm had been David's mother's birthplace; it had been her idea to buy it back. With an ingenuity and persistence unparalleled in her life, she had gained that end, and moved them all here—her son, her husband, her mother. Granmom, in her prime, had worked these fields alongside her husband, but now she dabbled around the kitchen futilely, her hands waggling with Parkinson's disease. She was always in the way. Strange, out in the country, amid eighty acres, they were crowded together. His father expressed his feelings of discomfort by conducting with Mother an endless argument about organic farming. All through dusk, all through supper, it rattled on.

"Elsie, I know, I know from my education, the earth is nothing but chemicals. It's the only damn thing I got out of four years of college, so don't tell me it's not true."

"George, if you'd just walk out on the farm you'd know it's not true. The land has a *soul*."

"Soil, has, no, soul," he said, enunciating stiffly, as if to a very stupid class. To David he said, "You can't argue with a femme. Your mother's a real femme. That's why I married her, and now I'm suffering for it."

"*This* soil has no soul," she said, "because it's been killed with superphosphate. It's been burned bare by Boyer's tenant farmers." Boyer was the rich man they had bought the farm from. "It used to have a soul, didn't it, Mother? When you and Pop farmed it?"

"Ach, yes; I guess." Granmom was trying to bring a forkful of food to her mouth with her less severely afflicted hand. In her anxiety she brought the other hand up from her lap. The crippled fingers, dull red in the orange light of the kerosene lamp in the center of the table, were welded by paralysis into one knobbed hook.

"Only human indi-vidu-als have souls," his father went on, in the same mincing, lifeless voice. "Because the Bible tells us so." Done eating, he crossed his legs and dug into his ear with a match miserably; to get at the thing inside his head he tucked in his chin, and his voice came out low-pitched at David. "When God made your mother, He made a real femme."

"George, don't you read the papers? Don't you know that between the chemical fertilizers and the bug sprays we'll all be dead in ten years? Heart attacks are killing every man in the country over forty-five."

He sighed wearily; the yellow skin of his eyelids wrinkled as he hurt himself with the match. "There's no connection," he stated, spacing his words with pained patience, "between the heart—and chemical fertilizers. It's alcohol that's doing it. Alcohol and milk. There is too much—cholesterol—in the tissues of the American heart. Don't tell me about chemistry, Elsie; I majored in the damn stuff for four years."

"Yes and I majored in Greek and I'm not a penny wiser. Mother, put your waggler *away*!" The old woman started, and the food dropped from her fork. For some reason, the sight of her bad hand at the table cruelly irritated her daughter. Granmom's eyes, worn bits of crazed crystal embedded in watery milk, widened behind her cockeyed spectacles. Circles of silver as fine as thread, they clung to the red notches they had carved over the years into her little white beak. In the orange flicker of the kerosene lamp her dazed misery seemed infernal. David's mother began, without noise, to cry. His father did not seem to have eyes at all; just jaundiced sockets of wrinkled skin. The steam of food clouded the scene. It was horrible but the horror was particular and familiar, and distracted David from the formless dread that worked, sticky and sore, within him, like a too large wound trying to heal.

He had to go to the bathroom, and took a flashlight down through the wet grass to the outhouse. For once, his fear of spiders there felt trivial. He set the flashlight, burning, beside him, and an insect alighted on its lens, a tiny insect, a mosquito or flea, made so fine that the weak light projected its X-ray onto the wall boards: the faint rim of its wings, the blurred strokes, magnified, of its long hinged legs, the dark cone at the heart of its anatomy. The tremor must be its heart beating. Without warning, David was visited by an exact vision of death: a long hole in the ground, no wider than your body, down which you are drawn while the white faces above recede. You try to reach them but your arms are pinned. Shovels pour dirt into your face. There you will be forever, in an upright position, blind and silent, and in time no one will remember you, and you will never be called. As strata of rock shift, your fingers elongate, and your teeth are distended sideways in a great underground grimace indistinguishable from a strip of chalk. And the earth tumbles on, and the sun expires, and unaltering darkness reigns where once there were stars.

Sweat broke out on his back. His mind seemed to rebound off a solidness. Such extinction was not another threat, a graver sort of danger, a kind of pain; it was qualitatively different. It was not even a conception that could be voluntarily pictured; it entered him from outside. His protesting nerves swarmed on its surface like lichen on a meteor. The skin of his chest was soaked with the effort of rejection. At the same time that the fear was dense and internal, it was dense and all around him; a tide of clay had swept up to the stars; space was crushed into a mass. When he stood up, automatically hunching his shoulders to keep his head away from the spider webs, it was with a numb sense of being cramped between two huge volumes of rigidity. That he had even this small freedom to move surprised him. In the narrow shelter of that rank shack, adjusting his pants, he felt—his first spark of comfort—too small to be crushed.

But in the open, as the beam of the flashlight skidded with frightened quickness across the remote surfaces of the barn and the grape arbor and the giant pine that stood by the path to the woods, the terror descended. He raced up through the clinging grass pursued, not by one of the wild animals the woods might hold, or one of the goblins his superstitious grandmother had communicated to his childhood, but by spectres out of science fiction, where gigantic cinder moons fill half the turquoise sky. As David ran, a gray planet rolled inches behind his neck. If he looked back, he would be buried. And in the momentum of his terror, hideous possibilities—the dilation of the sun, the triumph of the insects, the crabs on the shore in *The Time Machine*—wheeled out of the vacuum of make-believe and added their weight to his impending oblivion.

He wrenched the door open; the lamps within the house flared. The wicks burning here and there seemed to mirror one another. His mother was washing the dishes in a little pan of heated pump-water; Granmom fluttered near her elbow apprehensively. In the living room—the downstairs of the little square house was two long rooms—his father sat in front of the black fireplace restlessly folding and unfolding a newspaper as he sustained his half of the argument. "Nitrogen, phosphorus, potash: these are the three replaceable constituents of the soil. One crop of corn carries away hundreds of pounds of" —he dropped the paper into his lap and ticked them off on three fingers—"nitrogen, phosphorus, potash."

"Boyer didn't grow corn."

"*Any* crop, Elsie. The human animal—"

"You're killing the *earth*worms, George!"

"The human animal, after thousands and *thou*sands of years, learned methods whereby the chemical balance of the soil may be maintained. Don't carry me back to the Dark Ages."

"When we moved to Olinger the ground in the garden was like slate. Just one summer of my cousin's chicken dung and the earthworms came back."

"I'm sure the Dark Ages were a fine place to the poor devils born in them, but I don't want to go there. They give me the creeps." Daddy stared into the cold pit of the fireplace and clung to the rolled newspaper in his lap as if it alone were keeping him from slipping backwards and down, down.

Mother came into the doorway brandishing a fistful of wet forks. "And thanks to your DDT there soon won't be a bee left in the country. When I was a girl here you could eat a peach without washing it."

"It's primitive, Elsie. It's Dark Age stuff."

"Oh what do *you* know about the Dark Ages?"

"I know I don't want to go back to them."

David took from the shelf, where he had placed it this afternoon, the great unabridged Webster's Dictionary that his grandfather had owned. He turned the big thin pages, floppy as cloth, to the entry he wanted, and read

> s o u l . . . I. An entity conceived as the essence, substance, animating principle, or actuating cause of life, or of the individual life, esp. of life manifested in psychical activities; the vehicle of individual

existence, separate in nature from the body and usually held to be separable in existence.

The definition went on, into Greek and Egyptian conceptions, but David stopped short on the treacherous edge of antiquity. He needed to read no further. The careful overlapping words shingled a temporary shelter for him. "Usually held to be separable in existence"—what could be fairer, more judicious, surer?

His father was saying, "The modern farmer can't go around sweeping up after his cows. The poor devil has thousands and *thou*sands of acres on his hands. Your modern farmer uses a scientifically-arrived-at mixture, like five-ten-five, or six-twelve-six, or *three*-twelve-six, and spreads it on with this wonderful modern machinery which of course we can't afford. Your modern farmer can't *afford* medieval methods."

Mother was quiet in the kitchen; her silence radiated waves of anger. "No now Elsie; don't play the femme with me. Let's discuss this calmly like two rational twentieth-century people. Your organic farming nuts aren't attacking five-ten-five; they're attacking the chemical fertilizer crooks. The monster firms."

A cup clinked in the kitchen. Mother's anger touched David's face; his cheeks burned guiltily. Just by being in the living room he was associated with his father. She appeared in the doorway with red hands and tears in her eyes, and said to the two of them, "I knew you didn't want to come here but I didn't know you'd torment me like this. You talked Pop into his grave and now you'll kill me. Go ahead, George, more power to you; at least I'll be buried in good ground." She tried to turn and met an obstacle and screamed, "Mother, stop hanging on my *back!* Why don't you go to *bed?*"

"Let's all go to bed," David's father said, rising from the blue wing chair and slapping his thigh with a newspaper. "This reminds me of death." It was a phrase of his that David had heard so often he never considered its sense.

Upstairs, he seemed to be lifted above his fears. The sheets on his bed were clean. Granmom had ironed them with a pair of flatirons saved from the Olinger attic; she plucked them hot off the stove alternately, with a wooden handle called a goose. It was a wonder, to see how she managed. In the next room, his parents grunted peaceably; they seemed to take their quarrels less seriously than he did. They made comfortable scratching noises as they carried a little lamp back and forth. Their door was open a crack, so he saw the light shift and swing. Surely there would be, in the last five minutes, in the last second, a crack of light, showing the door from the dark room to another, full of light. Thinking of it this vividly frightened him. His own dying, in a specific bed in a specific room, specific walls mottled with wallpaper, the dry whistle of his breathing, the murmuring doctors, the nervous relatives going in and out, but for him no way out but down into the funnel. *Never touch a doorknob again.* A whisper, and his parents' light was blown out. David prayed to be reassured. Though the experiment frightened him, he lifted his hands high into the darkness above his face and begged Christ to touch them. Not hard or long: the faintest, quickest grip would be final for a lifetime. His hands waited in the air, itself a substance, which seemed to move through his fingers; or was it the pressure of his pulse? He returned his hands to beneath the covers uncertain if they had been touched or not. For would not Christ's touch *be* infinitely gentle?

THROUGH ALL THE EDDIES OF ITS AFTERMATH, DAVID CLUNG to this thought about his revelation of extinction: that there, in the outhouse, he had struck a solidness qualitatively different, a rock of horror firm enough to support any height of construction. All he needed was a little help; a word, a gesture, a nod of certainty, and he would be sealed in, safe. The assurance from the dictionary had melted in the night. Today was Sunday, a hot fair day. Across a mile of clear air the church bells called, *Celebrate, celebrate*. Only Daddy went. He put on a coat over his rolled-up shirtsleeves and got into the little old black Plymouth parked by the barn and went off, with the same pained hurried grimness of all his actions. His churning wheels, as he shifted too hastily into second, raised plumes of red dust on the dirt road. Mother walked to the far field, to see what bushes needed cutting. David, though he usually preferred to stay in the house, went with her. The puppy followed at a distance, whining as it picked its way through the stubble but floundering off timidly if one of them went back to pick it up and carry it. When they reached the crest of the far field, his mother asked, "David, what's troubling you?"

"Nothing. Why?"

She looked at him sharply. The greening woods cross-hatched the space beyond her half-gray hair. Then she showed him her profile, and gestured toward the house, which they had left a half-mile behind them. "See how it sits in the land? They don't know how to build with the land any more. Pop always said the foundations were set with the compass. We must try to get a compass and see. It's supposed to face due south; but south feels a little more *that* way to me." From the side, as she said these things, she seemed handsome and young. The smooth sweep of her hair over her ear seemed white with a purity and calm that made her feel foreign to him. He had never regarded his parents as consolers of his troubles; from the beginning they had seemed to have more troubles than he. Their confusion had flattered him into an illusion of strength; so now on this high clear ridge he jealously guarded the menace all around them, blowing like a breeze on his fingertips, the possibility of all this wide scenery sinking into darkness. The strange fact that though she came to look at the brush she carried no clippers, for she had a fixed prejudice against working on Sundays, was the only consolation he allowed her to offer.

As they walked back, the puppy whimpering after them, the rising dust behind a distant line of trees announced that Daddy was speeding home from church. When they reached the house he was there. He had brought back the Sunday paper and the vehement remark, "Dobson's too intelligent for these farmers. They just sit there with their mouths open and don't hear a thing the poor devil's saying."

"What makes you think farmers are unintelligent? This country was made by farmers. George Washington was a farmer."

"They are, Elsie. They are unintelligent. George Washington's dead. In this day and age only the misfits stay on the farm. The lame, the halt, the blind. The morons with one arm. Human garbage. They remind me of death, sitting there with their mouths open."

"My *father* was a farmer."

"He was a frustrated man, Elsie. He never knew what hit him. The poor devil meant so well, and he never knew which end was up. Your mother'll bear me out. Isn't that right, Mom? Pop never knew what hit him?"

"Ach, I guess not," the old woman quavered, and the ambiguity for the moment silenced both sides.

David hid in the funny papers and sports section until one-thirty. At two, the catechetical class met at the Firetown church. He had transferred from the catechetical class of the Lutheran church in Olinger, a humiliating comedown. In Olinger they met on Wednesday nights, spiffy and spruce, in the atmosphere of a dance. Afterwards, blessed by the brick-faced minister from whose lips the word "Christ" fell like a burning stone, the more daring of them went with their Bibles to a luncheonette and smoked. Here in Firetown, the girls were dull white cows and the boys narrow-faced brown goats in old men's suits, herded on Sunday afternoons into a threadbare church basement that smelled of stale hay. Because his father had taken the car on one of his endless errands to Olinger, David walked, grateful for the open air and the silence. The catechetical class embarrassed him, but today he placed hope in it, as the source of the nod, the gesture, that was all he needed.

Reverend Dobson was a delicate young man with great dark eyes and small white shapely hands that flickered like protesting doves when he preached; he seemed a bit misplaced in the Lutheran ministry. This was his first call. It was a split parish; he served another rural church twelve miles away. His iridescent green Ford, new six months ago, was spattered to the windows with red mud and rattled from bouncing on the rude back roads, where he frequently got lost, to the malicious satisfaction of many. But David's mother liked him, and, more pertinent to his success, the Haiers, the sleek family of feed merchants and innkeepers and tractor salesmen who dominated the Firetown church, liked him. David liked him, and felt liked in turn; sometimes in class, after some special stupidity, Dobson directed toward him out of those wide black eyes a mild look of disbelief, a look that, though flattering, was also delicately disquieting.

Catechetical instruction consisted of reading aloud from a work booklet answers to problems prepared during the week, problems like, "I am the _____, the _____, and the _____, saith the Lord." Then there was a question period in which no one ever asked any questions. Today's theme was the last third of the Apostles' Creed. When the time came for questions, David blushed and asked, "About the Resurrection of the Body—are we conscious between the time when we die and the Day of Judgment?"

Dobson blinked, and his fine little mouth pursed, suggesting that David was making difficult things more difficult. The faces of the other students went blank, as if an indiscretion had been committed.

"No, I suppose not," Reverend Dobson said.

"Well, where is our soul, then, in this gap?"

The sense grew, in the class, of a naughtiness occurring. Dobson's shy eyes watered, as if he were straining to keep up the formality of attention, and one of the girls, the fattest, simpered toward her twin, who was a little less fat. Their chairs were arranged in a rough circle. The current running around the circle panicked David. Did everybody know something he didn't know?

"I suppose you could say our souls are asleep," Dobson said.

"And then they wake up, and there is the earth like it always is, and all the people who have ever lived? Where will Heaven be?"

Anita Haier giggled. Dobson gazed at David intently, but with an awkward, puzzled flicker of forgiveness, as if there existed a secret between them that David was violating. But David knew of no secret. All he wanted was to hear Dobson repeat the words he said every

Sunday morning. This he would not do. As if these words were unworthy of the conversational voice.

"David, you might think of Heaven this way: as the way the goodness Abraham Lincoln did lives after him."

"But is Lincoln conscious of it living on?" He blushed no longer with embarrassment but in anger; he had walked here in good faith and was being made a fool.

"Is he conscious now? I would have to say no; but I don't think it matters." His voice had a coward's firmness; he was hostile now.

"You don't."

"Not in the eyes of God, no." The unction, the stunning impudence, of this reply sprang tears of outrage in David's eyes. He bowed them to his book, where short words like Duty, Love, Obey, Honor, were stacked in the form of a cross.

"Were there any other questions, David?" Dobson asked with renewed gentleness. The others were rustling, collecting their books.

"No." He made his voice firm, though he could not bring up his eyes.

"Did I answer your question fully enough?"

"Yes."

In the minister's silence the shame that should have been his crept over David: the burden and fever of being a fraud were placed upon him, who was innocent, and it seemed, he knew, a confession of this guilt that on the way out he was unable to face Dobson's stirred gaze, though he felt it probing the side of his head.

Anita Haier's father gave him a ride down the highway as far as the dirt road. David said he wanted to walk the rest, and figured that his offer was accepted because Mr. Haier did not want to dirty his bright blue Buick with dust. This was all right; everything was all right, as long as it was dear. His indignation at being betrayed, at seeing Christianity betrayed, had hardened him. The straight dirt road reflected his hardness. Pink stones thrust up through its packed surface. The April sun beat down from the center of the afternoon half of the sky; already it had some of summer's heat. Already the fringes of weeds at the edges of the road were bedraggled with dust. From the reviving grass and scruff of the fields he walked between, insects were sending up a monotonous, automatic chant. In the distance a tiny figure in his father's coat was walking along the edge of the woods. His mother. He wondered what joy she found in such walks; to him the brown stretches of slowly rising and falling land expressed only a huge exhaustion.

FLUSHED WITH FRESH AIR AND HAPPINESS, SHE RETURNED from her walk earlier than he had expected, and surprised him at his grandfather's Bible. It was a stumpy black book, the boards worn thin where the old man's fingers had held them; the spine hung by one weak hinge of fabric. David had been looking for the passage where Jesus says to the one thief on the cross, "Today shalt thou be with me in paradise." He had never tried reading the Bible for himself before. What was so embarrassing about being caught at it, was that he detested the apparatus of piety. Fusty churches, creaking hymns, ugly Sunday-school teachers and their stupid leaflets—he hated everything about them but the promise they held out, a promise that in the most perverse way, as if the homeliest crone in the kingdom were given the Prince's hand, made every good and real thing, ball games and jokes and pert-breasted girls, possible. He couldn't explain this to his mother. There was no time. Her solicitude was upon him.

"David, what are you doing?"

"Nothing."

"What are you doing at Grandpop's Bible?"

"Trying to read it. This is supposed to be a Christian country, isn't it?"

She sat down on the green sofa, which used to be in the sun parlor at Olinger, under the fancy mirror. A little smile still lingered on her face from the walk.

"David, I wish you'd talk to me."

"What about?"

"About whatever it is that's troubling you. Your father and I have both noticed it."

"I asked Reverend Dobson about Heaven and he said it was like Abraham Lincoln's goodness living after him."

He waited for the shock to strike her. "Yes?" she said, expecting more.

"That's all."

"And why didn't you like it?"

"Well, don't you see? It amounts to saying there isn't any Heaven at all."

"I don't see that it amounts to that. What do you want Heaven to be?"

"Well, I don't know. I want it to be *some*thing. I thought he'd tell me what it was. I thought that was his job." He was becoming angry, sensing her surprise at him. She had assumed that Heaven had faded from his head years ago. She had imagined that he had already entered, in the secrecy of silence, the conspiracy that he now knew to be all around him.

"David," she asked gently, "don't you ever want to rest?"

"No. Not forever."

"David, you're so young. When you get older, you'll feel differently."

"Grandpa didn't. Look how tattered this book is."

"I never understood your grandfather."

"Well I don't understand ministers who say it's like Lincoln's goodness going on and on. Suppose you're not Lincoln?"

"I think Reverend Dobson made a mistake. You must try to forgive him."

"It's not a *question* of his making a mistake! It's a question of dying and never moving or seeing or hearing anything ever again."

"But"—in exasperation—"darling, it's so *greedy* of you to want more. When God has given us this wonderful April day, and given us this farm, and you have your whole life ahead of you—"

"You think, then, that there is God?"

"Of course I do"—with deep relief, that smoothed her features into a reposeful oval. He had risen and was standing too near her for his comfort. He was afraid she would reach out and touch him.

"He made everything? You feel that?"

"Yes."

"Then who made Him?"

"Why, Man. Man." The happiness of this answer lit up her face radiantly, until she saw his gesture of disgust. She was so simple, so illogical; such a femme.

"Well that amounts to saying there is none."

Her hand reached for his wrist but he backed away. "David, it's a mystery. A miracle. It's a miracle more beautiful than any Reverend Dobson could have told you about. You don't say houses don't exist because Man made them."

"No. God has to be different."

"But, David, you have the *evidence*. Look out the window at the sun; at the fields."

"Mother, good grief. Don't you see"—he rasped away the roughness in his throat—"if when we die there's nothing, all your sun and fields and what not are all, ah, *horror?* It's just an ocean of horror."

"But David, it's not. It's so clearly not that." And she made an urgent opening gesture with her hands that expressed, with its suggestion of a willingness to receive his helplessness, all her grace, her gentleness, her love of beauty, gathered into a passive intensity that made him intensely hate her. He would not be wooed away from the truth. *I am the Way, the Truth . . .*

"No," he told her. "Just let me alone."

He found his tennis ball behind the piano and went outside to throw it against the side of the house. There was a patch high up where the brown stucco that had been laid over the sandstone masonry was crumbling away; he kept trying with the tennis ball to chip more pieces off. Superimposed upon his deep ache was a smaller but more immediate worry; that he had hurt his mother. He heard his father's car rattling on the straightaway, and went into the house, to make peace before he arrived. To his relief, she was not giving off the stifling damp heat of her anger, but instead was cool, decisive, maternal. She handed him an old green book, her college text of Plato.

"I want you to read the Parable of the Cave," she said.

"All right," he said, though he knew it would do no good. Some story by a dead Greek just vague enough to please her. "Don't worry about it, Mother."

"I *am* worried. Honestly, David, I'm sure there will be something for us. As you get older, these things seem to matter a great deal less."

"That may be. It's a dismal thought, though."

His father bumped at the door. The locks and jambs stuck here. But before Granmom could totter to the latch and let him in, he had knocked it open. He had been in Olinger dithering with track meet tickets. Although Mother usually kept her talks with David a confidence, a treasure between them, she called instantly, "George, David is worried about death!"

He came to the doorway of the living room, his shirt pocket bristling with pencils, holding in one hand a pint box of melting ice cream and in the other the knife with which he was about to divide it into four sections, their Sunday treat. "Is the kid worried about death? Don't give it a thought, David. I'll be lucky if I live till tomorrow, and I'm not worried. If they'd taken a buckshot gun and shot me in the cradle I'd be better off. The *world*'d be better off. Hell, I think death is a wonderful thing. I look forward to it. Get the garbage out of the way. If I had the man here who invented death, I'd pin a medal on him."

"Hush, George. You'll frighten the child worse than he is."

This was not true; he never frightened David. There was no harm in his father, no harm at all. Indeed, in the man's steep self-disgust the boy felt a kind of ally. A distant ally. He saw his position with a certain strategic coldness. Nowhere in the world of other people would he find the hint, the nod, he needed to begin to build his fortress against death. They none of them believed. He was alone. In that deep hole.

In the months that followed, his position changed little. School was some comfort. All those sexy, perfumed people, wisecracking, chewing gum, all of them doomed to die, and none of them noticing. In their company David felt that they would carry him along into the bright, cheap paradise reserved for them. In any crowd, the fear ebbed a little; he had reasoned that somewhere in the world there must exist a few people who believed what was necessary, and the larger the crowd, the greater the chance that he was near such a soul, within calling distance, if only he was not too ignorant, too ill-equipped, to spot him. The sight of clergymen cheered him; whatever they themselves thought, their collars were still a sign that somewhere, at some time, someone had recognized that we cannot, *cannot*, submit to death. The sermon topics posted outside churches, the flip, hurried pieties of disc jockeys, the cartoons in magazines showing angels or devils—on such scraps he kept alive the possibility of hope.

For the rest, he tried to drown his hopelessness in clatter and jostle. The pinball machine at the luncheonette was a merciful distraction; as he bent over its buzzing, flashing board of flippers and cushions, the weight and constriction in his chest lightened and loosened. He was grateful for all the time his father wasted in Olinger. Every delay postponed the moment when they must ride together down the dirt road into the heart of the dark farmland, where the only light was the kerosene lamp waiting on the dining-room table, a light that drowned their food in shadow and made it sinister.

He lost his appetite for reading. He was afraid of being ambushed again. In mystery novels people died like dolls being discarded; in science fiction enormities of space and time conspired to crush the humans; and even in P. G. Wodehouse he felt a hollowness, a turning away from reality that was implicitly bitter, and became explicit in the comic figures of futile clergymen. All gaiety seemed minced out on the skin of a void. All quiet hours seemed invitations to dread.

Even on weekends, he and his father contrived to escape the farm; and when, some Saturdays, they did stay home, it was to do something destructive—tear down an old henhouse or set huge brush fires that threatened, while Mother shouted and flapped her arms, to spread to the woods. Whenever his father worked, it was with rapt violence; when he chopped kindling, fragments of the old henhouse boards flew like shrapnel and the ax-head was always within a quarter of an inch of flying off the handle. He was exhilarating to watch, sweating and swearing and sucking bits of saliva back into his lips.

School stopped. His father took the car in the opposite direction, to a highway construction job where he had been hired for the summer as a timekeeper, and David was stranded in the middle of acres of heat and greenery and blowing pollen and the strange, mechanical humming that lay invisibly in the weeds and alfalfa and dry orchard grass.

For his fifteenth birthday his parents gave him, with jokes about him being a hillbilly now, a Remington .22. It was somewhat like a pinball machine to take it out to the old kiln in the woods where they dumped their trash, and set up tin cans on the kiln's sandstone shoulder and shoot them off one by one. He'd take the puppy, who had grown long legs and a rich coat of reddish fur—he was part chow. Copper hated the gun but loved the boy enough to accompany him. When the flat acrid crack rang out, he would race in terrified circles that would tighten and tighten until they brought him, shivering, against David's legs. Depending upon his mood, David would shoot again or drop to his knees and comfort the dog. Giving this comfort to a degree returned comfort to him. The dog's ears, laid flat against his skull in fear, were folded so intricately, so—he groped for the concept—*surely*. Where the dull-studded collar made the fur stand up, each hair showed a root of soft white under the length, black-tipped, of the metal-color that had lent the dog its name. In his agitation Copper panted through nostrils that were elegant slits, like two healed cuts, or like the keyholes of a dainty lock of black, grained wood. His whole whorling, knotted, jointed body was a wealth of such embellishments. And in the smell of the dog's hair David seemed to descend through many finely differentiated layers of earth: mulch, soil, sand, clay, and the glittering mineral base.

But when he returned to the house, and saw the books arranged on the low shelves, fear returned. The four adamant volumes of Wells like four thin bricks, the green Plato that had puzzled him with its queer softness and tangled purity, the dead Galsworthy and "Elizabeth," Grandpa's mammoth dictionary, Grandpa's Bible, the Bible that he himself had received on becoming a member of the Firetown Lutheran Church—at the sight of these, the memory of his fear reawakened and came around him. He had grown stiff and stupid in its embrace. His parents tried to think of ways to entertain him.

"David, I have a job for you to do," his mother said one evening at the table.

"What?"

"If you're going to take that tone perhaps we'd better not talk."

"What tone? I don't take any tone."

"Your grandmother thinks there are too many pigeons in the barn."

"Why?" David turned to look at his grandmother, but she sat there staring at the burning lamp with her usual expression of bewilderment.

Mother shouted, "Mom, he wants to know why!"

Granmom made a jerky, irritable motion with her bad hand, as if generating the force for utterance, and said, "They foul the furniture."

"That's right," Mother said. "She's afraid for that old Olinger furniture that we'll never use. David, she's been after me for a month about those poor pigeons. She wants you to shoot them."

"I don't want to kill anything especially," David said.

Daddy said, "The kid's like you are, Elsie. He's too good for this world. Kill or be killed, that's my motto."

His mother said loudly, "Mother, he doesn't want to do it."

"Not?" The old lady's eyes distended as if in horror and her claw descended slowly to her lap.

"Oh, I'll do it, I'll do it tomorrow," David snapped, and a pleasant crisp taste entered his mouth with the decision.

"And I had thought, when Boyer's men made the hay, it would be better if the barn doesn't look like a rookery," his mother added needlessly.

A BARN, IN DAY, IS A SMALL NIGHT. THE SPLINTERS OF LIGHT between the dry shingles pierce the high roof like stars, and the rafters and crossbeams and built-in ladders seem, until your eyes adjust, as mysterious as the branches of a haunted forest. David entered silently, the gun in one hand. Copper whined desperately at the door, too frightened to come in with the gun yet unwilling to leave the boy. David stealthily turned, said "Go away," shut the door on the dog, and slipped the bolt across. It was a door within a door; the double door for wagons and tractors was as high and wide as the face of a house.

The smell of old straw scratched his sinuses. The red sofa, half-hidden under its white-splotched tarpaulin, seemed assimilated into this smell, sunk in it, buried. The mouths of empty bins gaped like caves. Rusty oddments of farming—coils of baling wire, some spare tines for a harrow, a handleless shovel—hung on nails driven here and there in the thick wood. He stood stock-still a minute; it took a while to separate the cooing of the pigeons from the rustling in his ears. When he had focused on the cooing, it flooded the vast interior with its throaty, bubbling outpour: there seemed no other sound. They were up behind the beams. What light there was leaked through the shingles and the dirty glass windows at the far end and the small round holes, about as big as basketballs, high on the opposite stone side walls, under the ridge of the roof.

A pigeon appeared in one of these holes, on the side toward the house. It flew in, with a battering of wings, from the outside, and waited there, silhouetted against its pinched bit of sky, preening and cooing in a throbbing, thrilled, tentative way. David tiptoed four steps to the side, rested his gun against the lowest rung of a ladder pegged between two upright beams, and lowered the gunsight into the bird's tiny, jauntily cocked head. The slap of the report seemed to come off the stone wall behind him, and the pigeon did not fall. Neither did it fly. Instead it stuck in the round hole, pirouetting rapidly and nodding its head as if in frantic agreement. David shot the bolt back and forth and had aimed again before the spent cartridge had stopped jingling on the boards by his feet. He eased the tip of the sight a little lower, into the bird's breast, and took care to squeeze the trigger with perfect evenness. The slow contraction of his hand abruptly sprang the bullet; for a half-second there was doubt, and then the pigeon fell like a handful of rags, skimming down the barn wall into the layer of straw that coated the floor of the mow on this side.

Now others shook loose from the rafters, and whirled in the dim air with a great blurred hurtle of feathers and noise. They would go for the hole; he fixed his sight on the little moon of blue, and when a pigeon came to it, shot him as he was walking the ten inches of stone that would have carried him into the open air. This pigeon lay down in that tunnel of stone, unable to fall either one way or the other, although he was alive enough to lift one wing and cloud the light. It would sink back, and he would suddenly lift it again, the feathers flaring. His body blocked that exit. David raced to the other side of the barn's main aisle, where a similar ladder was symmetrically placed, and rested his gun on the same rung. Three birds came together to this hole; he got one, and two got through. The rest resettled in the rafters.

There was a shallow triangular space behind the cross beams supporting the roof. It was here they roosted and hid. But either the space was too small, or they were curious, for now that his eyes were at home in the dusty gloom, David could see little dabs of gray popping in and out. The cooing was shriller now; its apprehensive tremolo made the whole volume of air seem liquid. He noticed one little smudge of a head that was especially persistent in peeking out; he marked the place, and fixed his gun on it, and when the head appeared again, had his finger tightened in advance on the trigger. A parcel of fluff slipped off the beam and fell the barn's height onto a canvas covering some Olinger furniture, and where its head had peeked out there was a fresh prick of light in the shingles.

Standing in the center of the floor, fully master now, disdaining to steady the barrel with anything but his arm, he killed two more that way. He felt like a beautiful avenger. Out of the shadowy ragged infinity of the vast barn roof these impudent things dared to thrust their heads, presumed to dirty its starred silence with their filthy timorous life, and he cut them off, tucked them back neatly into the silence. He had the sensation of a creator; these little smudges and flickers that he was clever to see and even cleverer to hit in the dim recesses of the rafters—out of each of them he was making a full bird. A tiny peek, probe, dab of life, when he hit it, blossomed into a dead enemy, falling with good, final weight.

The imperfection of the second pigeon he had shot, who was still lifting his wing now and then up in the round hole, nagged him. He put a new clip into the stock. Hugging the gun against his body, he climbed the ladder. The barrel sight scratched his ear; he had a sharp, garish vision, like a color slide, of shooting himself and being found tumbled on the barn floor among his prey. He locked his arm around the top rung—a fragile, gnawed rod braced between uprights—and shot into the bird's body from a flat angle. The wing folded, but the impact did not, as he had hoped, push the bird out of the hole. He fired again, and again, and still the little body, lighter than air when alive, was too heavy to budge from its high grave. From up here he could see green trees and a brown corner of the house through the hole. Clammy with the cobwebs that gathered between the rungs, he pumped a full clip of eight bullets into the stubborn shadow, with no success. He climbed down, and was struck by the silence in the barn. The remaining pigeons must have escaped out the other hole. That was all right; he was tired of it.

He stepped with his rifle into the light. His mother was coming to meet him, and it tickled him to see her shy away from the carelessly held gun. "You took a chip out of the house," she said. "What were those last shots about?"

"One of them died up in that little round hole and I was trying to shoot it down."

"Copper's hiding behind the piano and won't come out. I had to leave him."

"Well don't blame me. *I* didn't want to shoot the poor devils."

"Don't smirk. You look like your father. How many did you get?"

"Six."

She went into the barn, and he followed. She listened to the silence. Her hair was scraggly, perhaps from tussling with the dog. "I don't suppose the others will be back," she said wearily. "Indeed, I don't know why I let Mother talk me into it. Their cooing was such a comforting noise." She began to gather up the dead pigeons. Though he didn't want to touch them, David went into the mow and picked up by its tepid, horny, coral-colored feet the first bird he had killed. Its wings unfolded disconcertingly, as if the creature had been held together by threads that now were slit. It did not weigh much. He retrieved the one on the other side of the barn; his mother got the three in the middle and led the way across the road to the little southern slope of land that went down toward the foundations of the vanished tobacco shed. The ground was too steep to plant and mow; wild strawberries grew in the tangled grass. She put her burden down and said, "We'll have to bury them. The dog will go wild."

He put his two down on her three; the slick feathers let the bodies slide liquidly on one another. He asked, "Shall I get you the shovel?"

"Get it for yourself; *you* bury them. They're your kill. And be sure to make the hole deep enough so he won't dig them up." While he went to the tool shed for the shovel, she went into the house. Unlike her, she did not look up, either at the orchard to the right of her or at the meadow on her left, but instead held her head rigidly, tilted a little, as if listening to the ground.

He dug the hole, in a spot where there were no strawberry plants, before he studied the pigeons. He had never seen a bird this close before. The feathers were more wonderful than dog's hair, for each filament was shaped within the shape of the feather, and the feathers in turn were trimmed to fit a pattern that flowed without error across the bird's body. He lost himself in the geometrical tides as the feathers now broadened and stiffened to make an edge for flight, now softened and constricted to cup warmth around the mute flesh. And across the surface of the infinitely adjusted yet somehow effortless mechanics of the feathers played idle designs of color, no two alike, designs executed, it seemed, in a controlled rapture, with a joy that hung level in the air above and behind him. Yet these birds bred in the millions and were exterminated as pests. Into the fragrant open earth he dropped one broadly banded in slate shades of blue, and on top of it another, mottled all over in rhythms of lilac and gray. The next was almost wholly white, but for a salmon glaze at its throat. As he fitted the last two, still pliant, on the top, and stood up, crusty coverings were lifted from him, and with a feminine, slipping sensation along his nerves that seemed to give the air hands, he was robed in this certainty: that the God who had lavished such craft upon these worthless birds would not destroy His whole Creation by refusing to let David live forever.

CHARLES WILLIAMS

BORN IN LONDON IN 1886, CHARLES WALTER STANSBY WILLIAMS received his education at St. Alban's School and at University College, London. In 1908 he began his association with the Oxford University Press, first as a reader, and later as a literary adviser, remaining a member of the staff until his death. In 1912 his first book of verse, *The Silver Stair*, appeared, followed by a profound list of publications, including over thirty volumes of fiction, poetry, biography, plays, literary criticism, and theological reason.

Williams was a devoted member of the Church of England and a writer concerned with the preeminence of Christ, believing that the role of the "doubting Thomas" was an integral one to the deepest understanding of the mystery of God. He lectured extensively throughout his life, and cultivated to a fine degree the art of conversation, developing in his meetings with others what would become and continue to be his high, indeed extraordinary facility for reasoned argument regarding the necessity of faith in God.

A member along with J.R.R. Tolkien and C.S. Lewis of the small but extraordinarily influential Oxford group The Inklings, Williams wrote novels he described as "psychological thrillers," and gave such well-crafted lectures on literature that he was awarded an honorary MA by the university of Oxford in 1943; he died unexpectedly in 1945.

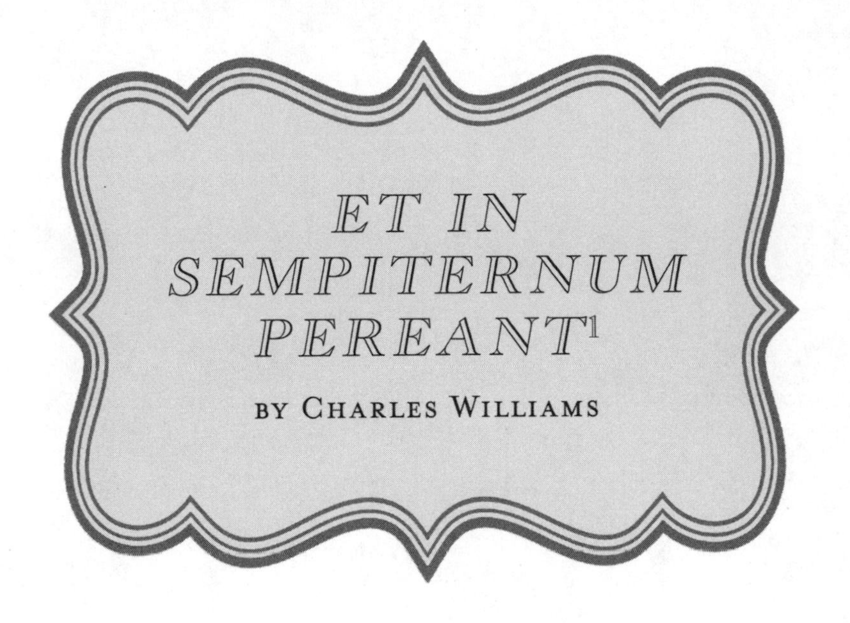

ET IN SEMPITERNUM PEREANT[1]

BY CHARLES WILLIAMS

1. "And They Would Perish Eternally," the antithesis of John 3:15, "That whosoever believeth in him should not perish, but have eternal life."

Lord Arglay came easily down the road. About him the spring was as gaudy as the restraint imposed by English geography ever lets it be. The last village lay a couple of miles behind him; as far in front, he had been told, was a main road on which he could meet a motor bus to carry him near his destination. A casual conversation in a club had revealed to him, some months before, that in a country house of England there were supposed to lie a few yet unpublished legal opinions of the Lord Chancellor Bacon. Lord Arglay, being no longer Chief Justice, and having finished and published his *History of Organic Law,* had conceived that the editing of these papers might provide a pleasant variation upon his present business of studying the more complex parts of the Christian Schoolmen. He had taken advantage of a week-end spent in the neighbourhood to arrange, by the good will of the owner, a visit of inspection; since, as the owner had remarked, with a bitterness due to his financial problems, "everything that is smoked isn't Bacon." Lord Arglay had smiled—it hurt him a little to think that he had smiled—and said, which was true enough, that Bacon himself would not have made a better joke.

It was a very deserted part of the country through which he was walking. He had been careful to follow the directions given him, and in fact there were only two places where he could possibly have gone wrong, and at both of them Lord Arglay was certain he had not gone wrong. But he seemed to be taking a long time—a longer time than he had expected. He looked at his watch again, and noted with sharp disapproval of his own judgment that it was only six minutes since he had looked at it last. It had seemed more like sixteen. Lord Arglay frowned. He was usually a good walker, and on that morning he was not conscious of any unusual weariness. His host had offered to send him in a car, but he had declined. For a moment, as he put his watch back, he was almost sorry he had declined. A car would have made short time of this road, and at present his legs seemed to be making rather long time of it. "Or," Lord Arglay said aloud, "making time rather long." He played a little, as he went on, with the fancy that every road in space had a corresponding measure in time; that it tended, merely of itself, to hasten or delay all those that drove or walked upon it. The nature of some roads, quite apart from their material effectiveness, might urge men to speed, and of others to delay. So that the intentions of all travellers were counterpointed continually by the media they used. The courts, he thought, might reasonably take that into consideration in case of offences against right speed, and a man who accelerated upon one road would be held to have acted under the improper influence of the way, whereas one who did the same on another would be known to have defied and conquered the way.

Lord Arglay just stopped himself looking at his watch again. It was impossible that it should be more than five minutes since he had last done so. He looked back to observe, if possible, how far he had since come. It was not possible; the road narrowed and curved too much. There was a cloud of trees high up behind him; it must have been half an hour ago that he passed through it, yet it was not merely still in sight, but the trees themselves were in sight. He could remark them as trees; he could almost, if he were a little careful, count them. He thought, with some irritation, that he must be getting old more quickly, and more unnoticeably, than he had supposed. He did not much mind about the quickness, but he did mind about the unnoticeableness. It had given him pleasure to watch the various changes which age tended to bring; to be as stealthy and as quick to observe those changes as they were to come upon him—the slower pace, the more meditative voice, the greater reluctance to decide, the inclination to fall back on habit, the desire for the familiar which is the first skirmishing approach of unfamiliar death. He neither welcomed nor grudged such changes; he only observed them with a perpetual interest in the curious nature of the creation. The fantasy of growing old, like the fantasy of growing up, was part of the ineffable sweetness, touched with horror, of existence, itself the lordliest fantasy of all. But now, as he stood looking back over and across the hidden curves of the road, he felt suddenly that time had outmarched and out-twisted him, that it was spreading along the countryside and doubling back on him, so that it troubled and deceived his judgment. In an unexpected and unusual spasm of irritation he put his hand to his watch again. He felt as if it were a quarter of an hour since he had looked at it; very well, making just allowance for his state of impatience, he would expect the actual time to be five minutes. He looked; it was only two.

Lord Arglay made a small mental effort, and almost immediately recognized the effort. He said to himself: "This is another mark of age. I am losing my sense of duration." He said also: "It is becoming an effort to recognize these changes." Age was certainly quickening its work in him. It approached him now doubly; not only his method of experience, but his awareness of experience was attacked. His knowledge of it comforted him—perhaps, he thought, for the last time. The knowledge would go. He would savour it then while he could. Still looking back at the trees, "It seems I'm decaying," Lord Arglay said aloud. "And that anyhow is one up against decay. Am I procrastinating? I am, and in the circumstances procrastination is a proper and pretty game. It is the thief of time, and quite right too! Why should time have it all its own way?"

He turned to the road again, and went on. It passed now between open fields; in all those fields he could see no one. It was pasture, but there were no beasts. There was about him a kind of void, in which he moved, hampered by this growing oppression of duration. Things lasted. He had exclaimed, in his time, against the too swift passage of the world. This was a new experience; it was lastingness—almost, he could have believed, everlastingness. The measure of it was but his breathing, and his breathing, as it grew slower and heavier, would become the measure of everlasting labour—the labour of Sisyphus, who pushed his own slow heart through each infinite moment, and relaxed but to let it beat back and so again begin. It was the first touch of something Arglay had never yet known, of simple and perfect despair.

At that moment he saw the house. The road before him curved sharply, and as he looked he wondered at the sweep of the curve; it seemed to make a full half-circle and so turn back in the direction that he had come. At the farthest point there lay before him, tangentially, another path. The sparse hedge was broken by an opening which was more than footpath and less than road. It was narrow, even when compared with the narrowing way by which he had come, yet hard and beaten as if by the passage of many feet. There had been innumerable travellers, and all solitary, all on foot. No cars or carts could have taken that path; if there had been burdens, they had been carried on the shoulders of their owners. It ran for no long distance, no more than in happier surroundings might have been a garden path from gate to door. There, at the end, was the door.

Arglay, at the time, took all this in but half-consciously. His attention was not on the door but on the chimney. The chimney, in the ordinary phrase, was smoking. It was smoking effectively and continuously. A narrow and dense pillar of dusk poured up from it, through which there glowed every now and then, a deeper undershade of crimson, as if some trapped genius almost thrust itself out of the moving prison that held it. The house itself was not much more than a cottage. There was a door, shut; on the left of it a window, also shut; above, two little attic windows, shut, and covered within by some sort of dark hanging, or perhaps made opaque by smoke that filled the room. There was no sign of life anywhere, and the smoke continued to mount to the lifeless sky. It seemed to Arglay curious that he had not noticed this grey pillar in his approach, that only now when he stood almost in the straight and narrow path leading to the house did it become visible, an exposition of tall darkness reserved to the solitary walkers upon that wearying road.

Lord Arglay was the last person in the world to look for responsibilities. He shunned them by a courteous habit; a responsibility had to present itself with a delicate emphasis before he acceded to it. But when any so impressed itself he was courteous in accepting as in declining; he sought friendship with necessity, and as young lovers call their love fatal, so he turned fatality of life into his love. It seemed to him, as he stood and gazed at the path, the shut door, the smoking chimney, that here perhaps was a responsibility being delicately emphatic. If everyone was out—if the cottage had been left for an hour—ought he to do something? Of course, they might be busy about it within; in which case a thrusting stranger would be inopportune. Another glow of crimson in the pillar of cloud decided him. He went up the path.

As he went he glanced at the little window, but it was blurred by dirt; he could not very well see whether the panes did or did not hide smoke within. When he was so near the threshold that the window had almost passed out of his vision, he thought he saw a face looking out of it—at the extreme edge, nearest the door—and he checked himself, and went back a step to look again. It had been only along the side of his glance that the face, if face it were, had appeared, a kind of sudden white scrawl against the blur, as if it were a mask hung by the window rather than any living person, or as if the glass of the window itself had looked sideways at him, and he had caught the look without understanding its cause. When he stepped back, he could see no face. Had there been a sun in the sky he would have attributed the apparition to a trick of the light, but in the sky over this smoking house there was no sun. It had shone brightly that morning when he started; it had paled and faded and finally been lost to him as he had passed along his road. There was neither sun nor peering face. He stepped back to the threshold, and knocked with his knuckles on the door.

There was no answer. He knocked again and again waited, and as he stood there he began to feel annoyed. The balance of Lord Arglay's mind had not been achieved without the creation of a considerable counter-energy to the violence of Lord Arglay's natural temper. There had been people whom he had once come very near hating, hating with a fury of selfish rage and detestation; for instance, his brother-in-law. His brother-in-law had not been a nice man; Lord Arglay, as he stood by the door and, for no earthly reason, remembered him, admitted it. He admitted, at the same moment, that no lack of niceness on that other's part could excuse any indulgence of vindictive hate on his own, nor could he think why, then and there, he wanted him, wanted to have him merely to hate. His brother-in-law was dead. Lord Arglay almost regretted it. Almost he desired to follow, to be with him, to provoke and torment him, to . . .

Lord Arglay struck the door again. "There is," he said to himself, "entire clarity in the Omnipotence." It was his habit of devotion, his means of recalling himself into peace out of the angers, greeds, sloths and perversities that still too often possessed him. It operated; the temptation passed into the benediction of the Omnipotence and disappeared. But there was still no answer from within. Lord Arglay laid his hand on the latch. He swung the door, and, lifting his hat with his other hand, looked into the room—a room empty of smoke as of fire, and of all as of both.

Its size and appearance were those of a rather poor cottage, rather indeed a large brick hut than a cottage. It seemed much smaller within than without. There was a fireplace—at least, there was a place for a fire—on his left. Opposite the door, against the right-hand wall, there was a ramshackle flight of wooden steps, going up to the attics, and at its foot, swinging on a broken hinge, a door which gave a way presumably to a cellar. Vaguely, Arglay found himself surprised; he had not supposed that a dwelling of this sort would have a cellar. Indeed, from where he stood, he could not be certain. It might only be a cupboard. But, unwarrantably, it seemed more, a hinted unseen depth, as if the slow slight movement of the broken wooden door measured that labour of Sisyphus, as if the road ran past him and went coiling spirally into the darkness of the cellar. In the room there was no furniture, neither fragment of paper nor broken bit of wood; there was no sign of life, no flame in the grate nor drift of smoke in the air. It was completely and utterly void.

Lord Arglay looked at it. He went back a few steps and looked up again at the chimney. Undoubtedly the chimney was smoking. It was received into a pillar of smoke; there was no clear point where the dark chimney ended and the dark smoke began. House leaned to roof, roof to chimney, chimney to smoke, and smoke went up for ever and ever over those roads where men crawled infinitely through the smallest measurements of time. Arglay returned to the door, crossed the threshold, and stood in the room. Empty of flame, empty of flame's material, holding within its dank air the very opposite of flame, the chill of ancient years, the room lay round him. Lord Arglay contemplated it. "There's no smoke without fire," he said aloud. "Only apparently there is. Thus one lives and learns. Unless indeed this is the place where one lives without learning."

The phrase, leaving his lips, sounded oddly about the walls and in the corners of the room. He was suddenly revolted by his own chance words—"a place where one lives without learning," where no courtesy or integrity could any more be fined or clarified. The echo daunted him; he made a sharp movement, he took a step aside towards the stairs, and before the movement was complete, was aware of a change. The dank chill became a concentration of dank and deadly heat, pricking at him, entering his nostrils and his mouth. The fantasy of life without knowledge materialized, inimical, in the air, life without knowledge, corrupting life without knowledge, jungle and less than jungle, and though still the walls of the bleak chamber met his eyes, a shell of existence, it seemed that life, withdrawn from all those normal habits of which the useless memory was still drearily sustained by the thin phenomenal fabric, was collecting and corrupting in the atmosphere behind the door he had so rashly passed—outside the other door which swung crookedly at the head of the darker hole within.

He had recoiled from the heat, but not so as to escape it. He had even taken a step or two up the stairs, when he heard from without a soft approach. Light feet were coming up the beaten path to the house. Some other Good Samaritan, Arglay thought, who would be able to keep his twopence in his pocket. For certainly, whatever was the explanation of all this and wherever it lay, in the attics above or in the pit of the cellar below, responsibility was gone. Lord Arglay did not conceive that either he or anyone else need rush about the country in an anxious effort to preserve a house which no one wanted and no one used. Prematurely enjoying the discussion, he waited. Through the doorway someone came in.

It was, or seemed to be, a man, of ordinary height, wearing some kind of loose dark overcoat that flapped about him. His head was bare; so, astonishingly, were his legs and feet. At first, as he stood just inside the door, leaning greedily forward, his face was invisible, and for a moment Arglay hesitated to speak. Then the stranger lifted his face and Arglay uttered a sound. It was emaciated beyond imagination; it was astonishing, at the appalling degree of hunger revealed, that the man could walk or move at all, or even stand as he was now doing, and turn that dreadful skull from side to side. Arglay came down the steps of the stair in one jump; he cried out again, he ran forward, and as he did so the deep burning eyes in the turning face of bone met his full and halted him. They did not see him, or if they saw did not notice; they gazed at him and moved on. Once only in his life had Arglay seen eyes remotely like those; once, when he had pronounced the death-sentence upon a wretched man who had broken under the long strain of his trial and filled the court with shrieks. Madness had glared at Lord Arglay from that dock, but at least it had looked at him and seen him; these eyes did not. They sought something—food, life, or perhaps only a form and something to hate, and in that energy the stranger moved. He began to run round the room. The bones that were his legs and feet jerked up and down. The head turned from side to side. He ran circularly, round and again round, crossing and recrossing, looking up, down, around, and at last, right in the centre of the room, coming to a halt, where, as if some terrible pain of starvation gripped him, he bent and twisted downward until he squatted grotesquely on the floor. There, squatting and bending, he lowered his head and raised his arm, and as the fantastic black coat slipped back, Arglay saw a wrist, saw it marked with scars. He did not at first think what they were; only when the face and wrist of the figure swaying in its pain came together did he suddenly know. They were teeth-marks; they were bites; the mouth closed on the wrist and gnawed. Arglay cried out and sprang forward, catching the arm, trying to press it down, catching the other shoulder, trying to press it back. He achieved nothing. He held, he felt, he grasped; he could not control. The long limb remained raised, the fierce teeth gnawed. But as Arglay bent, he was aware once more of that effluvia of heat risen round him, and breaking out with the more violence when suddenly the man, if it were man, cast his arm away, and with a jerk of movement rose once more to his feet. His eyes, as the head went back, burned close into Arglay's, who, what with the heat, the eyes, and his sickness at the horror, shut his own against them, and was at the same moment thrown from his balance by the rising form, and sent staggering a step or two away, with upon his face the sensation of a light hot breath, so light that only in the utter stillness of time could it be felt, so hot that it might have been the inner fire from which the pillar of smoke poured outward to the world.

He recovered his balance; he opened his eyes; both motions brought him into a new comer of that world. The odd black coat the thing had worn had disappeared, as if it had been a covering imagined by a habit of mind. The thing itself, a wasted flicker of pallid movement, danced and gyrated in white flame before him. Arglay saw it still, but only now as a dreamer may hear, half-asleep and half-awake, the sound of dogs barking or the crackling of fire in his very room. For he opened his eyes not to such things, but to the thing that on the threshold of this place, some seconds earlier or some years, he had felt and been pleased to feel, to the reality of his hate. It came in a rush within him, a fountain of fire, and without and about him images of the man he hated swept in a thick cloud of burning smoke. The smoke burned his eyes and choked his mouth; he clutched at it, at images within it—at his greedy loves and greedy hates—at the cloud of the sin of his life, yearning to catch but one image and renew again the concentration for which he yearned. He could not. The smoke blinded and stifled him, yet more than stifling or blinding was the hunger for one true thing to lust or hate. He was starving in the smoke, and all the hut was full of smoke, for the hut and the world were smoke, pouring up round him, from him and all like him—a thing once wholly, and still a little, made visible to his corporeal eyes in forms which they recognized, but in itself of another nature. He swung and twisted and crouched. His limbs ached from long wrestling with the smoke, for as the journey to this place had prolonged itself infinitely, so now, though he had no thought of measurement, the clutch of his hands and the growing sickness that invaded him struck through him the sensation of the passage of years and the knowledge of the passage of moments. The fire sank within him, and the sickness grew, but the change could not bring him nearer to any end. The end here was not at the end, but in the beginning. There was no end to this smoke, to this fever and this chill, to crouching and rising and searching, unless the end was now. *Now—now* was the only possible other fact, chance, act. He cried out, defying infinity, "*Now!*"

Before his voice the smoke of his prison yielded, and yielded two ways at once. From where he stood he could see in one place an alteration in that perpetual grey, an alternate darkening and lightening as if two ways, of descent and ascent, met. There was, he remembered, a way in, therefore a path out; he had only to walk along it. But also there was a way still farther in, and he could walk along that. Two doors had swung, to his outer senses, in that small room. From every gate of hell there was a way to heaven, yes, and in every way to heaven there was a gate to deeper hell.

Yet for a moment he hesitated. There was no sign of the phenomenon by which he had discerned the passage of that other spirit. He desired—very strongly he desired—to be of use to it. He desired to offer himself to it, to make a ladder of himself, if that should be desired, by which it might perhaps mount from the nature of the lost, from the dereliction of all minds that refuse living and learning, postponement and irony, whose dwelling is necessarily in their undying and perishing selves. Slowly, unconsciously, he moved his head as if to seek his neighbour.

He saw, at first he felt, nothing. His eyes returned to that vibrating oblong of an imagined door, the heart of the smoke beating in the smoke. He looked at it; he remembered the way; he was on the point of movement, when the stinging heat struck him again, but this time from behind. It leapt through him; he was seized in it and loosed from it; its rush abandoned him. The torrent of its fiery passage struck the darkening hollow in the walls. At the instant that it struck, there came a small sound; there floated up a thin shrill pipe, too short to hear, too certain to miss, faint and quick as from some single insect in the hedgerow or the field, and yet more than single—a weak wail of multitudes of the lost. The shrill lament struck his ears, and he ran. He cried as he sprang: "Now is God: now is glory in God," and as the dark door swung before him it was the threshold of the house that received his flying feet. As he passed, another form slipped by him, slinking hastily into the house, another of the hordes going so swiftly up that straight way, hard with everlasting time; each driven by his own hunger, and each alone. The vision, a face looking in as a face had looked out, was gone. Running still, but more lightly now, and with some communion of peace at heart, Arglay came into the curving road. The trees were all about him; the house was at their heart. He ran on through them; beyond, he saw, he reached, the spring day and the sun. At a little distance a motor bus, gaudy within and without, was coming down the road. The driver saw him. Lord Arglay instinctively made a sign, ran, mounted. As he sat down, breathless and shaken, "*E quindi uscimmo,*" his mind said, "*a riveder le stelle.*"[2]

2. "Where we came forth, and once more saw the stars," the last line of Dante's *The Inferno,* in which Virgil and Dante emerge from Hell.

ACKNOWLEDGMENTS

THE EDITOR WOULD LIKE TO THANK, ONCE AGAIN, AMANDA BOSTIC and Allen Arnold for their vision and patience and heart for God in putting this book together and bringing Christian literature to readers. He would also like to thank his wife, Melanie, for her wherewithal and typing skills and love, not necessarily in that order.

This book is dedicated to Conrad "Buster" Brown, pastor of East Cooper Baptist Church in Mount Pleasant, South Carolina, perhaps the most well-read man I have ever met. His enduring love of literature and, most importantly, God's Word has made him a continuing inspiration in my life.

DISCUSSION GROUP GUIDE

1. Which story in this collection was your favorite? Why?

2. Which story was the least compelling? Are you able to identify a particular element that didn't appeal to you?

3. This collection is one in which the stories hope to "challenge and inspire" their readers. Which story here perhaps challenged you most? In what ways did it challenge you? Which story inspired you most, and how?

4. The stories by Gina Ochsner, John Updike, and Frederick Buechner are more contemporary than the others gathered here. How do these stories differ from the older ones? What might these differences say about how our culture has changed since the older stories were written? In what ways are matters of faith still the same?

5. Given that a good short story has a fully developed theme but isn't as detailed or elaborate as a novel, which of the stories here seemed most "complete" to you? What made it seem so? Conversely, which story seemed most a fragment? Do you think that a short story can develop an idea as fully as a novel does?

6. Each of the stories in this collection was written by a Christian. What evidence of each writer's faith or faith journey do you see in these stories? Is it possible for a story to show us something about God without specifically mentioning his name?